A Lineage of
Deception

*For Windsong,
my special chone
sister*

*Love Marge
(B.Leaf) Hopper*

A Southern Novel

A Lineage of Deception

Maryann Hopper

MOUNTAIN ARBOR
  PRESS *an Imprint of BookLogix*
Alpharetta, GA

Copyright © 2022 by Maryann Hopper

All rights reserved. No part of this book may be reproduced or transmitted in any form or by any means, electronic or mechanical, including photocopying, recording, or any information storage and retrieval system, without permission in writing from the author.

ISBN: 978-1-6653-0384-2 - Paperback
eISBN: 978-1-6653-0385-9 - eBook

These ISBNs are the property of Mountain Arbor Press for the express purpose of sales and distribution of this title. The content of this book is the property of the copyright holder only. Mountain Arbor Press does not hold any ownership of the content of this book and is not liable in any way for the materials contained within. The views and opinions expressed in this book are the property of the Author/Copyright holder, and do not necessarily reflect those of Mountain Arbor Press.

Printed in the United States of America   0 3 1 8 2 2

∞This paper meets the requirements of ANSI/NISO Z39.48-1992 (Permanence of Paper)

Cover photo by Ria Coesel
Author photo by Lani Cartwright

*For those whose souls are gripped by the South
and need their stories told.*

"Everyone is filled with endless pools of unknowability."

—Elizabeth Strout

Contents

Acknowledgments   *xi*

A Summer Cracked Open	1
Bea's Choices	15
Courthouse Date	30
Rocky Marriage	35
Rocky Marriage Ends	47
Growing Pains for Maggie Lu	53
Maggie Lu's Teen Years	57
Early Thoughts of Baby	71
Dreaming Loss	80
News from Birdsong Farm	84
Fred's Last Mishap	90
Water Break	105
Orange Hollow Afternoon	113
Trouble at Birdsong Farm	121
The Losses Go Deeper	128
First Visit	139
The Risks	144
In the Long Run	159
Bea's Intrusion	164
Sunny's Confidences	175
Running Away	185
Ensnared in Crosston	198
Stopped by Shadows	209
Finding Leo	220
Leo's Reflections in Prison	228
The Last Ride with Bea	239

Maggie Lu and the Pup	248
Revelations at Birdsong Farm	258
Sunny's Pursuit	265
Edith Tells on Pearl	274
Still on the Hunt	281
Moving On	291

Acknowledgments

Writing is a singular activity, but I thank the following for their encouragement, insights, and inspiration. Carol Lee Lorenzo and the dedicated writers in her Fiction Intensives workshops, ever thoughtful and perceptive. Dykewriters, kind and courageous in sharing their musings. My editor, Susan Reu, for her expertise in all things grammatical, for her careful reading and keen suggestions. My life partner, Drea Firewalker, for her belief in me and her constant encouragement through the years. The folks at Booklogix for getting this work out!

A Summer Cracked Open

Perched on an old wooden sill, the small rotating fan fluttered the pages of Bea's journalism textbook. She placed a moist arm along the page to hold it in place and pressed hard on her yellow pencil, trying to make last-minute notes for the final exam. Struggling to push out a warm breeze, the fan made an annoying click on each rotation. Finally, Bea jerked the fan cord from the wall, stuffed out her cigarette in the overflowing ashtray, and threw herself onto the twin bed in her stifling dorm room, toppling an assortment of stuffed animals.

The green twill bedspread was scratchy against her naked back, not like the gentle touch of Evan's fingers "tracing a tree" along her spine. She wished for his call but knew he was dealing with exams, too. Squinting through the dirty screen covering the open window, she glimpsed heavy, gray clouds. A puff of steamy air floated through the room. Bea waited for asphyxiation, her only release.

"It's too hot to study," she moaned to the pink teddy bear that had tumbled over on its face after her pounce.

Her roommate cracked open the door to their room and said, "Talking to that bear again? You wanna talk to a human?"

"Not you," Bea replied, grateful the semester was soon

over, and she'd move away from her chatty roomie. She had to find a way to get off campus and be more available for Evan, her journalism professor, when he could get away.

"Your sister's on the hall phone," her roommate said, and slammed the door.

Rarely eager for her older sister Pearl's nosey calls, but glad for any study diversion, Bea slouched toward the pay phone in the hallway, clad only in her pink panties, chuckling at the shock her nudity might illicit. "Hi sis, I'm really studying for finals. Don't worry. I won't skip out like last term."

Pearl's perky voice rose. "Let's go to the beach to celebrate your school being out next week. See, I'm calling in something fun. I'm taking a couple days off work. Mama said I could borrow the good car, and we could spend the night at her friend's cottage in Biloxi. Come with me?"

Bea pulled the receiver from her ear and stared at it. Was this "nice" Pearl calling about fun? A rare gesture, indeed. "Gee, what a surprise," she managed to reply in between Pearl's awkward chatter. Bea's eyes moved to each open door along the dark hallway, hoping those inside were not listening. She hated the dorm girls prying, afraid she might slip up herself with a telling remark about Evan and get him in trouble. She shifted her attention back to Pearl's babbling about travel plans in a tone uncommonly pleading. Suspicious, Bea asked, "Are you okay?"

"Oh, little sister, I'll tell you all about it. You'll come, right?"

Bea considered her alternatives, a farewell keg party by a mosquito-infested riverbank or another rendezvous with Evan, only if his wife went to her family reunion, which she probably wouldn't. Then Bea would be stuck packing up her room in a dead town. "You're my best option. Pick me up Wednesday around 2PM." After hanging up the receiver, Bea lingered at the phone. Would Evan miss her if he called and got no response?

Trudging back to her room, Bea began to have second thoughts about spending a few days with Pearl. She'd have to be careful what she told her about her campus life to avoid Pearl's testy refrains. Bea stretched out on the bed and stared at a jagged, brown stain on the ceiling. When she and Pearl were youngsters and had to share a room, Daddy had "chosen" Bea for late evening "tucking in," causing that ceiling to swirl making her dizzy while enduring his calloused fingers groping her fragility. Pearl had rolled on her side in her bed across the room and faced the wall, pulling her pillow over her head, shutting out Bea's complaints. Pearl only shrugged when Mama asked her why Bea would say "bad things" about Daddy. She cringed now remembering how Pearl, tucking her dark home-permanent curls behind her ears, had smirked when Mama slapped Bea's face and told her to quit making up tales.

The dorm room was sweltering. Bea needed a cigarette. Her fingers wandered to her naked breasts and pinched each nipple. She told herself she loved being naked, but when she glanced at her long, thin body in the full-length mirror, she looked so small and unsexy.

* * *

"Maybellene," the unfaithful romance tune, blared from the nickelodeon at the wooden dance pavilion at the edge of the Biloxi beach. Bea imagined Evan holding her hand as they danced, but he never had enough time for outings. Eyes tight against the sun, she tapped her fingers, making tiny indentions in her beach towel, and stretched out her long legs, digging her heels into the warm sand. Full of small talk, Pearl slathered baby oil on her pale shoulders and sat against a red metal ice chest. "Ow, don't know how a hot metal chest keeps the drinks cold." Flipping her dark hair behind her ears, she straightened up and wedged a towel behind her back.

Bea winked open one eye and grinned. "Well, what's the big news? Have you and Fred finally done it?"

Making erratic, wiggly lines in the sand with her finger, Pearl sighed. "Yes, and I feel guilty, but I had to. I want to keep him. I suspect he's been with other women, but he swears I'm his true love. I'm worried now he won't marry me, since I . . . well, let him. Mama is furious with me, says I'll have a baby before I secure a man."

Bea sprang forward in shock. "You told Mama? Why?"

Pearl hung her head, letting her dark hair droop in her face. "She caught us in the bed at home. They were supposed to be gone for the weekend to Memphis, but Daddy got sick and had to come home to the doctor."

Almost holding her breath, Bea juggled glee at Pearl's earning their mother's disapproval with a tad of empathy. "Oh, that's terrible. I'd have to move out of the house and not face Mama. Is Daddy okay?" Bea turned her head from the wind and lit a cigarette. "Want one?"

Pearl shook her head. "It was just a scare—Daddy's heart, that is. I'm thinking about moving to Oxford. That's why I wanted to talk. Maybe we could rent a place, be roommates."

Nervously pushing back her long, golden hair, Bea blushed. "Oh, that's terrible. I mean, you'd be farther from Fred." A flash of the room they shared at home, Pearl putting a strip of masking tape on the floor to mark off her side, *Miss Neato*, brought on a warm flush behind Bea's ears.

Pearl laughed. "No, silly, he'd come, too. We just

wouldn't tell Mama we were all living together." Pearl adjusted her sunglasses and turned toward the beach. Bea knew her sister couldn't look her in the face when she was trying to be so coy.

"Wow, that's pretty bold for you, letting down that good-girl image." Bea took a long drag on her cigarette and let the smoke out slowly, trying to take in her sister's proposal.

"I never wanted to be as wild as you." Pearl picked at the pink nail polish on her toes. "It was Fred's idea. He's been down to Oxford for the football games, loves all the hangouts. I'm adjusting to his idea." She fluffed her shoulder-length dark curls and groaned, "I think I've been a disappointment to him, couldn't keep up, but I'll do what will persuade him."

Bea pulled on a wide-brimmed straw hat to make a shade for herself and searched for her sunglasses to hide her eyes. She tried for a firm response. "Of course, you will." She squinted at Pearl's high forehead and the coarse texture of her hair, their shared traits of sisterhood. Surprising herself, she felt a tinge of sadness for her sister. Pearl had been dating Fred Birdsong since high school. Pearl was the studious one who helped him cram for tests, though he always joked around, keeping them up late enough that Mama finally had to tell him to go home. His body muscular from farm work and football, he wore tight plaid shirts with his jeans. He always had a car that was running to drive them to town for Cokes and hot dogs, but not every weekend, which upset Pearl. Back then Pearl had liked that he invited her to the Mid-South Fair to see the ribbons he won for his FFA animal exhibits. Now, a few years after high school, she was still waiting for him to propose.

In high school Bea had rarely cracked a book and never went steady. She knew Pearl was stunned that she had even applied for journalism school at Ole Miss. Why not move to a swinging town? College anywhere was better than a boring job near home under their mama's watchful eye. Pearl was probably jealous after all of Bea's bragging about campus life, but it had been her own choice to take a job at the bank. Pearl wanted to save her money and get married. Bea found her sunglasses and popped them on. Stalling to collect her thoughts by taking several small puffs from her cigarette, she said, "Gosh it's bright out here."

Pearl said, "I know you've always been more independent with guys, but I've been with Fred so long. It's got to be inevitable. I do support myself. I'll have to give notice. In a few weeks, we'll both find new jobs. Fred has already talked to the Agricultural Extension agent, maybe find work with 4-H or the ag co-op."

Two working folks mostly paying the rent began to play well in Bea's head. "Gee, I might consider it. Gotta get out of that dorm and get a summer job. Would be cool to stay in Oxford close to . . . uh, friends and not to have to stay at Mama's all summer."

Pearl nodded quickly. "Yes, you're lucky you're already away from Mama's radar."

Bea laughed. "I can't believe we're talking this way. We might even learn to get along."

Giggling, Pearl pushed away from the cooler and whispered, "Have you gone all the way yet with any of the college boys?"

Bea's head was spinning with thoughts of staying near Evan over the summer. She took a breath, chortling, "Am I really saying this to you? Wow, mostly I like older men, more experienced, but I don't want to be tied down. I'm just experimenting."

"Oh, Bebe, maybe my baby sister can teach me what I might be missing out on."

"Don't call me *Bebe*." Bea cocked her head to one side. "What do you really want for yourself?"

"Not a big career like you, though I do want substantial money, farm life with a good man, some kids. Isn't that okay?" Her head bowed. Pearl traced a straight sand line along the edge of the cooler with her finger.

Bea stubbed out her cigarette in the sand and waved her hands in front of her. "Sure, sure, that sounds right for you." She could feel a worry line creeping into her forehead. "Writing about other folks' lives at a newspaper should keep me plenty busy."

Pearl dipped her head. "Will that be enough to satisfy you?"

Bea pushed the cigarette stub further into the sand. "Never certain I'll find a man to trust. Not sure about kids, maybe too time-consuming."

Her eyes still hidden, Pearl shrugged. "So, the rental plan sounds all right?" Then she jumped to her feet, saying, "Let's cool off in the water after all this kind of talk."

"All right, I'm for trying. Certainly can't afford a place on my own." Bea kept the rest of her thoughts silent about living with her sister's man in the house.

* * *

The months of sharing the little house on Green Street were still full of adjustments to work out. Fred was funny but too loud at the dinner table. Pearl complained about Bea's dirty ash trays left everywhere. Pearl was more like Mama with rules for bathroom cleaning, grocery contributions, and meal preparations. Bea hated Pearl's jangly alarm clock and how she stacked things in little piles. Bea declared they would all do their own laundry. Fred said he'd need a lesson in that.

Bea liked Fred's humor and his casual approach to most everything he encountered. From his work visiting farm families, he always had a story about dogs "making me leap a ditch" or farmers "nearly blind to the obvious" when he couldn't reason with them. On Wednesday nights they played poker and drank whiskey when Fred and Bea invited friends over who were fun. Looking at the mix of Fred's ag buddies and jocks and Bea's brooding, sometimes obnoxious girlfriends she met in classes, Pearl said her bank co-workers "wouldn't understand y'all." Bea enjoyed threatening to play a round of strip poker, but Pearl laid down the law. Winking at the rest, Fred always hung a thick arm on Pearl's shoulder and said, "My Pearl is keeping us all out of trouble." Pearl joined in the card game half-heartedly but rarely touched a drink, always reminding them of the hangovers that would result.

***

On a late summer Sunday not long after Pearl and Fred had left for an afternoon drive, Evan appeared at the front door of the Green Street house. His eyes were distant when Bea swung her arms around his neck, pulling his face closer to hers, whispering, "Aren't you the brazen one showing up here." She stood on tiptoe, but his lips barely brushed hers. A prickle shooting up her spine, Bea breathed, "What's wrong?"

His voice became that of the lecturer behind the class podium. "I've taken a new position down on the coast.

We've got to end this." After a hard, messy kiss, he tugged her arms away from his neck. "Let's always keep this our secret. I'll miss you so much. Let's not call for a while. Promise me you'll remember the good times." Was he trying not to make her angry? With the slam of the screen door came an "I'll miss you, baby." Bea collapsed into a flood of tears.

For two days Bea moaned and splashed whiskey over ice. Her golden hair stringy and uncombed, she dabbed at her damp eyes with Evan's handkerchief, burying her nose into the leathery scent of his cologne left behind. Bea moved between her bedroom and the porch swing, soaring in tirades of anger and groveling in fits of despair. She pressed her bare toes against the porch's rough floorboards, pushed back, and lifted them up to keep the porch swing going. Weariness still ached in her bones.

Now the odor of greasy fried chicken wafting through the screen door reminded her of Mama and how she wanted to curl up next to Mama and cry, but she knew she couldn't—and that Mama would probably say it served her right. When Bea looked up from the porch swing, Pearl was standing at the screen door shaking her head. They had argued earlier about Bea skipping work at the campus newspaper the last few days, but now Pearl was offering her baby sister her favorite meal. "I've made you a good supper." Fred held out an icy glass. "I've made you a good drink."

Once Bea sat at the kitchen table with Fred and Pearl, she spooned heaps of potatoes and green beans onto her plate and took big bites from a greasy chicken thigh. Relaxed by the comfort food, she surprised herself at revealing way more about her feelings for Evan than she meant to. She pounded the table in exasperation. "I am so mad that he's gone." Her table mates nodded in agreement. Fred's silver eyes seemed to glitter as he bounced his leg against his chair. Leaning a little too far over her plate, Pearl's mouth dropped open at the number of times Bea bragged about sleeping with Evan, another woman's husband. A drop of moisture slid along her cheek while her eyes danced in delight listening to how Bea found ways to make Evan always wear a condom. Fred made faces during the condom talk and told stories of his buddies refusing to even consider using them. He grinned at Pearl. "You're not worried if you get in a family way, are you?"

Pearl's shoulders stiffened, her face flushing a hot pink. "Not if I have a husband by my side."

Bea turned to Fred. "Well, what do you think of that, Mister Condomless?"

Fred pushed back his chair and ran his eyes between them. "You gals been talking, I see." Then he let the screen door slam, his work boots heavy against the wooden floor until the porch swing's chains groaned with his weight.

Bea sipped her whiskey and lit a cigarette while Pearl picked up the dishes in silence. Fred eventually called them out to the porch swing. "Hey, I'm ready for company." Each sister settled beside him, and he used his strongest push-off foot for the swing to press his thigh closer to Bea. After getting Bea and Pearl to laugh with silly songs and a touch more whiskey for himself and Bea, Fred nudged Bea's head against his shoulder to encourage one last cry over Evan that evening. His other arm occasionally nudged Pearl's neck. "Ouch," Pearl winced. "Morning will come early, and work will be waiting," she reminded them, jumping up from the swing.

***

Now that Evan had left, Bea was distraught the rest of the summer. No words from Pearl or Fred would soothe her for long. She did have to go back to work, though, and roamed the campus and town square following up stories for *The Daily Mississippian*, the school newspaper at which Evan had gained her a reporter's slot before he left. Some stories required a shot of whiskey at The Hideaway when evening fell.

Summer disappeared into the fall semester with few interesting stories under her belt. Bea was due to graduate by the end of the year. She hoped she could finish up her stint at the school newspaper with a memorable scoop. At The Hideaway one night the bartender let it slip that his cousin, Evan, was fired from the university for altering students' transcripts. All the changes were for men who did something illegal for him. Bea's voice shook. "You mean Evan who taught journalism?" The bartender nodded. "They moved the trial to the coast." Turned out that Evan might be the biggest story to report.

Bea ordered whiskey on the rocks and let the bartender light her cigarette. She thought of who else Evan might be, someone in trouble with the law. She had only taken one of his classes. She hoped her grade would not be one of those in question. Would she really investigate this story and expose him in *The Daily Mississippian*? She felt her heart race as she tried to recount her time alone with Evan. She had waited for him so many nights, and he had cancelled many more times than they got together. And were they always having sex in his car? She shuddered and let the whiskey burn her throat. Could the relationship she mourned have meant little to him? Her foolish swooning over him now embarrassed her. She added "Evan – fired" to her list of possible leads in her notebook. She took a long drag and blew a smoke ring.

Fred's voice called out behind her, "Oh, what a smoking talent." He slid onto the barstool next to her and ordered them both a drink.

He has no idea of my talent, Bea thought. She closed her notebook and tucked it in her bag. She was not in the mood for company, tired of thoughtless men, though she could always have one more drink. "Isn't Pearl waiting supper for you?" She tried to add a guilty tone.

"Nope, remember she was going to see your mama this weekend. Keep her from coming down here."

"So let's drink." Bea clinked her glass to his.

"I'm glad I'm good for something," Fred deadpanned.

"Just not in a joking mood, Fred." You men, she thought. You have no idea what I can do.

Fred struck a match for her next cigarette and lit a Camel for himself. After his second drink, he dropped a quarter in the nickelodeon. "Can you dance, Bea?"

"Can you keep up, Fred?" Bea laughed as she slid off the barstool and waved to a couple at the end of the bar. "Come out and join us."

Fred had chosen several lively songs, starting off with Jim Reeves' "Drinking Tequila." Both couples' feet flew across the smooth, wooden dance floor. They laughed and twirled, bumping into each other in the tiny space. Fred whispered jokes about the other couple's clumsy dancing, and they giggled more trying to suppress their silly glances. Between songs they all took quick drinks. Then Fred bought another round.

By the time a slow song began, Bea's moist fingers were slipping into Fred large palms. His warm arm around her waist nudged her closer to him. Watching the other couple steal long kisses as they moved slowly against each other, Bea sniffed Fred's salty cologne, then buried her head against his shoulder, missing Evan's touch. His words on a warm breath touched her ear, "We should go home."

* * *

Early morning sunrays warming her face made Bea open her eyes. She pulled the twisted sheet across her bare breasts and turned her head on the pillow toward Fred. She stretched and inhaled her exhaustion, realizing she'd opened up herself to enjoy her body again, this time with more intensity than she'd ever felt with Evan. She didn't want Fred. She sighed. Thanks to Fred, she now understood she hadn't wanted Evan either, just wanted their sex and how it made her feel.

Fred turned his head. "I felt you looking." He tugged the sheet off her body and smiled. "We're good."

Bea pouted. "We're bad."

"Dammit woman, don't make this complicated." Fred raised up on one elbow, his mouth wide and reverberating the word *complicated*.

Fluttering her eyelids toward him, Bea pushed toward flippancy. "I know, stay in the moment, right? That's what Evan always said."

Fred's eyes bored into hers when he moved closer. "Did you regret hurting Evan's wife?"

Meeting his stare, Bea snapped, "I didn't think about it." Her upper lip moved in and out, but she kept the words to herself. She just wanted to feel wild abandon with him, nothing more for now.

"It's who we are, Bea, no regrets." A thin smile crept under his steady eyes.

She turned away from him, considering that she and Fred could be regretless people. What would that feel like? Then her eyes blinked at the unused condom on the nightstand. She grabbed it, whirling around, and threw it at Fred's face. "You said you'd use it, damn you!"

"Oh, don't blame me. You opened it, then got in a hurry." He tugged the sheet further off her, then wrinkled his brow. "No regrets, remember?"

She pulled the sheet away and ran to the bathroom to wash. Towel wrapped around her, she returned to the bed, saying, "Don't let me give you regrets, Fred. Right now, you promise to marry Pearl by Christmas."

"I've been thinking about asking her."

"I could tell on us."

"No, don't go stirring her up. You know I love her."

"Good, last night didn't change that?"

Fred pursed his lips. "Nawww, honey, nothing's changed. We're just having fun. Let's not get into anything sticky."

Bea nodded. "Right, nothing sticky." She scooped up her slip from beside the bed. Turning her back to Fred, she dropped the towel and let the slip cover her. "You better clean up this room fast."

Bea's Choices

Bells attached to the front door jangled loudly when Bea pushed inside Cory's Hardware store. Running her wrist across her damp forehead, she wondered if she was catching a summer cold or probably worse. Frustrated to be chasing down errands for her mama, she was having second thoughts about having moved back in with her parents after graduating from Ole Miss. A parttime reporter and office lackey position at the *Crosston Gazette* didn't offer much alternative for a least a few months until she could get some rent money saved. It also allowed for too much free time, which her mama was quick to notice.

"Hey, Bea, how's your mama? Hadn't seen you here in a long while," came from a barrel-chested Mr. Cory, the proprietor, always behind the counter, whose teasing about her preoccupation with the gumball machine had lasted for years. Tensing, expecting a rejoinder about chewing gum, Bea gave a little wave and a quick, "She's a little under the weather today." Ducking down the first aisle, she cringed at so quickly being swept back into small town congeniality.

In Oxford she had enjoyed the anonymity of an Ole Miss college student when she entered the shops downtown. She'd loved her independence sharing a house on Green Street with her sister and her fiancée for the summer and fall semester. Now Pearl and Fred had married and moved to a shoddy home on acreage they named Birdsong Farm outside town on Hollyberry Road, which left Bea with only her mama's offer to move back into the childhood bedroom she had once shared with Pearl. What a drag for a twenty-year-old. After all, this was a new time. It was 1957.

Pushing back the blonde curls, Bea scanned the shelves for extension cords. She stopped short, almost losing her balance when a box of paint brushes slid into in her path. A stocky young man with a shock of dark, wavy hair and penetrating, light-brown eyes grabbed up the box. "Sorry, still learning how to stack this stuff." Shifting from one foot to the other, he began a stream of silly excuses, "Who knew paint brushes were different sizes. Cory is a character to work for" and ending with "I'm Leo, had to work somewhere."

Bea laughed as he stammered, enjoying his obvious pretexts to prolong a conversation with her. Finally, she said, "I'm Bea." Noticing a pack of cigarettes in the pocket of his plaid shirt, she said, "Can I bum a cigarette?" A grin slipped across his lips. He pulled the cellophane pack from his pocket and tapped a cigarette loose, offering it to her. Quickly he snapped his lighter for her while she stared at a hint of a moustache above his thick lips, hearing only, ". . . can't take a smoke break. Would you like to hear my band play at the Roadhouse Saturday night?" She took a quick puff and nodded. "If I can make it, we'll have to share a smoke there. Gotta go." Thrilled at his attention but suddenly queasy inside the dusty store, Bea made a quick stop at the register to charge the extension cords to her mama's account, then plopped on the bench on the sidewalk outside to finish Leo's cigarette. She wondered if his brand was stronger than hers. She coughed and her stomach flinched. She wished it was a summer cold.

On the drive home Bea leaned her head against the driver-side window discontentedly, missing the times she used to spend at campus haunts with her quirky friends. In those heated debates over their journalism assignments, she surprised herself with her enthusiasm in pursuit of a story. Her sister Pearl always acted snobbish around her friends, probably just not able to keep up, but Fred was a riot in any crowd.

Today she wasn't ready to go directly home. She didn't want to face her mama's interrogation about who she had seen in town and why Mr. Cory had told her the hardware store would close early for the funeral of a neighbor whose name she'd already forgotten.

In the rear-view mirror, she spied the cookie tin on her back seat. Mama had baked some sweets and instructed her to deliver them to Pearl and Fred yesterday. Bea turned her car onto U.S. 45 Highway, which led to their farm. She resented the increased favoritism Mama showed the married couple. Nothing new, except now Fred had joined the favored mix. Bea tapped the steering wheel, remembering Pearl as a teen, bossy and preening over Mama's praise of her looking after baby sister, "Blonde Bebe," that irksome nickname Pearl had given her. Mama wouldn't listen to Bea tattle that Pearl sometimes locked her in a dark hall closet all afternoon with only a peanut butter sandwich and tattered teddy bear while Pearl and her friends played records to drown out her screams. Bea squirmed against the car seat, considering that Mama would always favor Pearl. She'd even given her the prettier name. "Get over it," she hissed at the windshield.

Staring ahead at the empty roadway, Bea pressed her damp forehead with three fingers as if to stop her runaway memory. She drove on, snapping off an annoying Paul Anka tune Pearl liked with a fast twist of the radio knob. Bea accelerated, pushing the little vent window all the way open so she could feel the sting of the outside air. Pulling her tangled blonde curls from across her eyes, she glanced at the cookie tin again and wanted to hurl it out the window. Mama would ask her about the delivery. She wouldn't stay long at Pearl's. A tickle down her back made her shift against the seat. She *was* curious about their new home, though.

Bea turned on to Hollyberry Road and searched for the obscure driveway to Birdsong Farm. Her little Volkswagen wobbled over scant gravel and muddy ruts up to the house, which appeared weather-beaten by neglect. Bea urged the VW onto the scruffy grass in the front yard and stopped near patches of wild onions and dandelions. She made her way up the rickety steps and set the tin of sweets on the porch, her finger snagging a splinter. "Ouch." She stuck her finger in her mouth to ease the pain before pulling the splinter out.

Pearl kicked open the old screen door and greeted her with a glass of lemonade. "Hurt yourself, baby? Heard ya coming in that noisy little foreign car. Seems like another one that sounds foreign comes by here at night sometimes."

Bea frowned at her sister's observations, pushing out a flip response. "Foreign cars are becoming popular." She glanced at peeling paint on the porch ceiling. "Quite a place, here."

After offering the lemonade, Pearl's eyes dropped.

Mama had let slip that Pearl didn't even have a reliable car to drive to work, sometimes being stuck making last minute calls to a neighbor or Mama. Theirs was a poor life for now. Fred's talk was big.

"Got anything strong to put in that?" Bea held the cool glass straight in front of her while slumping into a plastic folding chair. She let her head fall back into the webbing. "I'm feeling woozy."

"You and Fred always need a doctored drink. It's a good thing he's in the field," Pearl said, taking the glass from Bea's hand. Over her shoulder she shouted, "Are you settling in at the homeplace?"

Was that a sarcastic tone? Bea knew better. Their parents' house would not be home to her for long. When Pearl returned, Bea pointed to the tin. "I'm the delivery gal for Mama's sweets. Be sure to tell her you love them."

Pearl scooped up the tin but didn't open it. "Mama is so thoughtful."

"Uh, huh." Bea bent over fast when a sharp pain pierced her stomach, wishing for sympathy, but never expecting it from her stoic sister. "I've got a bug that only good liquor will cure." She snickered, gladly taking a cool sip from the taller glass Pearl offered her. "Got to hide my fifth of whiskey in my room. Mama's such a Baptist."

"Free rent, don't complain," Pearl said, in her often-prissy tone. "You look sickly, can't be from overwork."

"Going to the doctor tomorrow. I just went to town for Mama, seems she needs one thing from a store every day. I wish I had a full-time job." At once, Bea held up her hand, "But not at the bank with you."

"No way," Pearl agreed. They both laughed.

Bea's idea of a job was tackling a reporting lead and being on her own to meet the challenge, using her wits to gain the facts. She couldn't imagine spending monotonous hours at the bank, but Pearl said she liked the methodical routine behind the comfort of her desk.

Bea took in long, tangy gulps and gazed out toward the road. "Got a big yard to tend."

Pearl shot back, "Fred got a used tractor with a Bush Hog. I'm going to drive it if he doesn't."

Bea raised an eyebrow at Pearl's exasperation that Fred maybe didn't want to keep the yard looking nice. Fred hadn't been raised to appreciate the cultivated flower gardens and trimmed lawns that were in their parents' neighborhood in Crosston. Mama let it slip that she and Daddy didn't think Fred was good enough for Pearl.

Pearl stood up and took the empty glass Bea held out. She returned with a glass of wine and another spiked lemonade. Smiling after a small sip, Bea teased, "I'm gonna tell Mama you're drinking wine."

Tugging at her dark hair, Pearl's lip curled. "Mama won't believe you."

"Never did," Bea whispered under her breath, unable to release childhood hurts. Feeling a tangy lemonade buzz behind her ears, Bea leaned forward, her tongue easy and slow in her mouth. "So how is married life different than when we were all down on Green Street?"

Pearl eyed Bea with a smirk. "Not so many crazy characters dropping in for late night card games."

Bea quipped, "So it's a boring country life?" Bea knew that Fred would tell her more. They talked about most everything when they saw each other without Pearl, which wasn't as often as Bea would have liked now that Fred and Pearl were married.

Pearl nodded uneasily. "I'm keeping my job, maybe try for a promotion. Fred's job at the county ag office and farming this place takes more time than he can manage well, at least for now. I've got simple tastes but decorating on a limited budget makes playing house less fun."

Bea wondered but her tone was not questioning. "But you still like playing house with Fred."

Pearl's blue eyes like Mama's sparkled, then grew dimmer. "He's a lot to handle, but he married me. We should have a baby before long, but sometimes I need to take a break from trying."

Bea winced, surprised at her sister's candor and her own reaction to their marital couplings. She touched her stomach. "Gotta keep him happy." Would a baby be what Fred really wanted? A queasy sympathy for her sister—and for herself—gripped her.

Frowning, Pearl said, "You think you know all about men and their desires."

"Some." Bea let her gray eyes twinkle a minute.

Pearl took a long drink of wine and giggled. "Oh, Bea, you know Fred's always got a lot of plans. We'll fix this place up before we have a family."

Bea cast an eye at the peeling paint and hoped Pearl was right. She wished she wouldn't have to stay too much longer at her parents' home but knew better than to impose in the newlyweds' home. It wasn't Green Street. Bea swallowed hard. Fred was Pearl's husband now. Taking another sip, she looked slyly over her glass. "I met a cute guy down at Cory's Hardware, going to meet him at the Roadhouse this weekend."

Pearl finished her wine and smiled, "You never miss an opportunity to meet a man."

***

Later that week Bea received the news about her condition

from the doctor and was still adjusting to it. Just after dark fell, she waited in her car alongside Hollyberry Road, fidgeting with the lighter until its orange coils singed the end of her cigarette. She took a long drag, but it didn't help settle her nerves. She told herself she knew what to say. The crunch of gravel turned her head, and she saw Fred's silhouette gliding down the long driveway. When he dropped heavily into her passenger seat, the scent of his aftershave drifted toward her. Her body warmed, but she held back when he leaned in for a kiss. She wanted to move further down the road and out into a field road before she let herself go.

"Hurry," he said, running his fingers through her long, blonde curls.

"Anticipation is good for us." Bea laughed when she barely pushed the accelerator to move the VW toward the familiar turnoff.

After the windows were steamed and their first flurry of passion subsided, Fred said, "You weren't hounding me about a condom tonight."

Relieved that he started that topic, she leaned her head onto his shoulder and said, "It doesn't matter. I'm pregnant."

Fred let out a long, "Ohhhh, now what?"

Bea said, "It's yours, but we can never tell Pearl."

"Of course not. I mean . . ."

Bea heard Fred hyperventilating. Feeling a sharp pressure on her shoulders from his palms forcing her away, she knew he wanted her to face him. "Okay, I mean it. Stay with Pearl."

Fred said, "It sounds like you're keeping this baby. I'll pay . . . to get rid . . ."

Bea cut him off, "No, I want something of yours."

"Mine?" His voice trailed off, sounding dubious.

She gasped, stunned at her adamant retort. Then she pressed her face back into his shoulder and released a deep moan. "I'm so sorry . . . for us." Her body shook, no longer able to hold back the sobs. She felt his arms tighten around her back, his fingertips almost piercing her ribs.

He whispered, "I never thought about this . . . this outcome." She listened to broken coughs between his attempts at words that never fully emerged, only the gurgle of his swallowing down breaths.

During the ride back down Hollyberry Road toward the driveway to Birdsong Farm, they were both quiet, interrupting sighs with hand clasps and uneasy shoulder rubs. Fred's tone became firm. "I'm staying with Pearl. That won't change now that you . . ."

Bea nodded, sniffing back anger and acceptance. "I'm mad that this happened. That first night without the condom when you laughed about it, I thought we'd be better. Rushing to be together, neither of us has been paying enough attention."

When Bea stopped the car, Fred said, "I'll do what I can, but you know this was never part of our game."

A shudder ran through Bea. *Game*. The evening air enveloped her when he opened the car door. "I know," she said, but she didn't. She let the car idle in the shadows and watched his silhouette slip in and out of view.

After an anguished sigh, Bea gunned the car and made a fast turn onto U.S. 45 Highway, letting one hand drop from the steering wheel onto her belly. Did she really want his baby but not him? She squeezed her eyes almost shut. Having his baby would make him always feel a tie to her. She wanted that to hold over him.

She slowed the car, not eager to get home, remembering

their first encounter on Green Street last year when Pearl had gone home for the weekend. She and Fred had agreed to continue "having fun" and to have no regrets about "being bad." She was pleased she could attract him, but she didn't want to settle for one man again after learning from Evan not to trust, no matter the passion.

On the slow drive to her parents' house, she pondered the changes. After Fred married her sister, Bea had felt the shift in their affair, trusting Fred less to be with her when he promised. Sometimes, he'd call and with a whisper say, "Gotta finish up the yard. Pearl's nagging me for days. Just got to the phone. Let's plan next week." Instead of their old banter and lewd jokes, he talked more about fixing up the farm, admiring Pearl's homey touch and her good cooking, all in a tone that sparked Bea's jealousy.

What if Pearl never conceived? Bea would always have the child they all would eventually know was his. Bea knew she and Fred had a bond, and she'd have his child, but she wanted someone else too, a man to count on more. That realization surprised her.

***

The next Saturday night the flickering neon sign outside the Roadhouse made her blink. Bea glanced into her rearview mirror for a final smoothing of her hair. Trying to take the edge off her excitement of being out on the town, she stood by her car and took the last drag on her cigarette, then let it drop by her foot and ground the smoldering tip into the parking lot gravel. A chubby man in a plaid shirt caught her eye and held the door open long enough to let out the twang of a country band's lead singer. Ignoring his offer of a drink, Bea let the music lead her straight up to the bandstand where she saw several bandmembers in identical blue silk shirts. One of the men tipped his hat to her when she approached but threw up his hands in disgust when she asked for Leo. "That character is late as usual."

Disappointed, Bea bit her lip and scanned for an empty table near the dance floor. She ordered a whiskey on the rocks to get herself loosened up for the wait. Leaning back in her chair, she lit a fresh cigarette and took long sips of the whiskey while she watched the band members banter and drag electrical cords across the stage. The chubby man in plaid eased into the chair beside her and slid another whisky next to her empty glass. "Didn't want you to get thirsty sitting here all alone." His grin showed a gap between two narrow front teeth, but his smile froze when the table was jostled by a stocky man in a blue shirt wielding a dolly laden with two speakers strapped to it. Bea pushed back quickly from the table, rescuing the fresh drink. Was it Leo? Bea squinted through the dark, smoky air. Chubby took her hand and led her to the dance floor. "Put the drink on a different table and let's get to know each other." Swallowing a stinging blast of whisky, Bea took his damp hand and decided a dance would do her good. When he pulled her close, his beer breath stung her nose. After he stumbled over her feet and the twostep went awry, she couldn't contain a shudder. Missing Fred's easy gait, she dropped Chubby's hand and twirled out of his grip on her waist. "Not tonight," she said, making swift steps toward the restroom sign.

The liquor swirling her vision, Bea leaned against the wall near the restrooms, telling herself she would have a good time because she was not stuck at home with her parents. Feeling a tap on her shoulder, she turned toward the stocky figure beside her. He fumbled to free a cigarette pack from his silky shirt pocket and offered her one, saying, "I'm glad you came to share a smoke."

Startled, Bea responded slowly, "Suuure." Then she stared a little too long at the outstretched pack.

"It's Leo, remember, from the hardware? Would you like to share my table, too?"

"Leo, oh, yes." Taking the cigarette and the light, she inhaled deeply, relieved that he'd shown up. Nerves tingled her neck. Tousling her long hair with a flirty hand, Bea nodded and followed Leo to a table next to the bandstand.

Leo's smile widened and one leg bounced continually, occasionally shaking the table. He talked about fishing with his brother, Kenny T, about his band and songs he was writing. "I'll write one for you." His eyes were liquid when he gazed at her. Enjoying his attention, Bea took little puffs and let herself listen to his exuberance. He bought her a drink and an appetizer, then jumped to the stage to join his band, making silly moves with his guitar and leaning toward her in swoons when it was his turn to sing, "Any place is paradise when I'm with you."

When the band took a break, she and Leo sat out back on a rickety bench and gazed at the stars, Leo pointing out Orion and Cassiopeia, Bea laughing because she only knew the Big Dipper. Hearing the band cranking out "Ready Teddy," they slipped back inside the smoky bar. Leo said, "Can we bebop a little just for fun?" Bea felt his thick fingers gently pull her onto the dance floor. His feet hurried hers as their bodies dipped and swayed and twirled to the beat. Bea gulped back a fit of nausea, then relaxed against his damp, silk shirt when the music urged them into a slow dance. "I like you, Bea," he whispered into her ear. She looked into his dark eyes and smiled, seeing only her reflection. "You're so easy, Leo."

***

Bea dropped by the hardware for a smoke break with Leo more days than not, sometimes stealing a quick kiss that stirred her for more. "Are you working on renting a place?" she'd say, eyes full of expectation. Bea's nausea was a daily occurrence that was getting harder to hide from her mama. One day they walked over to Baldwin's Drug Store and splurged on a grilled cheese sandwich and a milkshake for lunch. Leo's little moustache twitched against the cold liquid and Bea laughed more than she'd done in a long time at Leo's schemes to get rich. "I'll have a surprise before long," he announced.

Leo called every night. Bea dragged the phone down the hall and wound the phone cord into her room and shut the door so her mama wouldn't listen in, especially when she told him, "I'm ready." Laughing, he put her off. "I'm not going to play backseat bingo with you. You are just too special."

The next night when Fred called her for a quick rendezvous, with an urgent, 'I miss you," Bea held her breath, weighing her desire against the affection Leo had shown. She decided not to meet Fred on Hollyberry Road. "Maybe next time," she said, hoping he felt the sting of her rebuff.

Saturday night at the Roadhouse, Leo jumped from the band's stage and pulled Bea to her feet, moving slowly against her for the last dance, his warm breath urging, "I've got a place. Will you spend the night?" Bea had been waiting for his invitation, with dread that she'd forget he wasn't Fred and with anticipation that he would help her lessen her longing for Fred. "Are you ready?" she whispered in his ear. "I'll follow you." He squeezed her hand. "All right then."

Blinking back drowsiness, Bea followed the taillights of Leo's truck down a dirt path off U.S. 45 Highway. The liquor dulled her uneasy thoughts of never being sure about a man when he got you alone. Every Saturday night she told her mama she might spend the night with a girlfriend from the *Gazette*. This night it paid off. At the end of the path, she stopped in a clearing illuminated by a lone porch light from a small trailer, then eased her VW up next to Leo's truck. She stuck her keys under her seat for a quick getaway if needed but told herself, *he's crazy about me.*

In the next few weeks, she let herself start to become crazy about Leo, too. He fixed her simple meals of catfish or venison with beans and cornbread anytime she came out to his trailer. They always enjoyed a little whiskey or some moonshine he had swiped from his brother, Kenny T. She told him about the prizes she wanted to win for expose' reporting. He listened to her read her submissions to the *Gazette*, occasionally riding with her to some late-evening interviews, strumming his guitar in the car while he waited, singing little ditties about her all the way back to town. He sent in some of his songs to record companies every few weeks. He spun tales of the royalty checks he hoped would be coming from Nashville. "I'll buy you whatever you want," he repeated at the end of each conjecture. Before their prizes were won, she figured they could cut a few corners and get by. When the wooziness came over her, she gasped, wondering how much longer she had to keep her pregnancy secret. She still needed to get out of her mama's house.

A month after she had been coming to the trailer regularly, she said over dinner one night, "Would you like to have a family together?" Leo blinked. "Do you mean you're . . . ?" Making a slight nod, Bea let in a long drink of whiskey that burned her throat. She kept her gaze steady as the candle between them flickered in Leo's light brown eyes. She held her breath, not thinking he would hesitate.

"I'll be a daddy." He grinned. Surprised at his delight, she reached for his hand, but he leaned away. Stretching his arm toward a little desk, he pulled open the top drawer. His fingers moved to secure a small box, which he opened and offered her, the tiny diamond atop the ring glittering as it caught the candle flame.

"I've been wondering when to ask you . . . to marry me."

Her eyelashes fluttering back the tears, Bea bit her tongue hard, trying to hold in the shock of his responses. Her stomach twitched, the pain a sharp stab. Relieved that he would be with her when the baby came and that she'd be a married woman to avoid her mama's wrath, she dabbed her cheeks with a napkin. After a long breath, she tried to slip the ring on, then moved it to her pinky and laughed. "Yes, Leo, we're a fit."

Wide-eyed, he said, "I'll make it right."

Courthouse Date

Pregnancy was not anything like Bea had expected. Since it had caught her by surprise, she cursed Fred, the absent father often under her breath. She was bewildered by the morning nausea that slowed down her days. She had never felt such fatigue except from hangovers at Ole Miss or during that winter that she lay on her mama's plastic-covered couch for weeks with the flu. Just when she thought she couldn't drag herself out of bed another morning, she'd spy a single dandelion or other yard weed in a Coke bottle by the bed. She had stayed over at Leo's practically every night since their engagement. One morning Leo left a sketch of three stick figures, two tall, one tiny, holding hands. *Love us, Leo* was printed with big looping Ls below the drawing. Her eyes lingered on the tiny stick figure, and she let herself feel amazed, then uneasy about how this new life would change her and Leo, too.

Everyone thought their relationship was a bad idea, which made Bea and Leo know they had to stick together. Bea hesitated to invite Pearl and Fred to their courthouse marriage. Though Bea called her mama and daddy only the night before, her mama responded, "Late notice won't keep us away. We *are* your parents." After the call, Bea sat on a step outside the trailer blowing smoke rings toward the clouds, worry pinching her eyebrows. Marriage might not be what she was ready for; rules and expectations felt suffocating. When a pain throbbed inside her stomach, she gasped and took a long drag on the cigarette. She didn't know how long she could play house, but she was relieved that Leo was willing, for now.

The next morning rain tapped at their trailer windows. "Rain or shine, you're mine," Leo sang while he strummed his guitar in the living room, waiting on Bea to get ready. Leo wore his blue silk shirt and jeans, even polished his cowboy boots to a high sheen. Patting a constantly-damp forehead with a washcloth, Bea found a lacy peasant blouse and pulled it over a dark jumper, nothing tight. She draped a yellow knit shawl over her shoulder to ward off the chill, though lately her body was mostly burning up. She spied her short, red rubber rain boots, her solution to swollen feet. Leo held an umbrella over Bea and opened the VW door. Once inside the little car, they touched hands, both stunned, saying, "Are we really getting married?"

When they drove up to the Crosston courthouse, they saw Leo's brother and his wife inside the Tompkins' truck. Leo jumped from the VW and held the umbrella for Bea while she struggled from behind the steering wheel. Kenny T had driven over from the mill on his lunch hour in his overalls, a short cap perched on his head. His wife, Edith, still in her hairnet and white kitchen dress, on break from the high school cafeteria, ran up to them with a greeting. "Y'all aren't letting any grass grow under your feet. Why Kenny T took forever to propose and . . ." Kenny T touched Edith's arm and hurried her along the sidewalk. Leo patted his brother's shoulder. "You're my best man."

Bea's parents, in their Sunday church clothes, stood under the portico of the big stone building. "Glad y'all showed up," said her mama, offering a threatening glare. Her daddy squeezed Bea in his arms a little too long, whispering, "My baby girl, grown and getting married."

Hiding behind her parents, her sister Pearl popped into their path and whispered into her ear. "You've been holding out on me." Pearl and Bea kept a long stare until Bea felt Leo's fingers on her back, urging her forward. Bea balked, then stuttered, "Can you . . . will you be my matron of honor?" Eyes fluttering, Pearl's head bobbed while her pursed pink lips let out a quick, "I figured we'd do turnabout since you were mine. I wore your favorite color." Pearl soothed her yellow skirt of soft winter wool, and Bea pressed her lips in a slight smile, touching the arm of Pearl's matching blazer, saying, "Thanks, sister." She glanced around the portico uneasily, hoping Fred would not appear.

Inside the Justice of the Peace's office, a musty smell drifted over them all as they shuffled into the cramped quarters. The JP pulled on a black robe from a hat rack, waving his arms toward little masking tape x's on the floor and shouting directions, "You four upfront, other guests near the wall." Kenny T pointed for Edith to move off the x by Bea and stand with the parents. "I see plans change," Edith muttered. A few inches taller and leaner than his brother, Kenny T stiffened next to Leo and removed his cap, his palm patting down his dark hair. Pearl edged alongside Bea, nervously fingering one bulky earring. The JP's jovial expression flipped on like a light switch as he began, "Now join hands, Leonard and Beatrice." Flinching at these formal names, Leo and Bea smirked. By the time the *I dos* were said, Leo's eyes welled, and Bea squeezed his hand, their expressions moving between serious and silly when they exchanged thin silver bands. Leo wiped his eyes and Bea cleared her throat a few times while they exchanged speedy hugs with everyone before making quick steps through the misty rain to the VW.

"You drive," Bea said, then, "Where are we going?"

Leo made a shy smile. "Elvis' house in Memphis, Tennessee. My buddy in our band knows one of the Jordanaires and sang backup on that new record, "Hound Dog." They'll meet us there."

Bea felt a jolt of excitement she hadn't felt since Leo proposed. "Can we meet Elvis?"

Leo shrugged. "He should be there. We'll just drop in, maybe jam a little."

Bea began to imagine driving past the iron gate and up the long driveway she'd seen in "Photoplay" movie magazine. "Can we stay there?"

Leo flashed a smile, then a frown. "Naw, just grooving awhile."

Bea's shoulders drooped. "After we drive all that way, let's not drive the hundred miles back home tonight."

Leo popped the steering wheel with his palm in delight. "Got us a room at the Holiday Inn, fancy."

Bea leaned over and kissed his ear. "Have you got gas money, too?"

Leo shifted his gaze straight ahead. "I borrowed a little extra from Mr. Cory at the hardware, but he doesn't know it yet."

Bea gulped and straightened in her seat, then giggled, "Let's hope he never knows where it went."

Leo nodded his head. "Okay then. We're celebrating."

He drove along U.S. 72 Highway over small hills as

the road cut through cotton fields and cow pastures, humming little tunes to himself and wondering aloud if Elvis might sing one of his own songs. Bea rested her head against the cool window and listened to the putter of the little VW engine, steeling herself against an occasional wave of nausea. Drifting toward a nap, she closed her eyes and imagined Leo's first royalty check taped to Elvis' front door. Soon she was jolted awake when the little wheels bumped over a railroad track. Leo made a quick left into the Cotton Patch gas station and café. He pulled out a small stash of bills from his pocket and grinned. Bea leaned over for another kiss. Leo's lips met hers with a whisper-soft touch.

Rocky Marriage

The new baby girl came squalling to life late in the summer of 1957. When Bea and Leo brought her home all bound up inside a wicker clothes basket, they took turns shoving a pacifier and a baby bottle full of formula between her tiny pink lips to try to quiet her. The next few months they'd stand sleepily beside the little crib and stare at their creation when her lungs were finally spent and her diaper dry. When Leo ran a forefinger across the infant's tiny hand, he always said, "This little girl is perfect." With tired amazement, Bea had to say, "What did you expect?"

She had no answer herself to unprovoked bursts of crying when she held the baby girl or pounding headaches when she pushed Leo from their bed to attend to the piercing midnight screams from the little crib in the corner. Leo crooned, "Hush little Maggie Lu, don't you cry," cradling the infant in his arms all the way down the hall to the kitchen to heat the nighttime bottles.

"Maggie Lu" rang in her ears. Bea was getting used to it, but she heard her suggestion of Margaret quickly morph into a nickname Leo constantly included in every tune that whirled from his mouth. Bea's first-grade teacher, Miss Margaret, had quieted the mocking classmates who made buzzing bee sounds when roll was called. She'd been kinder to Bea than anyone at home. Leo liked the name, Margaret, and added with a flourish, "Margaret Lucelia. Let's name her for my favorite aunt." Bea watched Leo's eyes brighten, and she smiled to herself. At least her child would have a dignified name when she was grown.

Bea buried her head in her pillow and tried to remember the reporting assignments at the *Gazette* that she was eager to resume in one more week. If she hadn't been part time, she'd have been fired for getting pregnant, but the editor's daughter, Daisy, a former high school classmate, reminded her daddy that he wasn't paying for sick leave anyway. Bea owed her friend for helping her hang on to a meaningful job.

Elated to get out of the trailer a few days a week, Bea took on some human-interest stories around town assigned to her at the *Gazette*. Her first day out she ducked under an arch of honeysuckle and sat on a damp stone bench in Miss Uma Jackson's backyard listening to the wizened woman explain her mixture of red clay, sand, and lime poured into wooden molds she had constructed. Her bruised fingers pointed to rusty hand tools and makeshift platforms with wobbly wheels attached that helped her carefully remove her creations from their molds and move them along her fence line. Bea aimed her camera at several species of oddly formed prehistoric animals, trying to catch the marble eyes gleaming in the sun. "They guard me day and night," Miss Jackson declared. "I'm called to keep creating them, but don't mention in your story that I'm not a Christian." Bea wiggled on the bench and struggled to listen.

When she returned home in the evenings, her head was spinning from attempting to create articles from her interview notes. Leo sat across from her, nodding to her every detail. Then he recounted Maggie Lu's antics, exaggerating that she had caught a ball five times in a row or had sung all the words to "The Old Gray Mare." He talked about schemes too, creating his own tools to sell or mixing herbs into moonshine. He pulled out his notebook with lines of neat, hand-lettered lyrics in poetic form, little dashes and arrows up or down indicating his singing pace. On weekends he was exhausted from late night gigs at the Roadhouse. Bea was restless with motherhood, fascinated yet impatient. Maggie Lu's quick coo of recognition when Bea picked her up almost drew Bea into a dreamy coddling, but a sharp cry from the baby released her from the moment of almost-unnatural tenderness, bringing her back to the chores of attending to diapers and bottles. Bea recalled that her mama's arms had stiffened when a tearful young Bea ran for comfort. A maternal voice stern with warnings still echoed in Bea's ears. She shuddered at the thought of any affection from her mama.

Since Bea returned to the *Gazette*, she had spent the month poring over uninteresting research for her assignments. One afternoon, feeling the tiredness in her shoulders from endless baby chores, Bea twirled a pencil aimlessly over the list of potential interview subjects on her desk. She looked down and saw loopy letters, puzzling out the shapes into *F r e d* over and over. Infatuation came right up from pencil-point doodle on paper, finger to arm to a prickle on her neck. Bea snatched the receiver and dialed Fred at his ag office, the first time since the baby was born. His voice stirred her.

She surprised herself when she went into a flurry, "Maggie Lu has the cutest laugh, and she kicks her legs when she sees the bottle and . . ."

She heard Fred's infrequent "uh huh" growing more distant, sliding away, until he finally cut in with, "I don't want to see her, but I could see you."

Tightness coiled around her words. "Oh, well she doesn't favor you."

Fred's voice stretched into a silky murmur. "But I'd love a favor, honey."

A shiver jolted Bea to the quick. "I guess I thought I wanted to be with you."

Fred persisted with that pouty moan. "You knooow you do."

Pushing against a waning desire for his touch, Bea winced. "You could have called."

Fred exhaled. "Trying to hold out . . . but I miss it . . . miss you." His snigger did not titillate her.

Squeezing her pencil, Bea slashed through his name on her list, repeating, "You miss IT, IT."

His voice tensed. "Don't be like that. We could get together on . . ."

Finally, she cut him off. "Let's put some time between us." Her fingers loosened while the receiver dropped in place. Quickly she swept the list into her bag so she could get away from the office.

Slumping back into the VW on her way to her next assignment, Bea picked up one of Leo's guitar picks from the floor mat, fingering the smooth plastic, letting out a somber, "Leo should be enough." She remembered his smooth twang when he sang to Maggie Lu, when he lulled her into his dreams of finer things. Fred's rough edge was familiar, controllable, but sometimes not enough either.

***

Bea knew to keep Fred at a distance, to pursue what work was at hand at the *Gazette,* and try to be satisfied at home. The next few years Bea and Leo spent cheerful days loading young Maggie Lu in the back seat and riding through neighboring small towns admiring houses with white picket fences. "Just tell me which one you like," Leo promised. "We're making money." Bea wished Leo would find a better job than the one at the hardware, but he assured her he had "other sources" in addition to the gigs he and his band played at the Roadhouse. Catching sight of a swing set, they heard their daughter giggle, so they stopped at the city park to let Maggie Lu play and ate peanut butter sandwiches Leo had packed.

Some evenings Bea needed to research a story, so she left young Maggie Lu with her sister Pearl, who was full of anticipation of baby care. Holding up baby Maggie Lu to Pearl, Bea gazed at the pregnant Pearl, thinking Fred again was the reluctant father. Pearl gave Bea a sly smile, "Oh, you remember how this feels." Bea let out, "Fred's handiwork" before she thought, handing a squirming Maggie Lu into Pearl's arms. "Gotta go. Leo's helping me with leads."

Bea rode with Leo on the backroads to meet bootleggers with tips for Bea's "Crime Watch" column in the *Gazette*. Leo helped identify a few criminal haunts, but then he warned, "I know these are scary guys, can't be too pushy."

Bea laughed. "The bootleggers like to talk about what they do, could slip up." She thought Leo came along because he was thrilled by the stories told by some of the men who were rumored to be part of the Dixie Mafia. "Did you hear the guy talking about that local gas station robbery?" Bea was excited. "I'll get that story out quick."

Leo's voice was panicked. "No, I was driving the getaway car from that robbery."

Eyes narrowing, Bea was angry. "Dammit, you ruined my story."

Leo popped open the glove box and tossed three one hundred-dollar bills onto her lap, grinning. "We're flush, baby."

Thrilled at the newly found assets, she was amazed at his brazen feats. Keeping some details obscure, Bea couldn't resist submitting the robbery story for a front-page expose' in the *Gazette*.

***

When the sheriff's car pulled in front of their trailer a week later, Bea's heart pounded. Pulling on a t-shirt and slippers, Leo cast a worried smile toward Bea. Two officers swamped the small living room.

"Leo Lopez, one of the Dixie Mafia boys has pointed the finger at you for driving that getaway car. Gotta take you in."

The tall, barrel-chested officer tipped his hat to Bea. "Sorry ma'am." He pushed back his hat. "You're that crime reporter?"

Bea nodded, trying to bend her head forward when he said, "Just be careful who you associate with."

Leo's brown eyes moved around the living room and his shoulders sagged. "I thought we had it made."

Bea's stomach lurched when little Maggie Lu ran and grabbed Leo's jeans leg. "Daddy, don't go with that man."

Not looking at Leo, Bea said to the child, "Looks like Daddy's got himself in some trouble."

Leaning down for a kiss, Leo slipped his fingers inside Maggie Lu's tangled curls, seeming to hold on to her.

After the sheriff's prodding, Leo gently pulled her arms from his jeans. "I'll be back, baby girl." Arms flailing, Maggie Lu toppled backward, rolling on her side and let out a long wail.

Bea reached for the child but kept her eyes on Leo. "Guess you didn't think that out." He squinted toward Bea with eyes almost wet with awkward surprise, mouthing, *sorry*. Regret caught in her throat. Maybe she shouldn't have published the story. She wouldn't tell Leo, couldn't show him her true feelings. Fred was so much easier. True feelings didn't mean anything to him.

After Leo left with the sheriff, Bea slid down on the floor next to Maggie Lu, placing a comforting hand on the sobbing child's back and, with her own knees pulled to her chest, rocked against her anger and her frustration at Leo. Then it hit her. She was left alone with Maggie Lu.

***

She had to get Leo back. Pacing up and down the trailer hallway, she finally broke down and called her daddy for help. His brother Hugh had a law office in downtown Crosston. Dreading to face them, Bea drove with Maggie Lu to her parents' home. Mama only had a hug for Maggie Lu, and her greeting at the door was, "I never like dealing with Hugh and now I'm not sure about Leo acting a fool." Barely inside, Bea hugged her daddy, but he pulled away, his eyes fluttering. "So embarrassing." Her parents being reluctant babysitters, Bea glanced around with unease, pulling Maggie Lu into her lap. Finally, Mama waved Maggie Lu toward the kitchen to "get a treat." Daddy said, "I'll get Hugh on the line, but you do the talking." Steeling herself Bea took the phone. "Uncle Hugh, we can't let my husband go to jail.

Leo did drive the getaway car, but the robbery wasn't his idea." She was relieved hearing Hugh's response. "I'll see what I can do."

Because he'd gone to college with the judge, Uncle Hugh managed to gain a first-time offender reduction in Leo's sentence, but Leo was still headed to a central Mississippi corrections unit. The judge's voice was stern. "You are sentenced to serve eleven months." Leo's back hunched. His head dropped and loud gasps gushed out before he turned around with misty eyes and waved *bye* to Bea. Uncle Hugh had warned her there would be incarceration, but his words weren't real until the jolt of the judge's voice pierced her ears. She could only make a tiny wave back to Leo, fingers struggling to unfurl.

After Leo's sentencing, Bea lit out of the courthouse. Fishing a cigarette from her purse, she jay-walked across the empty street, stopping outside the *Gazette* to take a long drag. She'd write Leo's story before the general writer grabbed it. She signed the byline with her maiden name, *Bea Hopkins*. She decided right then to drop Leo's name and change both hers and Maggie Lu's to her family's name. She might as well have Uncle Hugh draw up the request. Leo would have to accept her decision. "We're on our own," she said to the mirror on her desk, flicking back a blonde curl with her finger.

* * *

Bea flung herself out of bed to calm three-year-old Maggie Lu's cries of "more story time" as she had nearly every night for the first few months that Leo was gone. Fatigue gnawing at her shoulders, Bea leaned her head against a brown and white teddy bear near Maggie Lu's pillow and propped *The Cat in the Hat* book on her knees.

Maggie Lu whimpered, "Daddy's gone." Bea tried for a smile and a "not for long" reassurance, but her throat tightened with resentment.

One night, listening for Maggie Lu's breathing to slow into an easy sleep, Bea slipped from beside her. Elbows propped on the Formica kitchen table, silver moonlight pouring onto the cracked linoleum, Bea lit a cigarette and shivered while she re-read Leo's latest scrawled note from prison: *Dear Loved Ones, I met a guy in here who's got a stash buried near a canon out at the old Shiloh battleground park. Hope he tells me more. Miss you both so that it tears at my heart. Love Leo and Daddy.* Bea tapped the ash from her cigarette, letting it fall onto the letter. She watched the burned-out embers drift across the page.

The next morning Bea called Fred from her office at the *Gazette*.

"Long time," he drawled. "I don't know how you sleep with a baby in the house. 'Course Pearl's elated with our little Sunny. That leaves me . . ."

While Bea let his voice prickle her neck again, she had to interrupt. "I'm ready, Fred."

His response was quick. "Me, too. Tomorrow night at sundown."

Bea and Fred stayed too long in Bea's VW parked in the field turnoff near Hollyberry Road. Flashing lights interrupted them, then came a tapping on the car window. Bea pulled a blanket over them.

The sheriff gave a stern look before his lips creased in the corners, "Thought you were teenagers. Best to move along, heard tell of some robberies down the road. I don't reckon you're investigating that though, Mrs. Lopez."

Bea shrank from the *Mrs. Lopez* moniker. She couldn't believe it was that same sheriff who'd come to the trailer months ago to get Leo. When the bright lights disappeared, Fred's laughter kept on until it was irritating. While they struggled to reassemble themselves, Bea let herself laugh as well. She could feel a lightness round out her defiant feelings of needing Fred still. The sheriff had interrupted her rant about wanting more time with him. When she drove him back to the driveway at Birdsong Farm, his kiss was brief, and his reminder calmed her. "We're keeping it fun, remember, nothing sticky."

***

By the time Leo spun into the front yard in a flashy little sports car after serving his eleven-month term, Bea was happy to see him, but wary. She had learned to manage on her own. "How'd you like this baby?" Leo pointed toward the two-seater. "Borrowed it from a buddy." His voice was as eager to please as a truant child. "A little small for us three." She couldn't hold back. Maggie Lu ran past her mama but hesitated until Leo beckoned. "It's Daddy." She inched into Leo's extended arms. He twirled them both round and round until the child's giggles came.

Once inside the trailer, Leo's plans began to spill out. "I know the canon at Shiloh where the stash is. I'll be trading this car quick." She was bowled over by his enthusiasm but warned, "Let's adjust to you being back, take it slow, find a job. I've talked to the owner of the Chevy garage about giving you a try." Leo took his time looking for work and stayed home with Maggie Lu. Bea did enjoy coming home to Leo cooking up spaghetti or grilling burgers outside over a makeshift grate. Within his first week back, Leo eased his way from the couch into their shared bedroom. Bea settled into his familiar embrace and set aside her stirring for more.

After a few weeks Bea asked about work. Leo was distraught. "I couldn't find the Shiloh stash, and the Chevy shop didn't hire me." His brother Kenny T had found some odd jobs for him, but Bea heard that he'd been spotted down in Hatchie bottom fishing more than once after Kenny T called her looking for Leo. Bea's VW was beginning to act up just when she had reporting assignments out of town. She guessed she'd have to find a way to get herself another car, not count on Leo.

One night Leo came home early. The minute he cut his engine, he was hollering, "Is this your truck in my yard, Fred Birdsong?" Bea heard a growling anger as Leo pounded the hood of Fred's truck. Fred emerged from the back door of the trailer. Bea watched both men stalk warily around the yard, Fred with a palm raised, whispering, "Just hold on, Leo, simmer down," until Fred made a quick move into the driver's seat and took off. Leo hurled a rock that bounced off Fred's tailgate.

Inside, Bea could only say, "You're gone a lot. Make some supper." Leo kicked doors down the hallway then returned with Maggie Lu on his shoulders. "We're outside for a while, playing." Bea slammed the door, angry at bad timing and doubting that she knew how to be married to this dreamer who provided for them on the fly. Back inside by sunset, Leo slumped into the couch, promising, "I'll get a job. We'll have money for what you want."

Friction eased up for a while between them. Leo talked Mr. Cory into giving him his old job at the hardware. Pearl was less critical lately, easier to visit now that she had her own child to fill her days. Pearl even offered for Bea to leave Maggie Lu at Birdsong Farm to play with her two-year-old cousin, Sunny, on Saturdays. Bea didn't always tell Pearl that she went out to the Roadhouse on those nights. Leo had rounded up a few of his old band to play some gigs at their former haunt. Bea and Leo smoked cigarettes on his break, and both threw back extra shots of whiskey. They sat out back, leaning into each other, staring up at the constellations Leo loved to name. On Sundays, their hangovers usually kept them in bed until after lunch. Sometimes their intimacy helped change the anxiety, sometimes not. When they picked up Maggie Lu at Birdsong Farm, Bea could usually tell that Leo was on edge, but she couldn't resist trying to draw a few meaningful glances from Fred.

***

Before long the sheriff was at their door. When Bea stood in the opening, she saw disgust in his eyes. "Step aside, Mrs. Lopez. Got to take Leo in for stealing checks from the Chevy dealer and attempting to cash them."

Bea gave an exasperated tug at a curl that sprung out from behind her ear while trying to take in Leo's latest blunder, calling down the hallway, "What a crazy scheme, Leo." She watched Leo slip into Maggie Lu's room, then heard a long bellow from her child. He pulled on his jacket and reached toward Bea. "I just wanted to get you a fine car." The sheriff grabbed his arm. "Not the way to get what you need, fella." Leo's head drooped, a little cowlick jutting from the back of his head as he shuffled toward the squad car. Reaching to smooth it, Bea nodded with a resigned stare.

Rocky Marriage Ends

Leo's jail sentence for forgery was two years, and the time away from him left Bea distant. Uncertainty crept in. Did she still want to be with him anymore? Maybe they could still have some fun at the Roadhouse, take some trips. She'd always have the tantalizing Fred affair. Leo did help with Maggie Lu and maybe still had some exciting ploys—preferably with legal proceeds this time. When Leo returned, he said he was antsy and unsure about a new start. Maggie Lu clung to her mama longer this time before warming to Leo again. Bea made no secret of her affair with Fred. Leo's eyes bulged when declaring, "We three have to stick together."

When they sat outside on the trailer steps, Bea wanted to tell of the articles she was getting published in big city papers. She had taken risks to expose a drug-smuggling gang based in Memphis. Leo no longer listened to her every detail, instead rambling about men who had threatened him in jail and how he learned to find the guys to watch his back. Anger, then fear flushed his face when he told of some embarrassing trades for survival. Bea heard that jail and disappointment had changed Leo's dreams. She was uneasy that he was quieter and had no plan. His moustache was shaggy around a mouth that trembled. "I know you want me to be more, give you more. I didn't even give you our baby girl, but I'm still her daddy."

After a few weeks with Leo at home and no help with a job from Kenny T, Bea told Leo she had begged his friend Roscoe for a job at the Ford dealer. His face ripened to red.

"I was going to ask him. I just needed time. Okay, I'll do it for you."

Leo tried the daily routine working at the Ford garage, but Roscoe just gave him the dirty jobs. He complained to Bea that Roscoe was harder on him than the other workers.

Bea reminded him. "Just got to take it in stride."

He pouted. "Maggie Lu and I get lonely for you on nights when you're out chasing interviews."

Bea glared. "I'm working to get some big stories, making some money."

Leo said, "I'm writing songs, but nobody's listening."

Bea never let up on urging him to "earn decent pay." One evening she turned to see Leo leaning against the kitchen door, having listened to her on the phone promising Roscoe "whatever you want in return" when she thanked him for his favor of a job for Leo. Leo's moustache twitched and his voice shook. "I hate that you're this way, Bea."

Bea heard from Roscoe that Leo started missing work, taking time off to fish, then to camp whole weekends. She called Kenny T, who said, "Roscoe's right about missing work. Leo's been hanging with a skinny loser from high school and a bearded guy he'd met in jail. He's nervous that the jailbird is pushing for some kind of heist for quick cash, but he's feeling desperate. Talking about going fly fishing in Montana with old buddies."

Not long after, Leo stormed into the trailer, announcing,

"Roscoe fired me. Maybe you didn't do him enough favors." Bea whirled around. "Nothing's working for you, Leo. Try another line of work."

* * *

A few weeks later, Bea got a hysterical call from the *Gazette* editor. "Big story, robbery at Ford garage. Found Roscoe dead. Talk to the secretary down there. Go quick."

Upset hit her. Roscoe had loaned her a car occasionally. She'd miss that. She cringed, hoping Leo wasn't involved. He hadn't been home for a few days. This absence was eerie, not like his other casual overnight jaunts with his buddies. Regardless, she wanted that front-page story.

By the time Bea turned her car onto Lee Street, flickering lights atop police cars made her blink. She scanned a small band of people huddled near crime scene tape that was blocking off the Ford Garage. Making a fast turn into a vacant lot, she grabbed her camera. She spotted the Ford Garage secretary at the edge of the crowd, pale faced and bleary eyed. "I've just got to see what happened to Roscoe," Bea said, convincing the shaken woman to slip away from the crowd and unlock a side door that led inside the garage.

When they pushed open the door, Bea gasped. In a pool of oily fluid, two jeans-clad legs at distorted angles were protruding from the narrow space beneath the hydraulic car lift. She lifted her camera and inched halfway around the lift, holding her lips tight against a bubbling throat when she encountered immobile eyes in Roscoe's crushed skull. After two camera shots that caught police attention, she pushed the secretary toward the oncoming officers at the side door and rushed by the tangled group.

She kept a fast pace back down Lee Street, clutching her camera, eventually having to duck into a yard and release the built-up bile. She circled back to her car and crawled inside, shaking and spent.

Later she was in the office typing up her notes and searching for more leads. When she called Kenny T, fear threaded her voice like a net. "I'm more worried than usual."

Kenny T's voice sounded nervous. "I think Leo was in on that robbery. They been talking about fishing in Montana, looking to find a good truck. Those buddies were dragging him down."

Bea's stomach churned. "I can't believe Leo would be a part of killing Roscoe." Her throat caught again, remembering Leo's anger at being fired.

Kenny T groaned. "Me neither. That's just not him, taking a life. Sheriff will be contacting Montana law enforcement. They'll find those guys somewhere, and we'll know then if he really did it."

Every few days Bea found more sources to get details about the investigation into Roscoe's death and the robbery. Eventually she heard that evidence showed Leo was implicated. Bea felt shaky but determined each time she typed up a follow-up of the story for the *Gazette*.

Exhausted from all the speculation about the accident, Bea couldn't believe it when her phone rang at midnight. Leo whispered on the line, "I'm sorry to have taken off like I did. We've stolen a good bit of cash. I'm sure you've heard about it."

Bea tried to shake off her grogginess. "Damn robbery is the talk of the town all right."

Leo's voice sounded giddy. "Me and the guys headed west in this fancy big old truck. I'll stash my share someplace safe and tell you where to meet me in a few weeks."

Bea didn't hold back. "Roscoe's dead. Y'all went too far. Leo, did you do it?"

"Dead?" reverberated into Bea's ear. "Naw, I tied him up to the pole holding the car lift and left him hollering to get loose. We barely twisted his arm."

Bea's voice was wobbly. "The car lift dropped on him, Leo. Fluid leaked out of the hydraulic pole overnight. There was a big car on the lift, so it inched down until it crushed him. Geez, it was a terrible sight." An uncontrollable shudder hit her like the day she had sneaked into the crime scene with the Ford secretary, listening to her spit out her horrific findings, in an instant her own eyes riveted on Roscoe's twisted legs under the car lift. She listened to Leo breathe like he'd run a mile.

Leo sounded ghostly. "Roscoe's dead?"

Bea's voice was firm. "It's true. The secretary found him under the lift."

Leo rambled endlessly until he just stopped. "We didn't mean to . . . Now we've really got to run. Don't know what else to do now."

Bea's voice dropped. "I don't either, Leo."

Leo's voice wilted. "I wasn't scared til now. Bye."

The phone clicked, but Bea let the dial tone beat against her eardrum. She was dazed by what consequences Leo would now face. She imagined his head pressed against the prison van window staring at the gate of the maximum-security prison at Parchman. She imagined his fear. She coughed and grabbed a cigarette.

After not too many days since she had talked to Leo, Bea received the call. "Leo's been extradited from Montana. We're holding him." *He didn't run far enough,* she lamented. Hesitating to face him, she forced herself to schedule a time to see him in the county jail.

Would she have enough time with him to ask for more details for the next installment of her story for the *Gazette*? Wishing for a cigarette while she waited at the jail, she gasped when she caught a glimpse of him. His brown eyes were listless. "I'm back," he said, apathetically. He sat down hard, his moustache bristly above hidden lips when he let out a hoarse declaration. "I failed us. I don't blame you for leaving me now." Bea reached for his hand, surprised at his cold and lethargic touch. An ache for what was lost between them tightened in her chest, then loosened when his hand slipped from hers. He wouldn't be telling her what happened.

***

Bea could barely sit through the trial, knowing this time Leo wouldn't be coming home for a long time. She watched him turn in his seat often, trying to catch her eye. She waved few times, worrying it looked like she was shooing gnats from her face. Even six rows of seats away, she could see his eyes were pinholes of fear when he turned for the last time after he was sentenced to the Mississippi State Penitentiary in Parchman for robbery, theft, and manslaughter. She caught a breath, but it blew past her lips. She covered it like it was a goodbye kiss. Now he was on his own, just like she and Maggie Lu were.

Growing Pains for Maggie Lu

Ten-year-old Maggie Lu heard the front door of the trailer squeak open and click shut. The car motor made an achy whine and then came to life over little pops of gravel in the driveway. Mama had to work late again.

When she was sure Mama was gone, Maggie Lu hung her head off her twin bed so she could glimpse the twinkling stars far up in the dark sky through the small window in her bedroom. She whispered "hello," and like a boomerang inside her, she heard a faint response. Her voices from outside sometimes sounded like her own, but then an owl would hoot to confirm she had been heard. "I'm telling you my secrets," she confided to the largest glittering orb in the sky. She remembered that Aunt Pearl's neighbor, Miss Edith, had given her a notebook to write down all her secret thoughts. No one had time to listen, anyway. She pulled the spiral edge from under her bed. Getting used to the dark was easy. She printed *easy* in small block letters, making a long, droopy tail on the *y*, but then underlined the word *afraid*—afraid of having no parents to come home to after school or after visiting her younger cousin, Sunny, at Birdsong Farm.

***

When Maggie Lu was six, her daddy left a hole in her heart when she watched the big men in dark uniforms lead him to a shiny car with piercing, flashing lights that made her eyes blink hard. Maggie Lu almost quit asking Mama when he would come back because Mama's eyes always flickered in a mean way, like she maybe didn't care when he was coming home. Mama didn't talk about how she missed him anymore either. Maggie Lu couldn't forget the day the house seemed to rock, and Mama started yelling, "He's not coming back." With her yellow curls all frizzed and her eyes big and crazy, Mama rushed through their trailer and snatched up every picture that had her daddy in it. The clattering frames all falling into a Budweiser box, Mama hurled the box outside into the back end of her new Chevy and slammed the trunk lid with a shriek, "He's gone!"

Maggie Lu had perched on the edge of the couch out of her Mama's way, her legs swinging and her palms sweaty watching though the open doorway. Jamming her tongue between her teeth, Maggie Lu kept her thoughts silent about the little black and white picture inside her notebook, her daddy and herself standing in the yard by his truck, his arm hugging her tight, a little grin showing under his moustache. She remembered his thumb tickling her neck while Mama fiddled with the Kodak.

Climbing the steps back into the trailer, all red-faced, Mama plopped down on the couch next to her. Mama crunched up her face with a really sad look and started talking in a strange tone. "Your daddy won't ever be coming home. He got himself killed hunting deer with his buddies over in Marshall County." Mama fell back into the couch, her left fist beating the cushion, repeating, "He's just gone, gone for good, Maggie Lu."

"Nooo," filled Maggie Lu's throat like too much cough medicine. Gagging and sliding onto the floor, she flailed her arms against Mama's legs until exhausted whimpers mesmerized her. He would never be really gone. Always when she looked out at the stars, she'd hear him on the wind, maybe feel a tickle on her neck.

* * *

Now Mama rapped on Maggie Lu's bedroom door usually on Sunday evenings at least once a month, announcing, "Get your stuff together. You're going to Aunt Pearl's." When ten-year-old Maggie Lu dropped her head, Mama's "Don't sass" came back fast. Maggie Lu always missed her own room when she was at Aunt Pearl's since she had to share one there with Sunny. To cheer herself while she scrambled to pack, Maggie Lu imagined the smell of Aunt Pearl's cornbread and the wild runs she and Sunny would make around the big yard at Birdsong Farm. Maggie Lu stuffed her paisley suitcase with school clothes and her secret notebook. She slung her book satchel over her shoulder and scrambled into the back seat of Mama's car next to boxes of file folders, empty cigarette cartons littering the floor. Mama chattered, "Glad I got rid of the VW. A Chevy is so much better. I'm following a story in Jackson. Gotta have something reliable to drive down there. This could be my big break."

In the back seat, Maggie Lu swayed when Mama made a fast turn up the long driveway to Birdsong Farm.

The porch light showed Uncle Fred's silhouette at the edge of the shrubs about halfway up the driveway. He waved their car to a stop. His head bent toward Mama's, a hint of hair oil and Listerine drifting inside the car.

"Bea, heard you were bringing the girl. Gonna be gone long?"

Mama was silly talking. "Will you miss me?"

Maggie Lu waved but was embarrassed by the feel of their funny talk.

Uncle Fred tapped on her window. "Run on up to the house, girl. Sunny's waiting on you."

Mama turned in her seat without offering a goodbye glance. "Go on. I'll call you in a few days."

A surge of liberation from the adult banter helping her push open the car door, Maggie Lu grabbed her satchel and little suitcase and ran up the gravel driveway. Out the back door, Sunny shouted "Wait for me." Dropping her bags in the carport didn't stop Maggie Lu's legs from propelling her out toward the open field. She wished she could run across the wide expanse to the edge of the sky where the clouds touched the earth at sunset.

Sunny caught up to her, panting. "Is your mama staying for supper?"

Maggie Lu kept her eyes on the last orange ray slipping behind the cloud. "I'm not sure where she's staying."

Maggie Lu's Teen Years

The summer before her fifteenth birthday, Maggie Lu started begging her mama to teach her to drive. "Can't risk you tearing up my Chevy," Bea responded too many times.

The next time she went to Birdsong Farm, Maggie Lu asked her aunt. Eyes narrowing into a daunting look, Aunt Pearl said, "Let me think about it. I guess your mama said no."

Maggie Lu's voice rose. "She's worried about her car. If you teach me, I'll help work in the garden the rest of the summer."

Aunt Pearl groaned. "She's got her worries all right." Then a little quiver showed at the edge of her aunt's mouth, flashing a glimmer of her eye tooth.

After Maggie Lu and Sunny had gone upstairs to their bedroom, raised voices floated up the stairway.

"Maggie Lu can't drive," came from Uncle Fred.

"The girl needs instruction her mama won't give," came from Aunt Pearl. "Somedays I wonder how much we've taken on with that girl."

Feeling anxious, Maggie Lu turned up the clock radio to listen to the Beatles. Sunny said, "Let's dance."

A few days later Aunt Pearl said after breakfast, "Let's try this." She opened the driver's door and let Maggie Lu behind the steering wheel of her Ford sedan and handed her the ignition key. Aunt Pearl offered a stern warning from the passenger seat. "Drive slow and don't kill me." With a few days of jolts, awkward turns, some loud engine whines, a tire stuck in the mud, Maggie Lu's "I'm trying" and Aunt Pearl's "Watch out," they struggled together to keep their tempers.

After a few lessons, Maggie Lu made endless trips up and down the long driveway most every day in August. She let the wheel twirl in her hand, pushed the accelerator hard for a minute and then stomped the brake after Sunny jumped into the passenger seat some days, squealing and poking fun.

"Two more years and it's my turn," Sunny repeated almost daily. "Daddy says I can drive his old truck."

Maggie Lu retorted, "Aunt Pearl says I might get a car for graduation."

Sunny laughed. "That's a hundred years from now."

***

Maggie Lu never knew what to do when Mama started pacing and speculating crazy ideas like wishing she could fly to New York City and win a journalism award. "That series on the Dixie Mafia should have gotten some attention." Then Mama got the full-time job with the *Clarion-Ledger* in Jackson, and she panicked. "Harder assignments. More people will read my columns. They've got to be good." They sat together outside on the trailer steps, Mama lighting up each cigarette from the previous stub. Maggie Lu barely sipped her Coke, the fizz burning her throat like her Mama's new job declaration.

"A reporter in Jackson will rent me a room so we've got to figure out your school."

Maggie Lu leaned back and pulled her knees against her. "I don't want to go to Jackson."

"Birdsong Farm then." Mama pursed her lips.

Maggie Lu pressed a thumb to her mouth, baby style. "Maybe."

Mama stubbed out the half-smoked cigarette and called Pearl. "This job is my big break. Can you take Maggie Lu, just for a few months till I get adjusted?"

Mama made some short gulps, holding out the receiver for Maggie Lu to hear Pearl catching her breath. "Well, that's news. Hold on." They listened to Pearl's and Fred's muffled voices. Pearl's tone cracked. "It would be nice to have two children in the house again. Losing baby Sonny . . ." Fred's voice bounded across the line. "Bea, we'll take her." Pearl finally said. "Better check on BHS."

Running inside, Maggie Lu threw herself onto the sofa. "I'll have to transfer to Bessieville High? My friends are at Crosston High. I was going to be on the debate team. Can't I keep riding the bus to town?"

Bea's face knotted into its few well-worn wrinkles. "Jeez, I hadn't thought of that being a big deal. Aunt Pearl can't keep up with you going into town for school."

Groaning, Maggie Lu couldn't imagine her life at Bessieville High.

* * *

Maggie Lu hated climbing on the school bus to Bessieville High with Sunny. "This is my older cousin. She lives with us," Sunny told kids, who mostly glanced over their shoulder for a good stare and resumed their own conversations. Maggie Lu dipped her head and stared out the window at the dusty, red clay roads leading through cotton and corn fields, pangs of anger and apprehension crowding her throat. She barely glanced up at some "country" kids gripping paper lunch sacks and shuffling along the aisle smelling of feed lots and sweat.

To get out of chores at Birdsong Farm and ride the bus less often, she wanted to join the basketball team because of after school practices. She told Aunt Pearl the teachers didn't know her, and the classes were boring with kids who acted crazy calling her "Maggie Lulu." Aunt Pearl's eyebrows knitted into a worry line. Maggie Lu pouted. "I just need a ride home till I know someone with a car." Aunt Pearl agreed. "Okay, I'll pick you up on my way from work at the bank . . . for a while."

The best part of being on the girls' basketball team was that the girls' and the boys' teams both rode on the same bus to out-of-town games. Riding back at night, cheers and chants and chatter filled the bus, making it easy for Maggie Lu and her new friend Inez to sneak to the back of the bus, singing with the Adair boys and sometimes stealing a kiss from those not too shy.

At the next out-of-town game, Maggie Lu and Inez sat in the gym bleachers watching the BHS boys team play the Water Valley Blue Devils. Maggie Lu couldn't take her eyes off a tall, blonde boy with a button nose. He trotted gracefully up and down the court, lobbing hook shots over the reach of the struggling BHS guard.

Inez slapped Maggie Lu's hand. "You can't clap for the other side."

Maggie Lu grinned. "He's cute." She grabbed the program and pointed to number 42. "His name is Karl Dees."

Inez feigned shock. "I dare you to go say hi."

Maggie Lu's eyes danced. "I'll show you."

With only fifty seconds left on the time clock, Maggie Lu bounded out of the bleachers and waited down by a door adjacent to the ball court. When the final buzzer sounded, she ran onto the court, waving at the BHS boys but chasing after number 42. She tugged at Karl's damp jersey, and he whirled around, his fierce gray eyes quickly softening.

"Who are . . . Uh, hi."

"Hi. Good game. I'm Maggie Lu. See you next week when you play in Bessieville."

His gray eyes fluttering, Karl stared down at her satin uniform. "You're on their girls' team." Then he beamed. "Sure thing. I'll look for you."

Maggie Lu fell into the bus seat next to Inez and chattered all the way home about what Karl must be like. She wasn't sure why she wanted to know him, but she was thrilled that he had smiled at her. He might really look for her at the next game.

Inez ventured, "Maybe he has a friend."

Maggie Lu elbowed Inez. "A girlfriend? You're mean."

Inez laughed. "No, a friend for me, silly."

At the next game in Bessieville, Maggie Lu heard a loud whistle when the BHS girls hit the court for warmups. She waved up into the bleachers toward the Water Valley boys' team all clustered together. Karl stood up and waved back, just when Maggie Lu missed catching a pass. She had to stay focused.

After the girls' game, Karl waved her over. "Meet me at our travel bus."

Maggie Lu was antsy throughout the boys' game, cheering for Karl too loudly whenever he scored points for Water Valley. She earned frowns from the Bessieville fans nearby. Inez shushed her a few times, eventually giving up.

His damp hair glistening, Karl ran up to Maggie Lu

outside by the Water Valley bus, saying, "What grade are you in? Can you date?" He shifted his gym bag from one hand to the other.

The word *date* sounded scary, grown up. She looked up into his anxious eyes, caught under the streetlight. "I guess so. I'm a junior."

Her breathing sped up when he asked for her phone number, pulling a scrap game ticket from his jacket pocket and fumbling in his bag for a pencil. Her fingers lingered on his warm palm after she wrote on the scrap and handed him her number. "I don't know what to say."

Karl ducked his head closer to hers. "Me neither, but we'll talk, okay?"

On the ride home, Maggie Lu announced to Aunt Pearl, "I like a boy from Water Valley. Can I date him? Can he call me?"

Aunt Pearl's head swung toward her. "What do you know about dating?"

Maggie Lu answered slowly. "Just what Inez and the girls say, going to the drive-in and stuff."

Aunt Pearl sighed. "Who is this boy? Why all the way from Water Valley? I need to meet him."

"He seems different. He doesn't know anything about me like the boys here."

"You've never been boy crazy like your mama, so just take it slow, get to be friends."

Ducking her head, Maggie Lu cringed at talk of her mama and men. "I know, Aunt Pearl."

***

When Karl first called Maggie Lu, she was reassured to hear that he was new to dating, too. He had to spend extra time helping his relatives at their nursery and hardware store. On the phone Karl acted silly, yelling at his twin, Karleen, and then his voice seemed quiet with understanding when Maggie Lu talked to him about living with her mama's sister's family. She surprised herself, admitting, "Mama is too busy to be home. That makes me feel weird." After a few weeks of regular phone chats, Maggie Lu looked forward to her first date with Karl.

When the shiny car turned toward Birdsong Farm, Maggie Lu peeked out the bedroom window. His friend Raymond was riding shotgun when Karl parked his uncle's Ford Galaxie in the driveway. Edgy, Maggie Lu ran downstairs into the living room. Sunny peeked around the corner, giggling. Aunt Pearl motioned Karl in through the front door and offered a glass of lemonade. He sat on the edge of a wingback chair, clutching the glass, but rose quickly when Uncle Fred stuck his head in.

"Well, a young fella after our Maggie Lu. Might have known something would happen at those basketball games."

Karl gulped. "A date, yes sir."

Maggie Lu interrupted. "He's my new friend."

Signaling her husband back into the kitchen with a toss of her head, Aunt Pearl said, "Fred don't say anything ugly to these young people."

Waving a palm to erase the embarrassment, Maggie Lu hurried Karl out the front door. "Going skating, bye."

On the drive to pick up Inez for their double date, Maggie Lu sat between Karl and Raymond, a flurry of independence surging like lightning inside her, way more exciting than driving with Sunny to the store on U.S. 45 Highway. Leaning to adjust the radio, Raymond brushed her knee and a warmth tingled down Maggie Lu's leg. The radio was cranked high. Karl raised his voice like Roger Miller and grinned at Raymond sticking his head out the window to sing a few lines from "Walking in the Sunshine." Maggie Lu smiled, tilting into the warmth of Karl's shoulder.

At the skating rink, with country tunes blaring overhead, Maggie Lu and Inez wobbled around slowly in their laced-up white rental skates, learning their footing, giggling and bumping into each other. Soon Raymond edged in close to Inez and they skated off alone, Inez looking over her shoulder with fluttering eyes. Karl skated backwards in front of Maggie Lu, slowly reaching his hands out to guide her, their eyes dancing while their feet struggled. By evening, with Karl's arm around her waist, Maggie Lu was leaning into the turns. Their bodies were damp from endless trips around the rink and their voices harmonized with duos by Loretta Lynn and Conway Twitty. She wondered if she had ever been so happy.

When the phone rang the next evening, Maggie Lu begged to answer it but was startled. "Well, you're answering now instead of the adults, making yourself right at home."

Maggie Lu's fingers tightened around the phone. "Hi, Mama." She braced for what was to come. "I'm back in Crosston staying at the trailer for a while. I was given the north Mississippi territory to report on." Maggie Lu's shoulders drooped, apprehensive that Mama might make her stay longer at the trailer. "Come over after school Friday to help me clean this place." Was cleaning all she wanted? Maggie Lu felt her stomach knot and was relieved to hear the phone finally click in her ear.

Birdsong Farm wasn't really home either, but Aunt

Pearl had welcomed her and was calmer, more reassuring. "We'll work it out," she often said, even when Uncle Fred gave Maggie Lu a harsh tone, never satisfied with how her chores got done. Now her mind raced with anxiety. Would Uncle Fred make her go home?

Hearing Aunt Pearl humming to the radio, Maggie Lu eased into the kitchen. "Mama's home for a while, new assignment. I'd really like to stay here . . ."

Dropping her paring knife with a quick wave of her hand, Aunt Pearl said, "And we want you here, honey. No telling how long Bea will stay put."

With a burst of grateful relief, Maggie Lu flung her arms around Aunt Pearl, their fluttering wet eyes surprising each other. Turning toward the window over the sink, they both watched Sunny emptying food in a pan for the prancing hound, Spot. Sharing a room with Sunny was better than being alone in the trailer with her mama.

Friday, Aunt Pearl let Maggie Lu borrow the Ford to drive to the trailer. After a brief hug from Mama, Maggie Lu sat on the edge of the old couch. Talking to her mama was like treading water, struggling to keep bobbing while Mama complained about her long hours on the job. Mama handed her a bottle of Coke and plopped in a kitchen chair, taking a long swig from a bottle of Budweiser beer. "What's going on with you?"

When Maggie Lu recounted her school projects, Mama clucked at any grade not an A. Mama's eyes took on a strange glint when she asked about her life on the farm, her tone eerie. "Is Uncle Fred treating you like one of his own?" Afraid to tell about her wariness of him, Maggie Lu only nodded. Yet when Maggie Lu mentioned Karl, her stomach tightened at Mama's response. "Well, bring that fella over. I want to see if you've got good taste."

The next weekend, Karl and Maggie Lu drove up to the trailer. Mama, in jeans shorts and a formfitting halter top, was hunched on the front steps, clutching a Budweiser bottle, a thin stream of smoke rising from the cigarette perched on the edge of a step. Wincing, Maggie Lu pushed open the car door. Karl followed her into the yard. Mama rose, staggered a little, and reached out her arm for a hug. Maggie Lu patted her arm down and introduced Karl, who nodded with a little half bow. "Pleased to meetcha."

Mama fluffed her curls with a flirty flick of the wrist and leaned back with a long gaze at Karl. Resuming her seat on the step near her cigarette, Mama crossed her legs, sandal dangling from a bare foot. "Likewise, son."

Perturbed, Maggie Lu glanced up at Karl, who raised questioning eyebrows.

"Tell Karl about your work, Mama."

Mama shifted her gaze to Maggie Lu, "Oh, this handsome boy has probably read my columns."

Maggie Lu feigned a glance at her imaginary watch. "We better go."

Mama reached for the cigarette on the steps and took a long drag, then pointed it toward Karl. "Take care of my girl. Make time for a little visit before long, you hear?"

Maggie Lu sunk into the car seat, her fingers pressing against her face. "I'm so embarrassed."

Karl patted her knee. "Your mama is a little scary, tries to act young, not like most other mamas I've met. Now I understand. It's better for you at Birdsong Farm."

***

Maggie Lu found Karl to be her joy and her rock the last years of high school. Little glimpses of the delight she'd felt as a child riding with her daddy would flare when Karl gave her a knowing glance. If they weren't cruising the streets of downtown Crosston, waving to friends, they went to a drive-in movie. A few times Karl pulled out a pint of moonshine from beneath the car seat, and they mixed it with sodas and scared themselves when his hands slid under her blouse, and she waited sometimes too long to push them away. Later she wondered how close she should let herself get to Karl.

For special occasions they drove the hundred miles to Memphis to see the Rolling Stones and country stars in concerts, singing until they were high on the music on the late-night return to Birdsong Farm. Sometimes Karl slept on the couch, but he often slipped out early just as Maggie Lu was coming down from her room. He tried to avoid Uncle Fred's taunting. "A country boy like you hardly deserves a good looker like Maggie Lu." Later Maggie Lu would remind him, "Just pretend Uncle Fred's joking around." Karl would respond. "He's odd."

During their senior year they confided their dreams and their secrets. Karl talked of marriage and each of them having jobs in Water Valley at the hardware and nursery that he and his sister would inherit. He would say, "We'll be on our own soon, and we'll have each other." Maggie Lu told him of her struggle to feel close to her mama and how she felt a hole in her heart since her daddy had died, clinging to a few sweet memories. Though Maggie Lu was uneasy about Karl's plans after graduation, she melted into intimacy with him while struggling with the depth of her longing for independence and understanding.

By the end of their senior year, Maggie Lu had gained scholarships to several colleges. When she chose to go to

Pennsylvania, Karl was confused. "Why would you go so far from me?" Maggie Lu tried to face his flickering gray eyes. "I have a chance to learn how it feels to be on my own and go to a great school, meet people from no-telling-where." Maggie Lu knew he was not hearing her need for exploring a life beyond Mississippi or accepting her rejection of marriage and work in Water Valley. She tugged at the silver bracelet with engravings of frolicking animals he had given her at prom. Biting words sprang from her mouth. "You cannot be everything to me anymore. We're growing up, probably apart."

***

When Maggie Lu arrived in Pennsylvania, the first few months she was lonely, no Sunny to throw a pillow and wake her in the morning. Instead, her dorm roommate slept in, left her messy clothes everywhere, and hung out with girls down the hallway. She was surprised at missing Aunt Pearl's home cooking and Karl's warm embraces. She felt out of place around big-city kids with smug attitudes and sharp accents. She was not used to such demanding professors who barely knew her name. Her heart skipped a beat when Karl drove up unexpectedly for the weekend near Thanksgiving to beg her to come back and attend Ole Miss. His touch was so welcoming that she spent the whole weekend holding on to him.

A week after Karl went back home, Maggie Lu's confidence lifted by their familiar talk, she started exploring the campus and hanging out after late classes in the rec hall, realizing she was settling into her independent life. The vision of a life with Karl in Water Valley seemed even more improbable. She didn't return many of his phone calls, since they were now having more arguments. He wasn't content to be just her friend.

After Christmas, she discovered the birth control pills had failed, she'd forgotten to take them only once, and now she was pregnant. Her longing for a new college-educated life wavered because of her own weakness. She felt sick to her core. Walking out of the doctor's office, she slipped into a pay phone booth and hesitated to call her mama, but facing Aunt Pearl would be worse. Maggie Lu shuddered at the embarrassment of letting her down after Aunt Pearl had taken her into her home.

"Oh, I can tell you're worried." Mama sounded hurried. "I know all about bad timing. I got no money for an abortion. He'd marry you, right?"

"None of those options make me feel better, Mama. Couldn't you come up for the weekend, help me think this out?" She avoided saying she had no mothering skills, that birthing a child who might grow up to feel as homeless and unloved as she had was unbearable.

Maggie Lu heard the flick of a cigarette lighter and the long exhale on the other end of the line before Mama said, "My schedule's a little tight, got an editor breathing down my neck to wind up this series of investigations. Have you talked to Karl?"

Maggie Lu ran exasperated fingers through tangled hair, enduring the little tingles of pain. "I don't want to tell Karl and have to . . ." Her voice was breaking up . . . "move to Water Valley and tend his hardware store."

Maggie Lu listened to her mama's incessant tapping of a pencil, maybe. Finally, Mama said, "Should I call Fred? Probably more decisive than Pearl."

Pounding the back of her head against the phone booth, Maggie Lu shouted, "No, never!" She flinched at the shame she would feel if Aunt Pearl knew. "Uncle Fred is the last person I would call. You're not listening to me. I'm sorry I ever called you."

"Well, girl, I was just thinking..."

Maggie Lu slammed the phone hard to stop her mama's voice. She pushed herself out of the tiny phone booth into the gray winter air, damp cheeks tingling. Her fingers plunged into her coat pockets, grasping at tissues and the stiff medical report folded inside. Glancing back at the phone booth, she knew there was no one else to call, not now. Legs wobbly, she needed to get back to her room. Habit forced each step forward, and panic walked her all the way back to the dorm.

Early Thoughts of Baby

Pearl Birdsong had never felt so elated and so terrified in her entire life when she received her niece's phone call. She wanted Maggie Lu to have that baby. Her daughter Sunny probably wasn't going to give her any grandchildren since she constantly announced that animals were always going to be her only kin, so this was the closest she was going to get.

"Aunt Pearl, I can't believe the birth control pills didn't work. I need an abortion quick." Maggie Lu's voice rose, anxious on a crackly phone line. Since being away from Mississippi, her cadence was taking on an edge.

"Abortion is a callous word, honey, life changing."

"Well, a baby would take up my whole life. My God, what have I done? What can I do?"

"Lord, abortions are dangerous. They haven't been legal long. Probably expensive."

"I've heard." Maggie Lu's voice dipped. "What can I do now?"

Aunt Pearl's tone was piercing. "How could you bring shame to this family? I'll take care of this."

"I'm sorry to cause you more heartache." Pearl heard more emphasis on *ache* than *heart*. Maggie Lu's voice sped up, disorienting her. "Karl is so confused, dazed really, but won't help. I'm pretty far along, didn't believe the symptoms. All of this is taking a lot out of me. I want to finish college."

"Karl Dees drove all the way up to Pennsylvania to see you? Dammit."

"I was lonely before the holidays. It's not like it's our first go, crazy. The damn defective pills. Mama says she has no money to loan me before summer, and then it's too late."

"I'm not surprised at Bea. Due in lat in the summer? Hmmm."

Maggie Lu's breath came in short bursts. "I'm on my own, Aunt Pearl, being so far from home. My roommate is freaking. Sometimes I feel locked in my room alone." Pearl detected an unfamiliar rasp.

Her own voice picked up once she'd decided. "I'll come up there and stay with you this summer till you have it."

"I dunno. What will I do with a baby?" Maggie Lu exploded. "Geeze, this wasn't part of the plan." Pearl heard pounding, like a fist punishing a table. Her niece began to wheeze, then exhaled a steady, long breath. "Gotta get through this one way or another."

"What if I raised the baby?" Pearl turned quickly and gazed on her wall at a black-and-white picture of her daughter Sunny propped up in her lap, wearing a tiny organdy gown. Then her eyes lingered on the wooden frame enclosing her lost young son, Sonny, standing next to her husband, both in plaid flannel shirts. A thin smile touched her lips.

"Yikes, you've raised too many of us already. I won't put you through more misery."

"What? I hope you never thought I was miserable

when you stayed with us. Kids are a joyful challenge. Your mama missed out on our good times."

"Being on the farm with you and Sunny, that was the best time in my life, right, Aunt Pearl? On this campus, I'm not the same as at home. The professors see me, kids at the rec hall, we talk about all we're learning, cool stuff. I don't want to lose that and have a baby now."

Pearl held firm. "Some ideas will gel. Give me time to think tonight."

"Hurry, and I'll call back tomorrow."

***

Pearl was weeding her flower bed when she caught sight of her husband puttering into the yard. Fred Birdsong's green tractor sputtered into the barn and then quit. He jumped from the seat, started to jog, but said, "Just can't jog anymore, hurts my back," and turned to give the tire a kick. Spot, the red-and-white bird dog, raised her big head from her nestling place in the corner, her floppy ears attempting to perk up.

"What you looking at, Spot?"

The dog eased up from the mashed down straw and walked with her head down toward Fred's calloused hand. He gave her a pat on her long back, causing her stick tail to speed up the wag.

Fred looked down at his shirt half stuffed into his overalls. Pearl's eyes were quick, watching his hands jerk down to button his fly. Mildred Adair's sister had alerted Pearl by phone that Fred had been over on Dumas Road visiting Mildred's little yellow cottage. She'd heard he couldn't get enough of Mildred Adair. Mildred's sister showed up and rang the doorbell way too long before Mildred came to the door.

The sister's voice had boomed across the phone line. "You won't believe what I heard down at Dees Nursery and Hardware Store." When Mildred swung open the door, her sister saw that she was still clutching her bathrobe around her. She saw Fred closing the back door without a clatter and jogging unevenly across Mildred's back yard.

Pearl just said, "Okay, I might have known," and hung up.

Fred bent down and hugged Spot around the neck. "You're my best girl, always loyal." The dog squirmed backwards and shook her floppy ears.

The sputtering of that tractor coming up through the field still echoed in Pearl's ears. "Tractor's running pretty hot," she couldn't resist saying. "How far you been today?" She wanted him to know the gossip phone line was active, but it didn't help her hurt feelings.

She missed the days when Fred plunked his straw hat on the table in the middle of the kids' homework, announcing a newborn animal in the barn, giving the kids and her an excuse to rush outside into the sweet-scented hay loft or paddock.

Pearl glared at Fred. "Go clean up for supper."

Awhile later Pearl set a big plate of fried chicken on the checked tablecloth in front of Fred. "Wouldn't it be fun if we had some grandchildren sitting around this table?"

"Sunny's barely out of high school. Don't rush things."

"You never change." Pearl looked disgusted. "She *is* engaged to Hamilton."

"Sunny's taking those pills, right?" Fred glanced up at Pearl. "It's just dogs that she wants for kids, the last I heard."

"Yes, I'm just dreaming." Pearl gulped at the thought of failing pills for Sunny too.

"Expensive and rash dreams." Fred took a long drink of iced tea.

Pearl barely gnawed her chicken leg, just pushed the butter beans around until the bottom of the cornbread sliver was soggy and disintegrating on her plate. Fred piled another chicken breast on his plate.

He said, "Why you not hungry?"

Pearl leaned across the table and touched his hand. When his hand carried hers toward the serving spoon, she revised her thoughts. "Maggie Lu's having a difficult time up in Pennsylvania."

Fred sat up in his chair, his silver eyes piercing her. "She's never had to work hard before; she'll learn to buckle down. You can't take her woes to heart."

"I might go up for a visit in a few months. She can't count on her own mama. Bea always puts herself first."

Fred clutched the chicken breast as it slid in his fingers to rest precariously on his plate. "How long you be away?" Fred blurted out. Pearl winced. He opened his mouth to take a bite, then reminded her, "You know Bea's got that career she can't lose sight of." Pearl drew in a breath to stifle the painful memory of discovering Fred's past rendezvous with Bea. His silver eyes took on a strange sparkle. "Maggie Lu's problems and you talking about that baby thing. I just thought . . . maybe."

"What?" Pearl looked at him intently.

"I'll bet something will turn up. Never mind." He got a strong hold on the meat, gnawed a couple big bites, and dropped the bone, then hurriedly cleaned his plate with the last bite of cornbread, popped it in his mouth and stood up. "Enough about that family, but I'm sure you're gonna go."

Pearl narrowed her eyes while he moved toward the

living room, adjusting tightness in his overalls, an expression pulling at his lips. Sometimes Pearl just ignored what folks told her about Fred. She didn't think about what she could do to make him turn his head back her way anymore. Instead, she weeded, went out to the hen house, called Sunny or Maggie Lu or drove over to the cemetery to talk to her dead son.

***

She made several long weekend trips to Pennsylvania to comfort Maggie Lu during the pregnancy. In midspring she convinced Maggie Lu to contact Inez. Her old friend was bored at Ole Miss and decided to transfer to the university in Pennsylvania and even agreed to help Pearl move Maggie Lu into an apartment. On each of Pearl's trips, Maggie Lu grew larger, but acted more distant, poring over her studies, even taking on a tutoring job for extra money. She told friends she and Karl had eloped.

"Why'd you go and do that?" Pearl hated lying, even to save face, though she suspected there would be more of it to come, maybe from both of them.

"Aunt Pearl, it's just easier to say you've got a man. I know I need your help, but this is all getting too tough. I wish I never agreed to having this child. It's making me crazy. With all this kicking, this baby is probably feeling crazy, too."

Pearl patted her shoulder and took Maggie Lu's clothes to the laundromat and washed sinks of dirty dishes. She rattled on about her garden. "Just giving life, fostering it is an honor." She gave a wistful glance toward her niece. "I'll do whatever you need me to do. Just tell me what you want."

Maggie Lu's eyes, clear and stern, took on a glint of

apprehension when she pointed at the calendar showing too many doctors' appointments and exam schedules crammed in, but then she nodded with a set chin. "I've resolved to see it all through." Her palm fell lightly on her belly. "I didn't know this living thing in me would change me this much."

Pearl gave a quizzical glance.

Maggie Lu groaned. "It's weird, giving life and giving life away, but I haven't changed my mind. Have you?"

Pearl shook her head *no*, yet her face flushed with unease. For a little while she'd enjoy the anticipation of holding the newborn. Surely it would be a boy. She straightened her back, tucking down the intimacy with the baby that would be hers again after so many years.

"Aunt Pearl..." Maggie Lu held her gaze, then turned away. "Never mind."

* * *

In later summer, just before the baby was due, Pearl packed a suitcase full enough for several weeks stay in Pennsylvania and rolled it out to the carport. Fred was leaning over the fender, wiping the oil from the dip stick. Pearl smiled at his concern for her safe travels. "Thanks, Fred, for checking out the car."

He twisted his neck and grinned, "I do want you back in one piece."

She sat down on the suitcase and watched him, then her eye caught the shiny edge of a combine behind the barn. She pointed. "New equipment?"

Fred glanced quickly. "Yeah, gonna need it, might lease the 200 acres next door."

"Sounds expensive." Pearl's lips were a thin line, disguising worry.

He replaced the oil stick, tugged at wires, and peered into the radiator, then slammed the hood. "All set." The noise had jarred her pondering of his latest leasing deal, and she pressed her palms to her ears. He opened his arms and she hurried toward him, snuggling inside his thick arms. He gave her ear a nibble. "Oh, Fred," she laughed, pushing against his embrace, but enjoying the shiver. She felt his breath then, hot and uncomfortable when he said, "I know you'll convince her. I'll find an adoption agency before you get back. I know some folks on the coast. They understand we'll need compensation in this kind of situation."

Despite Fred's uneasily sweet send off, Pearl hardly noticed the beautiful, rich crops and red barns along the way to Pennsylvania. The weight of worry over facing Maggie Lu and Fred taking on new debt was making her lean a little to the side as she drove. She gripped the steering wheel and let the hot wind blow into her face.

She recalled the day she finally told Fred about Maggie Lu's baby. He threw up his hands. "I want no part of it." She was shocked at his quick offer to find an adoption agency, the glint in his eyes unnerving, but it was him, truly. He loved mysteries that she wasn't in on. Nightmares plagued her about losing another baby those weeks after she argued with Fred about taking Maggie Lu's child as their own. "Adoption is expensive," he had repeated. Worry over debt sent a pang to her stomach, yet she could only say, "I guess loss is too painful to risk."

The closer she got to Pennsylvania, Pearl was almost nauseated, feeling guilty that she had ever wanted to take Maggie Lu's baby for her own self and promising Maggie Lu that she would adopt her child. Now she understood her sister Bea's desire to run from the hard decisions. At mid-forties Pearl had been caught up in a ridiculous grandmotherly fantasy. Finally, since she had agreed with Fred not to keep the baby, she hoped with all her might that the baby was not a boy, not another son to be lost. Now on this last trip she had to convince Maggie Lu that adoption was best for them all.

Maggie Lu was fanning herself on a bench outside of her apartment building when Pearl pulled into the little gravel parking lot. Her fingers were spread over her bulging belly. Pearl saw the fingers slip along her thighs, then curl into little fists beneath her swollen middle. Pearl straightened her shoulders and got out of the car, then sat down quietly on the bench beside her niece.

Dreaming Loss

Jerking into a run under the tiny blanket, Maggie Lu's legs pressed into the sofa cushion, but there was no kicking from inside her this time. The hum of the A/C window unit intensified. Maggie Lu's head popped up from the small throw pillow. From the clock, three-zero-three glowed red against the dark. Her squinting eyes gathered the dark into familiar shapes. Her fingers rested on her stomach, now flattened.

Glimpsing a rush of white paws scrabbling through the open window, she braced for the pounce. Instead, the stray thumped onto the scatter rug, claws making an unseen gash into hardwood. Maggie Lu clinched her eyelids in regret, fighting against the sleep that only sank her into a scrambled memory of Aunt Pearl's visit. Her breathing was getting ragged like those hours of labor.

A phone flipped over on the coffee table with the stern drawl of Aunt Pearl inside the receiver. "Do you hear?"

Maggie Lu stirred, then shouted out loud, "Why you telling me this again, Aunt Pearl? Just come on."

Maggie Lu watched the phone receiver float above her and blinked at the stray cat tip-toeing along the table's edge. Her aunt's voice still buzzed like it was on the phone. "I hear you breathing. You gave *her* life. That's enough, honey." In the dream, Maggie Lu's finger reached above her but couldn't find the phone button to make her aunt stop talking.

White paws gripped the pink blanket, then pushed down on four individual points of Maggie Lu's stomach. She lurched, thinking she might be awake, swinging a random arm to press the cat into her. Four thirty glowed red against gray windows. Who takes in all the strays? The tightness in her head tugged her into queasy regret of releasing not the stray but the tiny fingers wrapped around hers, fearing they'd strangle her eventually. The dream was an oncoming wave. She drifted in sleep, her fingers loosening into the soft fur, and the cat slipped away.

Blinking into the dreamy haze, Maggie Lu floated above the front window of her apartment, where Aunt Pearl's big four-door car limped into the parking lot below. Maggie Lu swayed, but her arms were too heavy to return a wave. Heavy footsteps moved up the stairs while a large straw basket padded with a white cotton quilt twirled around. Her aunt's arms grasping at the swinging basket made Maggie Lu's stomach queasy.

Aunt Pearl's big hands opened above her. The basket plopped onto the pink blanket on the sofa. Soft cries came from the next room. The cat crept across the sofa back, each paw easing into the basket until a living fur mound filled the basket.

Maggie Lu's arm struck the coffee table reaching for the crying bundle. She stared at a red five twenty-three glow. Her head fell back to the pillow. Too soon back in the dream, Aunt Pearl leaned forward over her plaid skirt, cooing at the bundle until she turned with a start.

"What is that?" she choked out.

Maggie Lu hissed. "Strays got their rights, but I can't take them all in, either." The cat leaped from the basket and crawled under the sofa, only a flicking dark tail brushing Maggie Lu's ankle.

Six fifteen glowed red against early morning shadows. Maggie Lu wiggled her feet against the soft blanket, pushing her side hard into the sofa over and over, then yawning back into sleep.

* * *

Aunt Pearl's eyes shifted. "Strays come and go" bubbled from her lips. "You'll be fine in time."

"Mama's not coming up to check on me."

Aunt Pearl grumbled, "Your mama left you with me a lot. She doesn't feel loss, honey."

Maggie Lu pushed against a damp pillow, feeling her mouth move against it. "I regret that I ever agreed to have this baby. I didn't know I'd feel this way." She reached for a silver bracelet splayed on a nearby table. "Take this silly thing, a baby trinket now." The engraving of animals frolicking across the gleaming band caught the light. She blinked and thrust the bracelet into Aunt Pearl's hand.

It hid in the dream, its wiggly legs kicking against Maggie Lu's stomach, a tiny fist gripping one of Maggie Lu's fingers. Aunt Pearl got in the dream, her thin arms slipping around the tiny body. The warm weight and tiny grip instantly vanished into the soft white quilt in the basket.

"Now you've got to take her?"

"You agreed."

Maggie Lu saw Aunt Pearl's arm quiver against the weight. The basket swung slightly in her hand. Maggie

Lu's breath barely came out of her tightened chest, but no words.

"Can I leave the door open for the stray?" Aunt Pearl asked, casting a stern glance over her shoulder.

"No." Maggie Lu waved her toward the door.

***

Nine thirteen glowed red in front of sundrenched curtains. Maggie Lu listened to the silent rooms in her apartment. Exhausted, she stretched out under the tiny blanket and ran her fingers across the ache it covered. She pulled the cat up onto her tender stomach. The white paws pressed an alternate rhythm between purrs. Maggie Lu returned the green-eyed empty stare.

"Do mamas ever make it better? Do you remember your mama?"

The stray pressed against her, its claws prickling her warmth.

She winced. "Keep purring."

News from Birdsong Farm

Finally, a break from the college grind, but Maggie Lu had to face some decisions she'd been putting off. Releasing her armload of textbooks onto the green Formica kitchen table, she leaned on the small refrigerator's open door, enjoying the cool air while she surveyed a few bottles of wine, a stack of lunch meat, wilted vegetables, and a mustard jar, before she grabbed a can of Tab. Plopping down in a wobbly lawn chair on her apartment balcony, she sipped the tangy soda and gazed between the trees at the red brick campus buildings spiking up where she had been confronted with enough new ideas and boring old ones to help her decide to enroll in law school next year, crossing her fingers that the LSAT wouldn't kill her. She imagined herself in a cozy, old office surrounded by the barrister bookcases she'd seen long ago when she and Mama had visited her granddaddy's brother in downtown Crosston. She didn't remember why they were even there. Was she ready to go to any law school that accepted her? She let her thoughts spin. She and Inez had been hashing out all their options, and it felt better to have her old friend as a sounding board. Mama or Aunt Pearl would probably worry about the cost, so she'd just get a loan. She and Inez both knew they'd return to the South to practice eventually, but Maggie Lu wasn't getting too close to Birdsong Farm.

Exhausted from end-of-the-semester exams, Maggie Lu let the irritating ring of the phone continue until she remembered it might be Inez. She took long strides and grabbed it before the ring ended, surprised to hear Cousin Sunny's plaintive tone. "Daddy's dead. I'm in shock. Hamilton's stuck at our house in Memphis. Mama found Daddy in the field, maybe a heart attack. Please come help. Mama's stunned and your mama's acting crazy."

Taking the last gulp of the fizzy drink, Maggie Lu squeezed the pink can and listened to its tinny resistance. Uncle Fred's steely eyes came to her mind and the memory of her unease in his presence sent a shiver. "I'm not finished with exams," she lied. "Oh, Sunny, I'm here for you." She tried to lend compassion, but since Sunny and Hamilton had snuck off to Memphis to marry right out of high school, Maggie Lu knew Sunny wouldn't be alone with her loss. A loud crash sounded in her ear, and Sunny said, "Gotta go. Spot broke through the screen door." Uncle Fred's bird dog must be antsy, wondering where Fred was. Sunny's voice ended with a click.

Maggie Lu had not been back to Birdsong Farm since she left for college. The last time she'd heard Uncle Fred's unwavering voice on the phone had triggered Maggie Lu's knees to buckle. "You got yourself pregnant. Say no more about it, gal." She heard low wails from Aunt Pearl in the background. Maggie Lu had let his disdain and the disappointment that they didn't adopt her baby work itself through the years into relief that she'd never have to face the child she had birthed. Though she talked to her mama, Aunt Pearl, and Sunny once a month, and only to Uncle Fred if he butted in with a smart remark, they made no mention of the child. Occasionally Sunny would confide that she longed for her own baby, but Hamilton wasn't ready. Maggie Lu was glad for the distance and the time to make her own way far from her relatives' entanglements.

Feeling more worry over Aunt Pearl, who'd soon to be living alone on the farm thanks to Uncle Fred's demise, Maggie Lu called the next day, immediately shocked to hear that his will declared that he be cremated. Aunt Pearl's tone tugged at her heart, "Please come. Can't believe he's gone. He never told me about cremation, I'm reeling, honey." Maggie Lu cringed, wondering why Uncle Fred would make such an unusual decision and not even tell his wife. Maggie Lu brought her thoughts back to Aunt Pearl's bereaved tones between Spot's barks. "Uh, huh, I'm listening" but didn't say maybe animal comfort would be better than Uncle Fred's. Holding her breath, Maggie Lu asked, "When's the service?" Aunt Pearl groaned before saying, "Just plan to stay for a while."

Hearing Aunt Pearl's urging sent a prickle of anxiety. Would Maggie Lu be sucked back into the role of the needy child, always beholden to her the aunt who had taken her in? Although Uncle Fred was dead, Maggie Lu felt a sense of dread about returning to Birdsong Farm. She had shut out the part of her teen years that she struggled against his unnerving behavior toward her. She had only told Inez, who agreed that Uncle Fred's eyes were often roaming uncomfortably. Returning to Mississippi meant being with her mama, too, who always made demands that she resented even while attempting to fulfill them. She'd have to struggle to maintain the stability she had so firmly constructed for herself while at college. No one questioned her right to be here. No one except Inez knew her past.

It had been a long time since she'd traveled, except for a jaunt to the coast during break, mostly spending her summers on campus enrolled for extra hours and working in the bookstore. Her friends were the workhorses like herself who spent long hours in the library, peeling away on the occasional evening for a movie or games and wine at someone's apartment. She stayed away from romance, letting closeness stay an intellectual match. She ignored the exceptions. Slip-ups, she called them. Maybe she had drunk too much wine.

When her mama called an hour later, Maggie Lu poured herself a glass of wine. Bea's voice was urgent. "You got the news about Fred? I'm just paralyzed by it. You're coming right?"

"Yes, I'm coming."

Bea kept talking. "His loss just puts a hole in our hearts."

After taking a long sip of wine, Maggie Lu couldn't resist interrupting her mama's lengthy, grieving torrents. "Why would Uncle Fred not tell anybody about wanting cremation?"

Bea didn't hesitate. "He told me he'd put it in his will. We even laughed that he'd just leave no evidence behind of his crazy life. Really he wasn't sure Pearl would bury him in the family cemetery."

"Why not?" Maggie Lu closed her eyes, struck by the strange tone in her mama's voice.

"They had their differences. Let's just say he wasn't a model husband." Bea stopped a snickered breath. "He knew Pearl wouldn't get it, but she would carry out his wishes. She wouldn't have to decide what to do with a casket."

Maggie Lu could hardly speak. "But Sunny . . ."

Bea said, "You kids are resilient. You have your own lives."

In so many conversations with her mama, Maggie Lu was stymied. Bea was often chasing a newspaper assignment, never really listening to Maggie Lu's responses or concerns. Now imagining Uncle Fred and Bea having that conversation was even more unsettling to Maggie Lu. She wished she did not care that her mama could not offer compassion for anybody, but she was disgusted.

"I've got to go, Mama."

"Come by the trailer before you go out to Birdsong Farm."

Shuddering at returning to the memories within Mama's trailer, Maggie Lu let the phone click in her ear, dazed more by her mama than the wine.

After a knock on the door, which was then pushed open, a familiar voice called out, "It's Inez. Your phone's been busy."

Maggie Lu waved her in. "Uncle Fred died."

Inez's eyes darted to the wine bottle. "Is that cause for drinking in the afternoon?"

"No, but Mama is. Just talked to her. Pour yourself a glass. Mama and Uncle Fred had a strange relationship."

"You're actually going to Mississippi to his funeral?" Inez's face mimicked horror.

Later in the evening, Maggie Lu dragged the big fabric suitcase from under her bed and opened it to a mass of black and white cat hair covering the inside. Her breath caught at the memory of the stray that had taken up residence a few years ago and then one night slipped out of the window into the moonlit street on its usual prowl and never returned. Her cheeks were wet while her fingers gathered the cat hair, its softness a deep comfort in that traumatic year.

Pulling clothes from drawers and the little closet, she wondered what was appropriate to wear. Do you have a funeral with no body? She had only been to her grandparents' funerals, then a child wearing patent leather shoes and a lacy, Sunday school dress. "He's really dead," she said aloud, but knew she was ready for him to be gone. His eerie harshness she would not miss. Yet more than once in the milk barn she had caught him staring with a keenness she hardly understood. Searching for appreciation, she told herself he was her only uncle, and he had let her live at Birdsong Farm. She had to go to Mississippi to comfort Aunt Pearl and Sunny, whom she did care for. She shuddered at the possibility of her old boyfriend, Karl Dees, coming to give his respects to the family. And then, of course, Mama would be there.

Fred's Last Mishap

The familiarity of driving up to the house at Birdsong Farm surprised Maggie Lu, as if all those years she'd let pass had not erased the roots she didn't know she'd put down at this place. In the front yard one of the Adair boys she and her cousin Sunny had hung out with as teens waved from a brush hog that he must have driven across the field from his parents' adjoining farm. Returning his wave, she opened her car window, letting the fresh-mown grass smell drift over her. "Helping out Mrs. Birdsong, with Mr. Fred just dying recently and all," he shouted and turned the sputtering machine to make a new layer of smooth, trimmed green. Gazing out at the yard, she almost glimpsed her younger self with Sunny close behind climbing those mimosa trees, leaping down into the lush grass beneath them to eat pimento cheese sandwiches for a summer lunch.

A *"beep-beep"* interrupted her reverie, and she turned to see her mama behind her, hanging a tousled, blonde head out her car window, fanning an arm toward her. Maggie Lu pulled further up the driveway close to the empty carport, and Bea's Chevy came to a stop beside her. Bea wrapped her arms tightly around Maggie Lu, holding on too long through grumbles of "My Fred . . .

our Fred is gone." When Maggie Lu wiggled uncomfortably, Bea quickly snapped her arms back, her hands flying to her own hips. "Damn him, dying so young, only 52. I'm glad you came home, Maggie Lu, to help deal with the investigation."

Maggie Lu offered a puzzled stare. "What investigation?" A bolt of disappointment shot through her. She had come to console, but instantly realized she needed a welcoming greeting, not an assignment. "Hello, Mama, glad to see you, too." Taking a long breath, she opened the car trunk and retrieved her bag, dreading to hear why she was not coming to a simple memorial service and family gathering.

The screen door popped open and cousin Sunny, her hair askew and her eyes puffy, walked awkwardly toward Maggie Lu and sniffed, "Let me help the college gal." Maggie Lu dropped her bag and hugged her cousin close, whispering softly into her fusty hair the compassion she knew Sunny needed to hear. Sunny reached for her bag, dabbing her eyes with a wad of tissue from her pocket and whispered, "Follow me," offering her Aunt Bea only a quick wave. Puzzled, Maggie Lu asked about Aunt Pearl. "Downtown," Bea spat, "in the center of it." Maggie Lu frowned at Bea pacing around the cars and taking long drags from a cigarette. She caught her mama's eye briefly before Bea waved her on toward the door, dismissed by that familiar air of her mama's self-indulgence.

Carrying her purse and a bag of fruit, Maggie Lu climbed the inside stairs behind Sunny. Exhaustion from the two-day drive from Pennsylvania tugged at her shoulders. Sunny hurled her suitcase on one of the twin beds in the room they had shared as teenagers and plopped down on the opposite bed, her eyes taking on a frantic glow.

"I'm in the middle of a nightmare, Maggie Lu. Daddy's dead and Mama—and no telling what other people—are suspected of killing him. They found a projectile in his heart so no heart attack, and no blow to the head ended his life like we thought, mysterious and scary."

"Could your mama have done it?" Maggie Lu rocked unsteadily, the spongy bed wobbling beneath her. "Wow, sounds horrible."

Engrossed in her rendition, Sunny touched her damp nose. "The doctor examined his body and said the police should be involved."

Sunny's head drooped toward her palms, and her mournful sigh shook Maggie Lu to the pit of her stomach. A nauseous burble erupted from Maggie Lu's throat, and she dashed down the short hallway into the bathroom to release the bile. Wiping her face with a fresh, pink cloth, she looked into the mirror and saw a face she had not seen in a long time, despair sinking into her eyes.

Maggie Lu crept into the hallway and peeked down the stairs at the family picture wall, remembering she had never been sure Aunt Pearl would make a place for her on that wall. She didn't want to see if her picture was still missing. Hesitating, she listened to the familiar lilting tones between her mama and Aunt Pearl, who dropped her keys on the hall table near the door, declaring, "My car's acting up, and Fred's left me with another thing to tend to."

Spot's tail offered a limp wag from her place near Aunt Pearl's chair, and a little whine slipped underneath the bird dog's whiskers when Sunny and Maggie Lu joined their mamas drinking iced tea in the kitchen. They listened to the women worry over what really caused Fred's death and how long before they had to do the cremation. "A burned-up body is worrisome," Sunny kept saying.

"Let's do the service at church before we send Fred's body to be cremated. I'll arrange it with Buck McPotter and Reverend Weedy." Aunt Pearl's lips were pressed firm like Maggie Lu had seen when her aunt made a decision. "I'm not ready for him to just disappear into the very air that we breathe."

Maggie Lu held her breath, eyes darting between Aunt Pearl and her mama.

Bea pressed her elbows into the table, chin in hand. "Did Fred have any Sunday clothes?"

"No, his red plaid shirt is fine, not his overalls, maybe his 'go out to eat' jeans," Pearl said. Sunny's bottom lip wiggled before her cheeks were wet.

"Can the memorial service be held this week?" Maggie Lu tried for a tone of concern but worried an investigation might cause a long delay. She had only prepared herself to be around her family for a few weeks.

"Not sure until we hear from authorities," Aunt Pearl said.

Maggie Lu urged, "What really happened out there?"

Aunt Pearl's lips were tight, her words slipping out slowly. "Fred said he'd be home for late lunch, first had to check on a fence line break along the Adair property line. He didn't come and didn't come. I finally put on my field shoes and walked the fence all the way to the old BB target range."

Sunny broke in. "Remember that spot we'd meet the Adair boys?"

Nodding, Maggie Lu felt her throat tighten when

Aunt Pearl's eyes began to blink, her voice a warble. "There he was on his side. I screamed *Fred* no telling how long. My knees gave out. I went down nearly on top of him, gave him a big shake, put my ear to his nose, nothing. The right side of his head had a big bruise. I thought he'd hit his head on a rock. I didn't want to leave him, but I had to, ran til my legs ached back to the house to call an ambulance, told them he might be dead. They must've called the police."

Sunny continued, "The police had the coroner do an autopsy. The autopsy report found a small projectile in his heart, a BB shot, said it was a rare occurrence."

"That's why they're grilling all of us. I'm hoping it was an accident, and somebody will just admit it. They kept the BB but didn't find the gun yet," Pearl said, regaining a little composure.

Bea tugged at a strand of unruly hair. "I couldn't believe they made me sit in that little room at the station for an hour, like a common criminal. What do I know about a BB gun?"

Sunny frowned, "So many farm kids get a BB gun for their birthday and they keep it forever. Sheriff took Daddy's BB gun from the gun closet."

Maggie Lu speculated, "The sheriff would have to check all the folks on farms around here, discouraging." She pushed down a worry over anything that would delay her planned departure.

Aunt Pearl scowled. "Come to think of it, Fred didn't have any tools with him, shouldn't have stayed out there that long."

Sunny leaned on the table. "Daddy wasn't far from the trail to the Adair's house. We used to go that way, and Mrs. Mildred would always have cookies."

Maggie Lu turned to her cousin. "You were out there?"

Sunny sat up taller. "Sure, Spot and I followed the EMTs through the field to Daddy. I was crying but couldn't leave him yet. Hard to look at him. One overalls strap was off his shoulder, his chest looked bloated. His shirt was ripped, something crumbly inside."

Pearl sniffed. "Oh, I couldn't look that close."

"Like being in a fight?" Maggie Lu asked, "Did you see a bullet hole?"

Sunny pouted. "Too early then to know he'd been shot. I was shocked to see Daddy lying there, his overalls all unbuttoned, stained down there, one shoe off."

"Could have stopped to take a leak." Aunt Pearl glowered.

Sunny's eyes flashed. "Spot found Daddy's shoe by the trail to the Adair's. Several heavy boot prints were near it, bigger than Daddy's. Odd, little indentions were pointing toward the Adair's, looked like there was a pink slipper further up the trail. I turned around, though. EMTs started moving Daddy."

Maggie Lu was agitated. "He encountered somebody out there near the trail."

Pearl exhaled. "First I heard of those prints. He shouldn't have been on that trail."

Sunny's eyes welled. "He looked so small when they rolled him over, his left hand all purply bruised. It was nearly sunset, the sun's glow was reflecting off something I'd stepped on and I backed up . . ." Sunny glanced at her mama, then to Maggie Lu. "Later."

"Better not have been intentional," Aunt Pearl warned.

"What would be their motive?" Dipping her head, Bea inhaled. "Why, Fred wouldn't have done anything . . ."

Aunt Pearl snapped, "Don't act a fool, Bebe."

After an annoyed snort at her baby name, Bea jumped from her chair, nearly knocking over her barely-touched tea glass, and made a beeline for the door, pulling a cigarette out of its pack with wiggly fingers, beneath her breath seething, "Fred at Mildred Adair's, no way." Aunt Pearl grabbed a hankie from her pocket and crept into the adjacent living room. "Leave me be," she said, leaving Sunny and Maggie Lu staring at their tea glasses and then at each other.

Stunned, Maggie Lu pushed back from the table. "Wait, don't go," said Sunny, who began a slow whimper. "The sun was reflecting off Daddy's wedding ring on the ground. Spot went right to it when the EMTs lifted him up." She stared at her feet while she told Maggie Lu of the threatening phone calls that had come to the house warning her daddy to stay away from the wives of several Bessieville men. She'd answered two calls herself, feeling scared when she told her daddy about them. He'd wagged his head funny and just laughed, "They've got the wrong number."

Maggie Lu gasped. "Did they threaten him?"

"Their voices were distorted, gargly. *Stay away or get what's coming to you.* Yeah, warnings were angry."

"I'm looking for a motive for Uncle Fred being shot."

"I told Mama I'd seen Daddy sneak down the driveway to a waiting car. Always on late evenings," Sunny lamented.

"Mama scared me that day, her eyes were wild with anger, and she told me in a nasty tone, "I don't ever want to talk about that."

Maggie Lu wrinkled her forehead. "Did you tell the police about the calls?"

Sunny gulped. "I told my husband back then, but

since Daddy was so casual about it, I didn't take it seriously enough until now."

Maggie Lu nodded. "Even in high school I'd seen him go out late, didn't really get it all then."

Sunny let out a blubber. "Daddy might have got himself killed over his craziness." She shook off Maggie Lu's hand on her shoulder and wiped her face with a paper napkin, the napkin ripping in her hand. Her expression was resolute. "I'm so mad at him and ashamed, too. I should contact the sheriff about those calls no matter what the consequences."

* * *

After the investigators had done all they could to Uncle Fred's body, they released it to Buck McPotter's Funeral Chapel. When the phone rang, Maggie Lu watched Aunt Pearl struggle for a hankie in her apron pocket and listened while she repeated facts about Uncle Fred that Buck would put in the obituary. "I didn't know Uncle Fred didn't graduate from high school," Maggie Lu said to Sunny. Aunt Pearl waved a "shush" at them, nodding and agreeing to Buck on the phone that later in the afternoon she would bring over Fred's clothes for an open casket memorial service.

When the call was over, Aunt Pearl slumped into her wingback chair. "Fred will have a loaner casket. Can you imagine?"

Sunny sniffed. "Open casket, oh, Daddy on display to everybody."

"I don't want him under a closed lid," Aunt Pearl huffed. "Get me some tea."

Sunny darted into the kitchen, rattling an ice tray, and brought out glasses of sweet tea.

"Got anything stronger?" Maggie Lu said to Sunny.

"Might make us crazier." Sunny was firm, then mouthed, *no liquor in front of Mama.*

"Buck is handling it all. Good." Maggie Lu switched topics and soothed her voice.

Relief that the services would be held soon helped Maggie Lu sink into the big recliner, rocking gently until a lingering scent of Uncle Fred's hair oil drifted from the headrest. One time in the milk barn, he had leaned in too close to her ear, his hair oil scent mixing with the sour milk splashed around her feet while he coaxed her with a guffaw to squeeze the cow's teat. Now she bounced forward from the chair with a shiver, uncertain if she would be able to hold steady for his memorial service.

***

On Saturday afternoon Maggie Lu and Sunny slid into the back seat of the black Ford behind Aunt Pearl at the wheel and Bea, who cracked her window immediately and lit a quick cigarette for the short ride to Redeemer's Chapel Baptist Church. Cars and a variety of farm trucks were already scattered throughout the church parking lot. With a halo of curly white hair surrounding his somber face, Buck McPotter, dressed in a shiny royal blue suit, waved them toward a parking spot near the front door. When they emerged from the car, Aunt Pearl clutched his sleeve. "It will be a long two hours," she lamented. Pointing to his shiny black hearse, he assured them in an unusually high voice, "I'll be taking Fred to Memphis to the crematory right after the service. I'll let you know when you can pick him up." He bowed with a flourish, a tiny pink bald spot appearing at the top of his head. Sunny took her mama's arm and steered her through the back door of the little white church.

Maggie Lu made her way up the aisle to the first pew in the church, nodding at familiar faces from her days at Bessieville High and touching her hair nervously, wondering what they thought of her now living up in Pennsylvania. Her eyes surveyed a few in the congregation suspiciously. Buddy and Mildred Adair both met her stare and shifted their eyes away. Several bearded men offered only cursory nods. Then she caught their whisper, ". . . only meant to scare him." Could Uncle Fred's killer be sitting among them? Two women, maybe former classmates, flipped little waves. Sunny turned and patted the open spot on the front row pew next to her and Aunt Pearl. Maggie Lu caught her eye. After strains of "Amazing Grace" groaned from the old organ, Bea nudged Maggie Lu's shoulder and plopped down at the end of the pew, a smoky scent rising from her tight pink jacket.

Maggie Lu's eyes riveted on the strangely pale lips of Uncle Fred, his head perched on a lumpy satin pillow thrusting his nose above the edge of the casket, his red plaid shirt stretched tightly across his boxy chest and his blue jeans stiff against legs that disappeared under a beige satin cover inside the dull metal container where he lay.

She watched Aunt Pearl gasp when her eyes darted to Fred. Her thin legs wobbled in her Sunday high heels as she inched toward the casket. Maggie Lu rushed from her seat to steady her aunt. Pearl's left hand, with glittering wedding band intact, reached tentatively to touch one of Fred's thick hands, ringless, still a hint of purple bruise near where his ring had been before it was pulled or fell off. His calloused hands rested on his chest. "You left us too soon, Freddie," she repeated, rocking over him until she seemed to shrink under Maggie Lu's encircling arm. Hearing the endearment, *Freddie,* gave Maggie Lu a start. Aunt Pearl's fingers pushed and pulled against Uncle Fred's flattened hair, trying to rearrange it "so it looks like him" she kept repeating.

Finally, Aunt Pearl's shoulders straightened, and she turned, glassy eyed, toward her niece, muttering. "His wedding ring is lost." Her fingers crawled along the edges of the satin that Fred rested on. Maggie Lu twisted her neck toward Sunny, miming *get the ring*. Sunny's mouth turned into a little *o*. Finally, Maggie Lu said, "We'll have Buck look for it when he takes Uncle Fred to Memphis." Aunt Pearl gave a stunned nod. Maggie Lu offered a sorrowful expression, escorting her aunt back to their pew and sitting down heavily beside Sunny, whispering, "Your mama's going to be asking Buck why your daddy's wedding ring isn't on his finger."

Sunny gasped. "Right, I forgot about it, didn't want to tell Mama where I found it. I'll talk to Buck." Her lip began to quiver. Sunny scooted in closer to her cousin, sighing. "Just like my husband not to get here on time to walk up there to see Daddy with me." Sunny's head hung over her lap, her loud wails encircling the room, and she moaned, "That's not my daddy anymore. He's gone forever."

Maggie Lu patted Sunny's shoulder, averting her eyes from Uncle Fred's final appearance. Instead, she watched her mama rise, almost toppling a spray of chrysanthemums when she edged toward the end of the casket, their petals continuing to tremble. Bea patted Fred's hand, her mouth moving a long time near his ear, then lingered to hold on to the end of the casket, her eyes pinched and hollow. Maggie Lu shuddered, remembering that uneasy laugh her mama made on the phone weeks ago when Bea told her that Fred had shared his cremation plans with her. What was she telling him now?

While some mourners shuffled up to the casket and briefly stood with heads bent to pay respect to Fred, others ambled unsurely in front of Aunt Pearl and Sunny. The rotund Reverend Weedy eventually squatted in front of Aunt Pearl and opened a worn Bible with several loose pages protruding, whispering as he read to her and nodding when she spoke.

Averting her eyes from Reverend Weedy's distracting overbite, Maggie Lu stared at the vase of roses on either side of the altar in front of the casket, where a few fallen petals already had drifted to the carpet nearby. Sprays of yellow and white chrysanthemums attached to metal frames were perched at either end of the casket and along the chancel rail. As a teen Maggie Lu had often knelt to take communion at that rail and had strained to feel spiritual enlightenment, expecting a quiver more holy than those that Karl Dees had aroused. Now her head jerked to the right to ensure he was not sitting in the sanctuary behind her. *No, no, all in the past,* she told herself.

Waving the Bible in an ominous swipe toward the congregation, the young Reverend Weedy reminded, "Your souls are at God's mercy. Mourn Brother Fred but pray for his soul. Forgiveness is always at hand if you accept God's ways." Sunny and Aunt Pearl passed tissues between tightly clinched hands, Sunny whispering, "Say something nice about Daddy."

A police siren whistled somewhere on a nearby road, seeming to draw closer. Maggie Lu turned to see Buddy Adair rise and drop his Bible in his wife's lap, saying brashly, "Take heed, Mildred. Our judgment is on the horizon." Mildred grabbed his sleeve, dragging him back down into his seat. Reverend Weedy wailed repeatedly, "We all need forgiveness. Come forward now." A number of the bearded men rose quickly and slipped out the back door, leaving it partially open.

Bea leaned toward Reverend Weedy, whispering, "This is about Fred Birdsong. May he rest in peace." The organist nodded at a cue from Reverend Weedy, and loud chords introducing "Worthy is the Lamb" poured over the congregation, but many were twisting their necks toward the sound of sirens.

Sunny's eyes blinked a revelation, and she tilted toward Maggie Lu's ear. "I wonder if some of those guys in the middle pews were Daddy's callers?"

Maggie Lu's eyes tightened almost shut. "Did you report those calls to the police? I heard one whisper . . ."

Sunny's eyes were anxious when she barely moved her head to confirm. She reached for Maggie Lu's hand and squeezed hard.

Maggie Lu couldn't stop her thoughts. "Where did Spot find Uncle Fred's shoe, Sunny?"

When the music stopped, Reverend Weedy instructed, "Come offer solace and prayer with the family."

Buddy Adair was the first in a line of congregants who filed past the pew where Bea, Maggie Lu, Sunny, and Aunt Pearl sat. "So sorry, so sorry," he repeated. Bea held his hand firmly, jerking his arm to keep his attention, leaning toward him menacingly.

Buddy wobbled and wrenched his hand free when Reverend Weedy steered him toward the reception hall. Maggie Lu glimpsed a uniformed man inside the hall. In a moment Buddy and the officer disappeared. As the congregants moved past, Bea fidgeted, barely returning "uh huh" and every few minutes repeated, "I need a cigarette," finally leaping up, making a fast pace into the reception hall after Buddy.

Maggie Lu glanced through the door at the tables holding punch with floating green sherbet balls and trays of homemade sugar cookies that reminded her of high school graduation parties. Those days and most of these people she had let fade from her memory.

After the last mourners had quickened their pace into the reception hall, Aunt Pearl stood first and wobbled toward Fred's casket. She leaned in toward Fred's face, her mouth moving quietly into a long, eerie wail. After a nudge from Maggie Lu, Sunny took small steps to her mama's side. She gasped, "Oh Daddy," before winding an arm around Aunt Pearl's shoulder while her mama's feet, seemingly not under her control, turned in a half circle. Taking Sunny's hand, Pearl stared blankly and seemed to glide toward the back door of the church.

Flashing lights from a police car spun across the walls of the sanctuary. Mildred Adair skittered in pink pumps behind Aunt Pearl and Sunny, nudging a shoulder as she pushed her way outside, shouting, "Don't take Buddy! It's all my fault!"

A commotion erupted in the reception hall with congregants pushing against each other in a surge toward the parking lot. A car motor revved, and gravel spun out front.

Buck McPotter shouted, "Wait, we need to move the casket!"

Blonde curls askew, Bea appeared at the back door of the church.

Shaken, Maggie Lu said, "Where have you been? An officer was waiting for Buddy in the reception hall."

Bea smirked. "I knew something was up when I

grabbed his hand, that guilty look in his eye. I went right in there to see them nab him. I wonder how the law figured it out?"

Her face motionless, Maggie Lu wasn't going to mention all that Sunny knew. Instead, she tapped her mama on the shoulder. "We should go find Aunt Pearl."

Bea looked puzzled. "Without Fred?"

Watching Buck lower the casket's metal lid over her uncle, Maggie Lu felt her chest open in relief. She pointed toward the bier. "Look, Uncle Fred is disappearing."

When the lid snapped shut, leaving only a metal cylinder, Bea emitted an awkward howl.

Four men, their white shirts damp from the weight of the casket, walked unsteadily down the aisle past them and slid the closed metal box inside the open doors of Buck's black hearse.

"There he goes," Maggie Lu said evenly. "I wonder how heavy that casket was?"

"Heavier than you can imagine," Bea replied.

Water Break

Pearl pulled her Ford too close to her old mailbox, leaning the leaf-stained box backward a few inches with her car mirror. "Can I get this right?" she breathed. She took her foot off the brake, scraping a little more paint, then letting the car bump forward. The mailbox door flopped downward on rusty hinges, revealing an AARP magazine, a pink envelope, and her bank statement from Crosston Fidelity. She snorted at the word "<u>fidelity.</u>" *No one has ever been loyal, leastwise a bank,* she thought. Even this long after Fred's death, she squirmed as a memory popped up of her husband sneaking down the driveway after midnight. She never really learned to live with his catting. She chuckled. Was he making up for his ways with a pink envelope for Valentines, sent from hell?

After she dropped the mail on the passenger seat next to her carton of milk and a brown bag not disguising a wine bottle, she turned onto her gravel driveway and shrieked. Large pools of muddy water were standing where only dry gravel patches had been when she'd left for the store in town two hours before. "Something's broke," she said to the windshield, then let the Ford slush through the gravel pools and on up the long driveway to the carport by the house.

Her mind buzzed, not sure what to do about the puddles, trying to think between tiny pants against panic. Should she call Sunny? She stared at Fred's mounted deer head hanging in the carport and wished for Fred to just come back from the dead and do something to help her out. She heard Fred's rebuke in her mind, *Can't trust the county to get anything right, leastwise the water.* The oily hot sauce she had dumped on her Wendy's chili for lunch gurgled in her stomach. Her hands went clammy on the steering wheel.

County Water Department, they were the culprits. They'd sent a blue postcard saying for her to sign up for service about the time her well pump was short circuiting. She was still trying to cook just for herself again, with Sunny having gone back to Memphis, getting used to her daughter's more limited weekend trips to check on her, and not used to making mechanical decisions. She told them yes, because she was afraid of the sizzle when she flipped the pump breaker back on. That was reason enough to sign up for county water.

A week after she had agreed to connect to the county water system, she was stricken when the big-wheeled road machines took over her front yard. After she got used to their noise, she sat on her porch fascinated by the fellows in sweaty work shirts who grinned and hollered orders to each other. They seemed to be showing off, moving the mechanical arms of the yellow machines up and down while they dug a long trench through the pretty grass in her big yard all the way from the road to the house, then filled it with pipes. She was still making payments on that decision. She liked seeing a man in the yard working, but a thought startled her that day. She didn't know if she was ready for one in the house quite yet. She glanced at the wine on the seat next to her.

Pearl was tempted to open the wine in the car, lean her head back, and enjoy the warmth and ease it offered. Instead, she gathered the mail, the wine, and the milk and pushed up out of the velour seat. Her left leg wobbled but she leaned against the fender and propelled herself across her covered patio, letting everything in her arms slip onto the green porch swing.

It was easier to use the key under the welcome mat. She clicked the lock, threw the key back under the mat, then listened. Was water dripping? She heard nothing but the ticking of the timer she had attached to her lamp to make the wrong people stay away at night.

She brought in her mail and groceries and turned on the kitchen faucet to wash her hands, afraid of a flood. A gurgle slipped up inside the faucet, but no liquid poured out. She twisted the hot water knob, then both knobs in the bathroom sink, nothing. All her water was going into the puddles that were expanding in wider circles up her driveway. She stood at her living room window and considered a pond with cows standing in the middle. Would those neighbor cows just crowd in her yard for a drink?

She bent over the worn oak desk pushed against a wall of framed pictures of her family. A few weeks after Fred's funeral, she moved his urn from the desktop to the tool shed in the carport. He had spent a lot of time out there anyway, and she decided he eventually needed burying, maybe near his favorite mulberry tree in the front yard.

Rustling through her bill drawer, she found a number for the County Water Department. "Water all over my yard, please come," she spoke into the phone before she forgot what needed saying. The lisping voice on the other end asked way too many personal questions, but Pearl had to answer. When she hung up, she stacked the mail on her side table and went outside, easing onto Fred's lumpy pillow, which she now had in her wicker rocker on the front porch. She sipped a Coca-Cola to wait.

After Fred was sent into the great beyond last year, Pearl started trying new things. She drank wine sometimes in the evenings and slipped into reveries about every man friend she had ever lusted after. She smiled to herself, pleased to feel a spark of warmth inside. After she dribbled the last sip of her Coke, she reached for a tissue and remembered the pink envelope.

When she tore open the envelope, two pink tickets fluttered to the porch floor, offering another free meal at Spaghetti Spoons on the town square in exchange for listening to someone tell her what retirement funds she should buy. The last time, she and the neighbor lady had groaned as they scraped the last of the tasty spaghetti from their plates. They had struggled to pay attention to the financial talk, disturbed that dessert had been withheld until the slide show was completed. Turning the tickets in her hand now, she speculated on who to call to join her for the next free meal.

She was gazing at the puddle ponds by the mailbox when the big white county truck lumbered into her driveway. The stooped man in the navy-blue shirt and pants did not look her way. He only took a long tool out of his truck, twisted the thin pole into the ground, and tossed it back into his truck bed. He taped a paper to her mailbox, climbed into his truck, and spun the gravel, making the truck slide onto Hollyberry Road. *Can't trust the county.* Fred's voice seeped into her mind. She wondered what the paper on the mailbox said.

In the carport, she found the grass-stained garden

shoes she would need to wear to get through the water to the mailbox. She pushed her bare feet inside onto grainy inner soles. The uneven walk down her driveway seemed long.

Her feet sank into the red mud floating around the mailbox. The water department card taped to the box held a check mark next to *Water has been turned off.* "What?" Another mark was next to *Call a plumber to repair your water line.* "Call who?" A yellow sticky note attached to the card displayed a phone number and in shaky script, *Or call me for a referral.* Pearl held the card and note in her hand as she made a wide path though spongy grass, feeling the wet seep through her canvas shoes. By the time she'd slipped off her soaked shoes in the carport, she'd decided to call the number on the yellow note, though it gave her a nervous twitch. Could she trust a sticky note?

"Yeah, this is Hershel," came over the line.

Pearl said, "You came to my house on Hollyberry Road, about the water, then left me this note. Oh, I'm Pearl Birdsong." She took a breath and her chest fluttered.

He said, "I did? I leave a lot of notes."

Pearl glanced at the pink envelope by her chair and sighed, "Do you ever go to the Spaghetti Spoon meetings?"

"Dunno about meetings. Going there tomorrow for lunch, Pearl. If your water's not fixed, maybe I'll see you there," he said with a chuckle. "Ladies like pink. Wear a pink hat so I'll recognize you."

"I guess I can make do till then." Pearl chewed her lip as she hung up the phone, pushing away worries of strangers creating more yard destruction like before, then holding their hands out with a detailed bill. She'd eat spaghetti, and she and Hershel could figure it out from there.

***

The next day Pearl tugged her pink scarf around her hair and jingled the bells hanging from the glass door of Spaghetti Spoons. Garlic and buttery French bread aromas floated over the cafe crowded with lunchtime locals nodding and chattering. Several gave her a quick wave of recognition. She surveyed each small table and booth for a navy-blue-uniformed man, then caught sight of one waving a hand from the back booth, and someone in a ball cap hunched across from him.

Pearl inched between the tables, tentatively zigzagging toward him, then away from him, taking little worrisome gasps, stretching her neck to see who else was sitting in the booth with him. He stood up, waiting for her, shuffling a bunched hat from hand to hand, his stooped shoulders making his arms look stringy. He took her hand as she came closer and bent into a little bow. "You must be Pearl. I'm Hershel Lopez." His small brown eyes peeked from under thick shocks of gray hair that fell on his forehead and hung over his ears.

Pearl swallowed and coughed, feeling the warmth from his hand travel up her arms into her neck. "I'm Pearl." She pulled the pink scarf down into her sweater pocket, then straightened her shoulders, and thought about pushing back the hair near his ears.

Hershel's smooth lips moved into a smile. "Let me help with your sweater." His thick fingers brushed Pearl's neck and slipped her sweater from her shoulders and onto a nearby coat hook. He swiveled on short legs and pointed to the empty booth seat. "Sit here next to me.

This is my boy, Hersh Junior, a fine plumber. He'll help you out if you haven't gotten anybody yet."

When Pearl slid across the red vinyl booth, a younger replica of Hershel removed his red cap and grinned. "Pleased to meet ya, Mrs. Pearl." Pearl's eye fastened to his light blue eyes. She breathed uneasily at his continuous blinking. Would it affect his work? "My water's shut off," she managed without sounding desperate.

Hershel pulled out a small legal pad and with quick pencil strokes sketched of her house, driveway, and mailbox. "I looked up your water record. Here's where the line's laid." He drew little x's along the driveway. She watched his thick, olive-skinned hands move across the page. She noticed he wore no wedding ring. "We can come out today after lunch, Okay?" Hershel leaned closer to Pearl and blinked his eyes slowly. She could smell a hint of aftershave that made her light-headed. Pearl turned to Hershel and forgot what he said but looked into his brown eyes and nodded.

After lunch the men drove behind Pearl's Ford all the way to Hollyberry Road. Pearl rolled through the puddles on up to the house and fluffed her hair in the carport. Inside she pulled back the living room drape to watch them climb out of their white van laden with pipes and ladders on top.

Hersh Junior waded into the water at the end of the driveway and pushed the shovel with his boot, heaving clumps of red mud onto the soggy grass. Hershel ambled toward the house, his stooped shoulders seeming to carry invisible pipes. He knocked lightly on Pearl's front door. Pearl tried to walk slowly to the door, letting him knock another time.

"Might take him awhile to find the break," Hershel

said, easing his short frame onto the bare wicker of Fred's rocker on the porch. Missing a chair pillow, Hershel's frame sunk low into the rocker.

Pearl's stomach lurched. She nodded, standing behind the screen door, and watched him lean his neck toward her and blink slowly. She opened the screen door slightly and stood on one foot, then the other.

Hershel pushed up. "This your chair?"

Pearl said, "That one," and pointed to the wicker chair with the cushion.

Hershel bent over and fluffed Fred's lumpy cushion, then moved back into the rocker, balancing on the edge for a moment, his small eyes expectant. Pearl slipped out the screen door and settled into her chair across from him. She smoothed her slacks with her palms, then tried to make a halo around her hair, pressing in unruly strays. She decided she liked someone sitting in Fred's chair.

They sat on her front porch watching Hersh Junior fling mud until he shouted, "Found the break. Got to drive to town for a fitting." Hershel waved a hand of approval, and they both gazed at the white van crawling up onto Hollyberry Road.

Pearl glanced at Hershel. She leaned toward him and, before she'd decided, said, "Would you like to come in the house for some afternoon wine?"

Hershel smiled. "I'm glad you asked. Let me hold open the door for you." His breath warmed Pearl's neck as she moved through the door.

Orange Hollow Afternoon

Pearl had done her daily yoga poses and written in her gratitude journal. Being alive was the easiest entry, but she eventually thought of her new shoes to add, and a Dove candy bar that Sunny, had brought her. Reverend Weedy had said three entries were enough.

After putting on the coffee pot, she pushed up the kitchen window. A warm breeze carried in bird tweets and claws scratching on bark. She wished for the energy of two young squirrels with fluffy tails larger than their bodies playing tag round and round the magnolia tree in her yard. Bright fall leaves glowed with the sun in the woods behind her farm home.

She took her coffee outside on the front porch and sat the wedding anniversary China cup on a wrought iron side table next to her wicker chair. When she sat down, her foot pushed over a wine bottle that was underneath the chair. She didn't remember finishing that wine last night under the stars. She moved a large white candle away from the edge of the singed trellis and pushed the matches into her housecoat pocket. She had never taken the time for wine and candles until those years that Hershel Lopez made frequent visits. Before that, when Sunny came home or Fred was always needing something, she rarely had a minute's peace. Since Hershel had a falling out with her, and Sunny was busy either fighting with Hamilton or dog rescuing, sometimes Pearl didn't know what to do with herself, especially in the evenings.

She sipped her coffee and glanced at the sagging wooden screen door. A turnbuckle rod attached horizontally would straighten that. She would go to Orange Hollow Discount Center and find one. That gave her focus for the day. She eased down in the chair to finish her coffee and let the sun stimulate her pineal gland. She had read about measures to help avoid depression in the *AARP Magazine*.

She pulled on her favorite slouchy blue cardigan and soft pants, inattentively slipping the matches in her pants pocket, and slid into new orthopedic sandals. Her feet stopped aching. She took in a full breath and her body seemed to float. She could walk the entire length of Orange Hollow Discount Center today.

* * *

Rows of brightly painted portable storage buildings enticed Pearl's eyes when she steered her black Ford into the parking lot at Orange Hollow. She craned her neck at the yellow one and absently shut off the car motor near a chain-link fence, away from the regular parking lot. She climbed up inside the yellow building, gripping the door frame until a dizzy spell passed. She ran her fingers along the rough plywood work bench and smiled at the cute little window cut into the wall. She slid it back and forth on its plastic runners, imagining the honeysuckle breeze that would drift in at Birdsong Farm. She saw herself pulling all of her old pots and garden tools out of the leaky milk barn and lining them up on wide shelves inside a clean building like this one. Glancing at the price on a small cardboard sign taped to the door, she winced. For today she would buy colorful garden gloves.

When she stepped inside the fenced garden section of Orange Hollow, she slipped off her clip-on sunglasses and carefully put them in her pocket. They were hard to keep up with and hard not to sit on or break. They weren't attractive like the rhinestone-encrusted ones she used to wear. Blinking to adjust her eyes, she stopped at the first register and asked the clerk, whose name tag spelled out *Franzeene* with a lot of extra letters, "Where's the stray cat, Tabby? Isn't that its name?"

The clerk laughed and pointed to a long, mottled cat stretched out in the sun near the edge of the fence. "People ask more about her than the plants. Whatcha after today?"

"A rod to level up my wooden screen door," she said. "And maybe some new garden gloves."

Pearl squatted near the sleeping cat and touched her warm side. The cat purred. Pearl's throat closed up for a minute when the cat under her hand transformed into a familiar barn cat, a stray that had been struck down by a giant wheel of her neighbor's tractor right before Christmas last year. Pearl leaned on the fence for support when she stood up.

Franzeene nodded. "Not sure about that rod. So many folks have these new metal doors now. The guys in hardware can probably help you out."

"I'm old fashioned I guess," said Pearl with a chuckle, but she knew she was just practical. "I'll check the begonias first." She took hold of the handle of a little red wagon and started toward the flower rows. She liked talking to the clerks. Many she recognized as Sunny's old high-school friends. Their kids played ball at the YMCA like Sunny had on Saturday afternoons. Little flashes of Sunny in years past—or was it her niece Maggie Lu in her red and white basketball uniform—popped in her mind. She could hardly replace those images with a coiffed-haired Sunny in a business suit always holding a phone at her ear now. No, it was her sister's daughter Maggie Lu in that lawyer's business suit. Sunny just cared about those rescue dogs. Pearl's head was foggy sometimes.

The concrete pushed against her new sandals. She missed the creaky floors and the tin ceiling of old Cory's Hardware in downtown Crosston. It was cozy, familiar. Someone used to call out her name when she slipped inside the front door with the little bell attached. The men all knew Sunny or Fred and always found whatever she needed, even helped her to the car with the heavy things. Cory's couldn't compete with the prices at Orange Hollow Discount Center. It was a shame that the downtown stores were all closing or turning into cutesy, expensive boutiques Pearl had no use for.

Pearl dragged the little red wagon up and down each aisle of the Orange Hollow garden shop, touching the soft petals of the pansies, stroking the long narrow leaves of the irises. She would clear out the rusted buckets of seeds and dried flaky plants that she had stored in the milk barn, maybe not even plant them, so she could make room for the new pots of yellow pansies she was wedging into the wagon.

She waved at Franzeene as she rolled the wagon past the checkout. "I've got twenty pots. I'll be right back," Pearl said, concentrating her gaze on a search for her car in the parking lot. She filled the back seat, the floorboards, and the passenger's seat with all her plants. She slammed the door too hard, straightened up slowly, and rubbed her hip. She watched the wagon roll into the fence, then walked back inside, but Franzeene was not at her register.

Pearl's eyes brightened at the garden glove rack. She tugged on a pair of yellow gloves with orange and pink flowers on them. They just fit. Her feet were comfortable in her new sandals, and she began humming a little tune from the radio. A young clerk hurried down the aisle. She waved to get his attention. "Oh, sir, can you help?"

A freckled, red-haired man slowly turned around, his shoulders sagging when he glimpsed her. He stopped with no expression and replied in a monotone, "Yes ma'am."

Pearl tried explaining, "I need a pull up rod." She couldn't think of the real term. "Maybe it's a door leveler." She coughed and tried to keep looking at the young man, whose stern eyes bored into and then past her. He wrinkled his nose while she talked when he noticed that she was wearing the yellow garden gloves.

"It's a metal rod. It levels up a wooden screen door." Pearl's new shoes were sinking into the floor. She held her breath while pictures of lopsided doors swung in her mind, but she didn't know how to tell him what they looked like. She tried to show him the length of a rod, but the little elastic string between her yellow gloves held her hands close.

He pushed a button on his portable two-way radio. "Metal rod, screen door. She *says* she bought one here before." His tone stung Pearl's ears.

A muffled reply said, "Never heard of . . . Doors are metal. What the f . . . oh, just send her to aisle two."

The red-haired man swung his arm over his shoulder

and pointed. "It's probably there," he said in an unconvincing breath. He jammed his radio into a leather pouch attached to his belt and strode in the opposite direction, leaving Pearl swimmy headed.

Her neck arched up at the 2 imprinted on a big banner high above the rows of shelves filled with boxes and paint cans. A beeping machine inched by her, balancing heavy garden timbers on an outstretched bar. "Step back, lady," came from the young person perched in the driver's seat. The screeching beep rung in Pearl's ears after the machine rolled on down the aisle. "Beep, beep, beep."

Her feet were heavy now in her new shoes, but she moved toward the aisle Red Hair had pointed toward. Disappointment hung inside her. Her mind searched for an explanation for this empty feeling. She had been dismissed by a man who was young enough to be her grandson. He probably doubted the existence of what she had asked for, so he made no time for a fruitless search. She was not worthy of his time. Pearl's chest tightened. Her eyes blurred over the metal devices in Aisle 2, and she strayed into another aisle.

A mirror in the designer bathroom aisle surprised her. She looked in at the pouches under her eyes, the tiny lines around her mouth. She pushed down her fluffy hair sticking out from both sides of her little cap, straightened her comfortably-stretched blue cardigan, and blinked. This is the woman Red Hair had been talking to. Inside she was the same Pearl she had always been.

She moved quickly back through Aisle 2, past chatting young employees with orange aprons on. One of them mechanically smiled and asked, "Find everything you need?" but then turned back to continue talking before she could reply. Pearl did not hesitate or think of answering, just willed herself toward the front of the store. She waited in front of the automatic doors until they slid open. A blast of wind propelled her into the parking lot. The maze of cars in the lot caused fuzzy clouds to drift in her mind. A horn honked at her. Then she glanced toward the row of storage buildings and saw her car parked by the chain-link fence. The yellow buildings from this view were pee yellow.

Her sandals flopped in ghostly steps across the asphalt. She fumbled for her keys, dropping them on the ground, before climbing inside her car and letting her head fall back against the headrest. The image in the rearview mirror startled her and little trickles began to slide down the outsides of her cheeks and inside the wrinkles along her neck. The inside edge of her cardigan felt damp and chilled her. She leaned forward and rested her head on the steering wheel.

She had parked wrong but didn't care. Pearl's black Ford was blocking the entrance to the garden area delivery gate at Orange Hollow. She glanced at the driver from Dees Nursery and Hardware Store with a load of seedlings in his truck when he tentatively honked his horn. Pearl's car didn't move. The driver popped out of his truck and slammed the door with a curse. He rushed toward Pearl's car, waving his arms, then tapped on the rolled-up window.

When he saw Pearl inside, he said, "Hey is that you, Mrs. Birdsong? Are you okay?" Karl Dees scrunched up his face, turning it from side to side and kicked a heel in frustration. Pearl watched him bend over and pick up a ring of keys lying outside her car door.

Inside the car Pearl pressed her forehead against her steering wheel. Her back and shoulders were arched, then shook when her sobbing hurt more. She was sorry Karl recognized her. A thousand sad details ran through Pearl's mind, all pushing down on her that she was just too old to go to Orange Hollow again. Then Pearl heard the tapping and tried to focus on the blurry figure standing outside her window. Pearl said, "I just need a little push."

"Aren't these your keys?" Karl's voice held frustration as he dangled the keys from one finger in front of Pearl's nose.

Pearl stared at the little "P" charm on the ring and tried to reach for it but her hand hit against the closed window. Her fingers were sticky inside the yellow gloves, and she struggled to crack open her window. An uneasiness crept up her back as she stared at Karl's confused face. Was he wearing a red cap and holding her keys? Then Pearl said, "Do you know what a turnbuckle rod is for a screen door?" A little fog from her breath covered part of her window.

Karl tugged on his faded cap and stared around the fog at Pearl, "Sure, my Grandma's house had them on the screen doors, but the house went up in smoke long time ago."

Pearl slipped one hand out of a glove and felt her matches in her pocket. "That's what I thought," she said.

Karl leaned toward her back window. "The last time I saw such a heap of flowers around someone was at my Grandma's . . . oh, never mind."

More fog from Pearl's breath covered her window when Pearl said, "I'm locked inside."

Trouble at Birdsong Farm

It wasn't five months after Aunt Pearl's passing that her home place near Bessieville, Mississippi, was struck hard by a tornado. Aunt Pearl had lived on Birdsong Farm for more than thirty years. Just her being there must've protected it all those years, but for once her magic didn't transfer to her daughter Sunny. That's what Maggie Lu thought first when Sunny called out of the blue about the disaster. She rarely called anymore.

Sunny's chattering about the storm's destruction stirred up mixed feeling for the farm. It had been Maggie Lu's home, too, for a few years, but Sunny never understood her choice to leave it behind and become an attorney. One of Maggie Lu's early legal cases did not go well when she tried to help Sunny and Aunt Pearl with farm debt. Today Sunny talked like that was all forgotten. She was wound up about the tornado. Maggie Lu listened on her cell phone.

"It was a miracle that I'm alive. I tell you, Maggie Lu, the Lord was watching over me."

"That's right," was what Maggie Lu knew to say when talk of the Lord was involved. She hesitated to ask but had to. "Is it still standing?"

"Oh my, yes. I'm so grateful for that."

"And Hamilton?"

"Storm didn't hit in Memphis. I was all alone at the farm. Just got a few cuts and bruises. You know we're having our differences, but thanks for asking."

Maggie Lu heard a little teardrop in Sunny's voice. Sunny was attached to that house and the whole farm, and now trouble with Hamilton had brought new heartache.

Maggie Lu fanned a fly from her windshield and reminded Sunny, "I'm sure your mama was watching out for you from above. You were the special one in her eyes." She tried to remind her cousin it all worked out fine.

"You're the one she always watched out for." Sunny's voice stabbed through the phone.

Sunny was always a little jealous because her mama had encouraged Maggie Lu to go to college. Aunt Pearl was the closest she had to a mother for a lot of years, especially when she ran into trouble in college.

"I sure did love your mama. I've always been mighty grateful for all she did for me." Maggie Lu teased, "And you know you are my best cousin."

"Maggie Lu, sometimes I think you know me almost as well as Mama did."

"Yes, I know." Feeling the childhood memories, that's what she and Sunny did best when they talked. Maggie Lu looked out the window of her sports car at the countryside zooming past.

"Aunt Pearl told me about how she and Uncle Fred moved to Birdsong Farm when it was really rundown right after they got married. She never got over not picking her own home, just fixed up the one that was there. She passed up the one chance she had in 1977 but wouldn't talk about it more. Her voice was so sad then." Maggie Lu bit her lip thinking of 1977, a painful year of pregnancy she couldn't have endured without Aunt Pearl.

Sunny started crying. "You knew Mama better than I did. She never told me any of that."

Maggie Lu reminded her. "You know you were her favorite girl."

Sunny sighed. "Mama was letting me drive more then and promised me Daddy's old truck. She bought you a car for college. I think that was when she built some new barns and repainted the house and bought a new Ford and a truck for Daddy. I do wonder where she got the money?"

Sunny made a funny clucking sound. Maggie Lu caught her breath.

"Wow, you're right. Maybe she inherited it from some of her old relatives. She called me more after Uncle Fred died. We got closer. That was the winter she covered the walls of every room from floor to ceiling with pictures of us all, and all her Hopkins relatives and some of the Birdsongs. I was relieved that she put my picture in with your family."

Sunny sniffled. "I barely remember that."

Maggie Lu sensed her cousin's anxiety. "Why were you out there at the farm during the tornado instead of at your house in Memphis?"

Sunny was excited. "I just felt like taking a road trip for the weekend, getting a little space from Hamilton. I'm thinking of building a kennel. The Adairs have livestock out there. There's still a few of Mama's chickens. I just felt obligated to check on the place. Oh, I wish I had never gone."

Then she started telling blow-by-blow how the big winds had come in the middle of the night. She had panicked when the window glass came pouring in with the rain in the bedroom they had shared in their youth. Maggie Lu winced, imagining her cousin's fear and a rain-soaked bed. Sunny's voice cracked when she told about hearing loud, whinnying screams from the neighbor's horses and the frantic chicken squawks piercing the night.

"Oh, poor animals," flew out of Maggie Lu's mouth. She couldn't think of what else to say. She glanced at the moon ring on her little finger. Aunt Pearl said it would protect her from the unknown.

She put her phone on speaker and laid it on her lap while Sunny droned on about the storm. She slipped the Nissan Z car to cruise and whizzed on down U.S. 45 Highway with the afternoon sun bouncing off her sunglasses. She had been on her way to Tupelo to visit a friend's mama in the nursing home. She started thinking about turning off at Bessieville, just to see what was left after the tornado. She didn't tell Sunny she was anywhere near the farm.

"You out there now dealing with cleanup?" Maggie Lu was halfway hopeful to see her and halfway relieved when she said she was back in Memphis.

Sunny admitted, "I hired a couple of those Adair boys to board up the house and start sawing up the trees that fell.

"Uh, huh," Maggie Lu said until an eighteen wheeler's taillights lit up in front of her. "Crazy driver ahead." She stomped the brake hard, jerked the wheel to the left, and the cell phone flew onto the floor in front of the passenger seat.

"Sorry cuz. Gotta go. Bye."

"Hello, hello, can you hear me?" came back from Sunny.

Maggie Lu gunned the motor and shifted back to fifth. The Z raced past the big truck stacked high with crates of feathers pressed against wooden slats. She glanced up in time to see a yellow beak and tiny eye inside a crate on the bottom row. "Ooooh, I don't want to see the little victims headed to slaughter."

"I wouldn't call it slaughter," floated from the phone on the floor. "I survived, with minor cuts."

Maggie Lu laughed. "No, not you. I'm passing chickens loaded on a truck."

Sunny responded, "I can barely hear you. Must be losing our connection. Bye, Maggie Lu."

"Yes, losing our connection," Maggie Lu sighed.

* * *

Once Maggie Lu caught sight of the fat water tower with *Bessieville* painted in big red letters, she flipped a quick right at the old Gulf gas station. Piles of brush lined each side of the road. Blue tarps stretched like plastic flags over the roofs of white farmhouses. She turned into the start of the gravel drive to Birdsong Farm and cut the engine. Pushing her sunglasses down just a little, she peeked over the top. Intense daylight assaulted her eyes as painfully as the sight before her.

The home place looked hunkered down after taking a bad beating, cringing with plywood nailed over the front door and the picture window. Twisted limbs full of withered leaves lay on the spring grass next to the spaghetti-like root balls protruding from gaping holes. She sat on a big fallen tree trunk and dabbed her eyes. Sunny didn't have the market on grief over this place. Her own childhood was caught up in it, too.

Maggie Lu gazed at the destruction long enough to feel the penetrating afternoon sun. An itchy resentment of her mama's abandoning her at this farm—and of Uncle

Fred's creepy behavior toward her—crept around her shoulders like a ghost. She stretched her arms to shake it off and decided to drive up to the house and get a closer look at the destruction.

Maggie Lu taunted herself. Why was she even here? Maybe just a curiosity seeker gazing at barely familiar relics. She picked her way around back. White and red feathers were matted into the wire. The coop had blown away. Poor chickens, she empathized, more for them than the relatives she had known so long. A scrawled *Do Not Enter* was duct-taped to the back of the screen door.

Her spine prickled. Would Aunt Pearl's ghostly self be inside to greet her? The screen door spring squeaked like it had always done. The inside door swung open easily. She held out her hands until her eyes adjusted to the dim light. A mouse skittered into the kitchen. A wobbly shelf leaned out from a wall that had once been covered by the refrigerator, revealing a small plank on the floor behind it. She gave it a kick. A closed-up smell drifted through the opening it had covered. Curious, she shone her key ring's laser pen light into the carved-out dark area.

A small cedar box sat in the corner of the hole in the floor. When she lifted the top of the felt-lined box, she recognized her own handwriting. Nervous sweat rose on the back of her neck. Aunt Pearl had kept the letters Maggie Lu had written to her from college. She felt air pushing down on her ribs. She thumbed quickly through the stack and indeed those from the summer of 1977 were included, and the month her baby was born. Shuddering, she remembered she had been in no place to raise a child then and hadn't wanted her education halted in midstream. Maggie Lu remembered being flooded with relief and gratitude when Aunt Pearl took the baby and promised it would have a good home. She stopped her memory of that time when her eyes stopped on the edge of an unfamiliar envelope.

A long envelope from Robinson's Adoption Agency protruded from the bottom of the stack postmarked September of 1977. A carbon copy of a check made out to Aunt Pearl for thirty thousand dollars was stapled to the letter. Maggie Lu's arms went limp as she read that the agency had completed its search and removed Pearl's baby "granddaughter" from the orphanage and placed the child with a "high bidder" from Biloxi. Aunt Pearl had *sold* her baby. Now all her kindness felt like callous greed. Dropping the envelope, Maggie Lu bent over in a dizzying lurch toward the kitchen sink, a nauseous metallic bile spewing from her mouth. Her arms pushing her upright against the sink, she stared out the window toward the open fields and gasped to stabilize herself. She turned to spy a tiny baby ring that fell from the envelope. Scooping it up, Maggie Lu slipped the ring on the tip of her little finger next to the ring Aunt Pearl had given her. She grabbed the box and pushed the letters down hard and put it under her arm. She stood up and leaned on the wall. Still feeling queasy, she edged herself out of the kitchen carrying more disappointment than she could have imagined.

The sky was pink when she stuck her head outside the screen door, nearly sunset. The air held an uncomfortable cool tint to the humidity. She shivered, depleted. The evening sun left silhouettes around the white and the red feathers stuck in the tangled pen wire. She thought she glimpsed a golden eye.

The Losses Go Deeper

Sunny's shorts were on fire. Glancing at the broken bench by the wrought iron fence, she sat on top of grandmother's tombstone, wiggling against the hot marble infused by the sun's afternoon rays. Maybe burning a little fat off her nearly thirty-something-year-old butt was the only way to get rid of it, she chuckled to herself. Her husband Hamilton told her more than once that he wasn't worried about it. Her mama, Pearl, always had said she was too skinny. She decided she could worry if she wanted to, no matter what came to her mind sitting out among the dead.

She could find comfort too, any way she chose to, even if it was often just with animals. She smiled at Spot when the old bird dog followed its stick tail twice around and settled into the grass a few feet from her. She patted the dog's bony ribs, then put her garden gloves back on.

After devoting an hour to pulling weeds from around her parents' tombstones and those of other relatives dotting the New Faith Community Cemetery, Sunny wasn't satisfied with her work. She eyed the insistent honeysuckle that crept up into a nearby holly bush and dangled over a shady smaller tomb, her younger brother's. She doubted she had brought enough plastic flowers for all the family graves. Her mama wasn't coming behind her to check if she skipped her brother Sonny's grave, but she might be looking down from the pearly gates. Tetchy resentment scratched Sunny's insides.

Long red-stemmed strands of poison ivy inched across the ground behind her parents' tombstones. She was allergic and decided she'd just let the vine crawl up Daddy's side, even if it stretched over the scripted *Fredric L Birdsong* etched into the marble tombstone. Daddy's urn rested under that side of the ground, though it had taken some years to get it planted under his stone. Under Mama's stone, inscribed *Pearl H. Birdsong*, sat a full-sized casket, grass wisps not fully covering the red earth that was parted for her funeral last year.

* * *

The first time Sunny ever heard of cremation was eight years ago when Mama sat on the couch in the front room, the day after he died, and read her daddy's real words requesting it in the will. At thirty, Sunny was in shock. Daddy had never warned her he'd considered cremation. Her fingers twisting against an imagined shadow of flames, she had let out a little "Oh, Oh, Oh." Mama responded to her concern with, "He didn't give me a reason, either."

At first Sunny just couldn't abide the idea of a burned-up body, not that she was bothered that his would ascend toward the pearly gates. He was her daddy. But to accept his wishes, she decided that his body was probably all used up by the time he died anyway.

Mama only worried that she'd disappoint Buck McPotter. He was the family mortician who had buried both sets of grandparents and no telling how many distant relatives spread all over New Faith Community Cemetery. Sunny had gotten him right on the phone. Mama was relieved when Buck said, "Now don't you worry Pearl. My brother in Memphis owns a crematory. He'll take care of Fred. Your needs are all kept in the family." Mama probably tried for reassurance when she said, "I'll be having the standard casket when it's my time to rest next to my mother at New Faith." To prevent their continuing conversation from reaching her ears, Sunny held her palms against the sides of her head, not wanting to consider another parental funeral any time soon.

After Mama read the will, Sunny squirmed in the wingback chair while her mama broke down over her embarrassment about her husband's indiscretions. When Sunny was younger Mama had only tightened her eyes and told her, "He must be doing his business again." The only business Sunny had shared with him was farm work. He'd let her drive tractors and trucks and wagons. His daring laugh urged her on.

When Mama laid the will in her lap, she declared she would not be buried near her husband. It was the first adult conversation they shared. Sunny knew it wasn't the time for her to reminisce her good times with Daddy. She wondered what they would talk about when the funeral was over.

In the years following Daddy's death, Sunny felt like a failure when she told Mama how she and Hamilton weren't close anymore, and that he never spoke about babies again after her miscarriage. That loss left haunted glances between Sunny and Hamilton at shared meals and long silences in the car. For months she still ached over their shared being who didn't stay. The one time Sunny told Hamilton about her disturbing dreams of gurgling cries from a nameless form, he said, "Your family's cursed with lost babies." Then Sunny realized this marriage held no joy for either of them. Mama should have told her trying harder to please didn't always work.

After Mama picked up what was left of Daddy's body at the crematory, Sunny asked her to at least place his urn on the mantle. Not long afterward though, Mama carried it out to the toolshed off the carport. "I couldn't stand him being so close," she said. Sunny didn't blame her for leaving his urn in the toolshed but urged her to bring him out before the rats knocked him over onto the concrete floor.

It took nearly six years before Mama had decided to move him over to New Faith. Mama finally told Sunny that she didn't really want to pay for a headstone when she could have shared Grandmother's headstone, but now she was considering putting her name next to his and lying beside him in death even though he had lain beside so many women in life. He was her husband. He was her children's daddy. The record would show she *had* survived him.

***

Now Sunny gazed at the twin tombstones again, glad at least that her parents were there together. Despite the heat, a shiver passed down her back. Mama had rarely been satisfied with much that Sunny had done. Was she prodding her from the grave? Sunny pulled an old dishrag from her back pocket and sponged her beaded face and neck, then tugged at a soaked red bandana wrapped around her head. She didn't mind the sweat. Finding a place for the loss of Mama and the trouble between her and Hamilton just kept her off balance. Thinking of the dreams scared her. Maybe Mama's dreams had passed on to her.

***

For a few years after Daddy died and Sunny was living in Memphis with Hamilton, Mama rarely kept in touch except to report that "those uneasy dreams made me call." Since Mama was busy joining the red hat ladies and the library book club, even running in to the nearby Redeemer's Chapel Baptist Church nearly every time the doors were open, Sunny decided it was the jumble of activities that overwhelmed Mama some nights.

But last year Mama started calling nearly every night, so Sunny couldn't keep herself away. She was in her truck barreling across U.S 72 Highway making a lot of trips between her home in Memphis and Birdsong Farm. She even began spending an occasional night in her old room upstairs to keep Mama company. Staying was not so bad at first since Hamilton was already getting on her nerves, too.

On most every overnight visit, a voice that didn't even sound like Mama's bawled loudly enough in the early morning hours that Sunny bolted downstairs. She would find Mama in a thin gown with her hand pushing at the bedroom window or sometimes struggling with the front door lock, repeating, "Don't take the baby." Usually, she never awoke as Sunny led her down the hallway, only fluttered her eyes as she sunk back into her feather bed, whispering "Yes, I know it's you, Sssssssuuuhhhh." Which name was she saying, *Sunny* or *Sonny*?

When she'd quieted Mama and returned to her own room, after drifting into sleep, sounds began to echo in Sunny's mind—growling dogs, creaking branches, and crying from the barn. Were her past nightmares of her gurgling miscarriage intermingling with the spirits that haunted Mama? Was it not only her dead brother that brought anguish to Mama? After Sunny returned to Memphis from stints at Birdsong Farm, the tiny cry from her own lost baby, who couldn't have ever cried, crept back into her dreams, now tangled with spirits of Daddy and brother Sonny from Birdsong Farm. Hamilton was no comfort at all.

* * *

Sunny swatted at a bee that dipped down from the holly bush, then looked toward the weathered stone carving of a lamb atop her brother's grave. She realized she had stared at the lamb's features longer than at the name etched in the stone. She remembered hiding by Grandmother's tomb as a child while Mama ran her fingers along the lamb's head and traced each letter, whispering like a rosary, "too soon, you were taken, my Sonny. Stay close by me, my angel lamb."

Sunny barely remembered this ghostly brother whose fat pink arms poked her through the slats of her crib in early mornings before Mama scooped him up and left her crying. Then one morning, Mama screeched over and over from his bedroom, "Sonny won't wake up!" Sunny watched her run to the phone, then outside to tell Daddy, and back through the house. From the barn Daddy emitted a howl Sunny never heard again. The yard dogs responded in kind until he had quit.

Then the screen door opened, and Daddy hurried toward Sonny's room. Doors slammed. Mama screamed. In silence, Daddy returned to lean against the door frame, staring up at the ceiling light a long time. He let out a long

"Ohhhhhhhhhh, my boy." Sunny sat at her tea table and stared up at him. He swiped a crinkled bandana across his swollen eyes and dabbed the wet under his red nose. Then he took her hand, saying "You're my only Sunny now."

They sat on wooden child's chairs whispering. Sunny grasped his hand, afraid he might break the chair, and she'd lose Daddy too. She set out four child-sized pink cups, but Daddy took one away. "Now there's three of us." Sunny grinned, then knew she shouldn't. He poured pretend tea in all three cups. They lifted their cups of pretend tea at the play table while Mama moaned and rocked the lifeless child in the front room until McPotter's black hearse crept up the driveway, silent as a cat in search of prey.

She always liked being called Sunny, hoping the dead brother's favor would filter from the nickname. Her daddy never mentioned his son to her after the child's death. "You're my baby forever," he'd say. Although she had been named a bright and stately *Sunita*, she only heard that name from Mama when criticism was imminent. She had never been an adequate replacement for the original Sonny boy in Mama's eyes. "You're almost grown," Mama would say during her childhood, leaving Sunny the kitchen chores while she took long afternoon naps. Sometimes Sunny would watch her mama sleep, sad that her brother had, in some ways, taken Mama with him to that other world. Staying in the barn and out in the fields with Daddy had been the happiest place most of the time. When Maggie Lu came to live at the farm, eager to please, Mama brightened, declaring her the smartest. Sunny became the outsider since Daddy was gone working at the ag office or in the fields so often during her teenage years.

***

A shiny red truck backfired out on the gravel road that ran past the cemetery, startling her. Sunny shifted her gaze over to her mama's tombstone. The memory of the loud organ music at her mama's funeral stirred her thoughts. Sunny had been uneasy inside Redeemer's Chapel Baptist Church, averting her eyes to avoid the parishioners' chatty condolences. She'd sat up straighter and smoothed her wrinkled jeans. It's what Daddy would've worn, she thought. Then she edged her folding chair, its legs scraping the narrow board floor, closer to Aunt Bea. Her aunt opened her palm to expose an extinguished half cigarette and showed gritted teeth, then leaned over and whispered. "We're all suffering, honey."

Maggie Lu slid into the chair next to Sunny, edging her large bag underneath the seat in front of her with a shiny black pump. Leaning in front of Sunny, Maggie Lu said, "Mama, can't you say something nice?"

Bea pursed her lips. "My sister's at peace now."

Sunny moaned. "What peace? She was haunted by a baby."

Maggie Lu's breath was short. "Her own, or the one she tried to get and couldn't? She lost a couple."

Sunny offered a blank stare, stretched and said, "You mean your baby, too, the adoption when you were up north?"

Sunny caught her breath at the reminder of her own loss that she had never shared with Maggie Lu. She was afraid of Maggie Lu's response to her miscarriage. Until just now, Maggie Lu had always avoided talking about the baby she willingly gave away.

"Turned into an easier adoption for some," Maggie Lu hissed, remembering that Aunt Pearl gave into Uncle

Fred's decision. She nodded toward them both, her lips tightening into a pink ribbon.

Sunny moved a little closer to Aunt Bea. Maggie Lu was unpredictable, touchy. Sunny didn't understand her sizzling response. Since Maggie Lu had passed the bar exam and opened that office in Memphis, she hardly returned Sunny's calls, except if they were quick and to the point. Maggie Lu looked older than the two years that separated them. All those college years away from Mississippi had changed her.

"Easy?" Sunny frowned at Aunt Bea.

Her aunt chewed her lip and whispered only to her. "I don't know, but I think I'll investigate if Fred found an agency so quickly. Don't tell."

Sunny winked an okay with both eyes to Aunt Bea, then glanced to see if Maggie Lu was looking. She wondered if Maggie Lu's lost baby was part of Mama's haunting dream, too. Bitterness had always been in Mama's tone when she talked of the adoption, while Daddy only responded, "It had to be done. It was done businesslike. I made sure. It's all in the past."

Sunny shifted her eyes back to Aunt Bea, trying to move away from the prickles inside. She hoped all this sadness wouldn't bring on those dreams again, dreams passed down like family heirlooms that nobody wanted.

Maggie Lu folded her arms against her suit jacket. "Losses are hard, cousin. I know you miss your mama."

Sunny leaned back, almost tipping her chair, then leapt straight up when the organ music blared a noisy introduction to "Worthy is the Lamb." Stung by that image at the cemetery, her mama's fingers that had kept touching the headstone lamb, she took long strides down the row of seats, the words from the congregation "slain to receive" piercing her temple, more strains of "honor and glory" bringing up forgotten reminders of her own unworthiness in her mama's eyes. Surprised to find herself at the back of the church, Sunny lingered by the door, distraught that Mama had picked that hymn for her service, still not giving up on the lamb. Now that Sunny was in the rear, could she stay for the rest of the funeral service?

Slipping into a chair in the back row when the music stopped, she turned toward a tiny "meow" coming from an orange fluffy kitten sitting by the door just outside her reach. Lost baby stories lurked in her family, and she kept running from all those unsettling losses of loved ones. Sunny bent toward the kitten. Animals were always true. Had they stirred the only love in her that she trusted since her own baby was lost? Her mama didn't even come to Memphis to be with her, just called and said, "Your loss could have been so much deeper."

* * *

Heat from the day and the memories had wearied her. Sunny wiped her brow and patted her mama's tombstone. She did miss her mama, whose backhanded love had always been a familiar presence in the big home place, but no one loved her like her daddy had. Hamilton tried, but time did not keep them close after her miscarriage. He took bigger sales routes and more golfing junkets. He didn't want another child, and she hadn't either for a long time. The ache from the dreams seemed to be more soothed this last year after Mama's death. Sunny began to consider becoming a mother again, with or without Hamilton, but she would need to hurry before her fruitful thirties slipped away. Still, she'd give herself to all the animals she fostered, too. She was torn with facing a new kind of life without Mama and probably without Hamilton.

Spot yelped near Mama's tombstone, but only her back leg twitched. Sunny watched her daddy's eleven-year-old bird dog dream, content to relax surrounded by grave sites. Finally the dog's head jerked up and her mouth stretched into a yawn, exposing brown teeth and a faded pink tongue. Her long, thin legs dragged her aging body toward Sunny's outstretched hand.

Sunny had known Spot so much of her life. It was easy to look after her at Birdsong Farm. Sunny had stayed for longer spates of time out there since Mama died. After the tornado came, she began to take in rescue animals, naming each stray not long after it arrived. Building the kennel at the farm was the best idea she had in a long time.

Leaning against her mama's tombstone, Sunny peeled a sweaty glove from her hand. She crooned to Spot, "Sweet animal, you're my baby for now. We'll make only the good dreams together."

First Visit

Gravel popped from under an old Chevy recklessly speeding up Sunny's driveway, heading for the back yard. Seeing two figures inside, one big and one small, caused Sunny to rush out to her front porch. She ducked inside to fluff her hair and slipped back through the house to the kitchen. She stood inside the screen door squinting to see who that driver might be. She wasn't expecting anybody.

The noisy engine wheezed and quit behind Sunny's old truck in the carport out back. A middle-aged woman with blonde hair pulled into a ponytail gave a little wave from the driver's window. It was Aunt Bea.

Uneasy over the arrival of her least favorite aunt, Sunny shoved her hands in her jeans pockets, moving slowly toward the car, careful not to brush against the steaming fender. "Aunt Bea, what a surprise."

Bea let out a final puff of smoke between lipstick-smudged lips and stubbed out her cigarette into a messy ashtray. She turned to the teenage girl next to her and said, "This is your cousin Sunny. See, I told you there's relatives up here in north Mississippi."

Leaning over to be level with the passenger window, Sunny squeezed her fingers inside her jeans. "Now who could this be?"

Sunny had to launch herself back, the girl had flung open the car door, and now right close to her, grabbed her in a hug. "You're my cousin. And that means I'm your cousin Tiffany. I've heard all about this farm." Tiffany gave a little pinch on Sunny's arm and said, "I didn't know cousins could be as old as my parents. Well, my adopted parents."

The girl leaned hard against the Chevy door, shifting her peculiar gray eyes up to Sunny and then to a sound coming from the kennels. She set off running toward the fences like a pup exploring new ground. The terrier that was stretched out behind the chain-link barrier leapt up to greet her with a yip.

Sunny nodded, "Cousins? Where'd she get that idea?"

Bea flashed an astonishing grin, "I've discovered my granddaughter, Tiffany."

Sunny blinked. "Maggie Lu's child? She gave it up. Oh, where did you find her?"

"She's living down on the Gulf Coast. Her adopted parents are out of town. I told the housekeeper I'd just keep her a week. She wanted to meet family."

Prickly with embarrassment, Sunny's mind raced back through those frantic days long ago when Maggie Lu made her tearful phone call about not wanting to continue her pregnancy. Sunny heard her mama being stern. "How could you bring shame to this family? I'll take care of this."

She gazed at her mama's rocker on the side porch and was grateful Pearl Birdsong had not lived to see this day. Sunny stepped back from the car, reeling at the appearance of this child no one ever talked about and pondered what was to come of this.

After a few moments she wondered how long they'd

stay. She didn't want to offer, but she knew she should. "Y'all are welcome to stay here." She hesitated. "We could catch up." She stared at Tiffany running toward the kennels, hoping she wasn't a rambunctious child.

Nodding, Bea pulled bags out of the back seat. "Listen, I need to drive over to Memphis. I'm investigating Robinson Adoption Agency, the one that placed Tiffany."

"Really, that sounds messy." Sunny struggled against a frown.

"Oh, this investigation could lead to something big, maybe a Pulitzer."

"Then why involve the child?"

"Just a whim to bring her." Bea almost giggled.

"That was okay, just to take her?"

"Got a notarized form written up swearing I was her grandmother. The housekeeper was wary but thought she had no choice since I had the form."

"You have your ways, don't you, Aunt Bea." Sunny was uneasy with the way Bea hurled through life.

Bea glanced across to the kennels where Tiffany was squatting next to a small dog. "I got attached to her a little after a couple visits to her home, thinking maybe I'd eventually rescue her from her circumstances. When I met her the first time, I was taken in by those familiar eyes, but gosh, now I've got to work. Can she stay here while I'm gone?"

"Okay, uh, you know I'm not out here full time?" Sunny had a hard time saying no to anyone. She was always relieved that the Adair neighbors never charged a lot to check the kennels and feed the dogs when she was gone a few days. She gave what they asked.

"Sure, sure, I'll be back soon."

"Are you going to see your daughter?" Sunny was unraveling Bea's plan.

"Yes, I do need some legal advice from Maggie Lu's law firm." Bea's jaw tightened.

"You'll tell her about Tiffany being here, right? That would be too much for me to put to her."

"Yeah, but I haven't said a thing about her to Tiffany. She gave this child away thirteen years ago, not sure how she'll react to this discovery of the kid."

Sunny cringed at the shock Maggie Lu would be faced with soon. Should she call her?

Bea picked up the bags. "A quick bathroom break and I'd better be off."

Unnerved, Sunny motioned toward the back door, realizing Aunt Bea was enthralled but too busy with work to keep track of the kid for now, nothing new since she hadn't taken much care of her own daughter, back when she and Sunny were kids. Tiffany's flashy gray eyes matched those of the mother she didn't know, but it was the profile as she tilted her head, striking and familiar in one glance, that Sunny kept trying to place while Bea had rambled on.

The screen door slamming behind her, Bea shouted to Tiffany. "You'll have fun here. I'll be back before long."

Tiffany ran toward the car. "Don't leave." Her wary eyes searched the back seat. "My stuff, wait."

Bea waved. "It's all inside the house."

Tiffany stepped back, glancing uneasily at Sunny. "It's okay for me to stay?"

Sunny put her arm around the worried teen. "For a little while. You can help me in the kennels." She tried to offer comfort when she only felt manipulated by Aunt Bea, and now she had to make a place in her farm routines, worse yet in her solitude, for this foundling. This intrusion into her day was already stirring up her feelings about kids in her life.

They gave Bea a wave and walked toward the barking dogs. Sunny leaned against her kennel gate watching her aunt's Chevy race out of her driveway. Frustrated that she'd let Bea just burst in on her life, she gripped the chain-link gate until she felt the painful pressure of the wire. She'd at least call Maggie Lu to warn her that Bea was headed to Memphis. She couldn't decide whether she'd mention Tiffany.

Tiffany squatted next to the little wire-haired terrier and talked to the dog as if she expected words of understanding to slip off its panting tongue. Sunny smiled, letting her heart open a little toward another animal lover. She caught herself staring at Tiffany and remembered she had to be the adult. "Are you hungry?"

Tiffany's unquenchable eyes widened. "Yes, but can I just play with the dogs for now?"

The Risks

"Your mother is on line two, Maggie Lu." The law assistant's voice had a quizzical tone.

Maggie Lu sipped some warm coffee, then stared at the blinking light on the speaker phone. "There must be a mistake." She glanced up at her framed law degree but withered into her chair like a toddler being chastised.

"Nope, she says she's Beatrice Opal Hopkins Birdsong and..."

A sickening gulp of coffee went down fast. Maggie Lu hadn't heard from her mama in a while. Yes, that was her birth name—except, where did she get the *Birdsong* part? That was her mama's sister Pearl's married name? Never mind.

"Well?" came from the assistant.

"Okay." Maggie Lu punched the line two button, and the light remained steady. She mustered a strong "Hello?"

"It's me, your mama, honey child. I know I haven't been good to keep in touch since Pearl's funeral, good we could all make it. Can't believe I still flash back on the funeral, been months since I'd seen my sister. None of us are getting any younger. Amazing I've got a daughter in her thirties. What does that make me?" A cackling laugh erupted, then was quickly cut off by a hacking cough.

"Still smoking, huh?" Maggie Lu twirled a number

two pencil on top of a legal pad on her desk. Her mama's voice turned on a heat valve all the way down her back. She pushed the remote to start the ceiling fan blades whooshing a hint of cool air overhead.

"I still like smoking, though the damn government is trying to boss me about it." A couple more coughs crackled through the speaker phone.

"Aunt Pearl died about six months ago, Mama, not that long." Maggie Lu barely tempered her disgust.

Sisterly love rarely showed up in how Mama acted toward Aunt Pearl, though her mama had counted on Aunt Pearl to take care of Maggie Lu when she had a chance as a freelance journalist to write in a number of newspapers and flirt with the men on staff. Maybe because Aunt Pearl was older, Maggie Lu always felt okay with just seeing her mama occasionally. Mama was more like a playmate that always took all the toys when she left.

Mama said, "I know that. I've been out to the cemetery, read the marker."

"Have you even thought of a burial plot? Where is Daddy buried?"

"I don't want to think about death. He's in south Mississippi. I hate to say I never really cared for Leo. Maybe the years right after you were born we did all right." Her voice gnawed at the line.

Maggie Lu drew a jagged heart on the pad, then two slashes across it making an X. "What do you want, Mama?" There was no reason to wait for her to express an interest in Maggie Lu's life.

Mama said, "Right before he died, your Uncle Fred told me he divorced Pearl and would leave me part of Birdsong Farm. I just found a paper he signed about it. I figured you were the family lawyer and handled the estate." Maggie Lu winced, assuming Aunt Pearl's will had settled all matters about the farm. Sunny would be as shocked as she was now to hear that the two of them might have to share ownership with her mama. Maggie Lu's mind whirled, determined to look carefully at Uncle Fred's document and check county divorce records, though she doubted most of what her mama said.

"Really and how did you get the Birdsong name?" Maggie Lu couldn't hide her surprise.

Mama laughed. "I just told your receptionist I was a Birdsong to get your attention."

Maggie Lu chewed her lip to keep from cursing.

Dropping her doodling pencil, Maggie Lu stood up, then bent over toward the speaker phone like she was talking to an ordinary client. "Just make a copy of that paper and send it to me."

Mama's voice changed to a whine. "Why, I'm wanting to know something pretty quick, kind of in a bad way financially just now."

Maggie Lu grabbed a tissue and touched her clammy neck. "Legal wheels grind slowly, Mama. I'll transfer you to my assistant. She'll handle your details. Bye."

"Wait, I've got news of your daughter here."

"Who?" Obviously, Mama was trying to shake up her world with that blindsiding quip. So many years since Maggie Lu had let her child go. She fell back into her chair. "How could you possibly . . . ?"

"Fred was drunk one night back in '77, told me Pearl had arranged the adoption for you. I let it lie a long time, Maggie Lu, but it's bedeviled me."

Now Maggie Lu felt like the tormented one. News? She didn't want any news about that child.

"Mama, when I called you to help me back then, you

suggested abortion, among other torments." Her fingers strained around the desk chair armrests. "If you're after that money paid to Aunt Pearl for the adoption, it's long been spent."

Maggie Lu still seethed thinking about discovering that hidden box full of the details around the adoption and the amount of money Aunt Pearl received for her baby.

"I *know* Fred spent it," Mama said evenly.

"And Aunt Pearl only told me fees had to be paid, not profits gained." Maggie Lu couldn't hide her disappointment in their profiteering.

Her head flopped forward onto her arms, exhaustion setting in over Mama's news. Now, desperation churning in her stomach, Maggie Lu turned her head to peek out the window and whisper. "Why are you doing this Mama?" Maggie Lu had not been prepared for a child in her life.

"I'm freelancing, investigating that adoption agency Pearl used, and several others in Jackson."

"Why?"

"I got a tip that the *Clarion-Ledger* was snooping around several of the agencies, sniffing for extortion practices. I wanted to get the scoop first. Now if the child was a pawn of criminal activity, that news story could win me a journalism prize—if I don't get killed."

"Mama, can't you find a safer story to pursue?" Maggie Lu tried to sound calm.

Mama's voice bounced against Maggie Lu's ear. "I have legal counsel in the family."

Maggie Lu kept an even tone. "No, let's not even consider that."

Mama switched to a concerned tone. "I had to find her, our own flesh and blood. She needs us."

"Needs us? We have no legal right to minister to her

needs. I didn't want her to ever know me . . . and still don't. And you took your own time to show concern."

"But listen, now that I'm learning more, I *am* concerned." Mama's voice was uneven.

Maggie Lu let a long breath explode. "What about when I needed a mama? It was all whiskey, men, and news scoops back then for you."

"I can't argue with you, Maggie Lu, about any of that. I didn't always do right by you. Couldn't we sit down and talk?"

Maggie Lu felt Mama's wheedling tone creep into her shoulders, poking and prodding. After her daddy was gone, Mama used to exchange promises for just one more concession like "borrowing" her savings to pay a bill so "we" could have a telephone or heat.

She slammed her hand on her desk. "I don't want to talk about any of this, not now, not ever." She punched the disconnect button on the phone.

In her thirties, Maggie Lu was happy with her life, which did involve too many hours working at her law firm. She was used to not much family connection anymore. Hearing from her mama was rare and usually stressful, but not ever to this degree.

Her assistant cracked the door to her office and stuck her head inside. "Your cousin Sunny is on line one, sounds frantic."

Maggie Lu punched the flickering button. "Sunny, what's wrong?"

"Maggie Lu, did you tell your mama to bring a teenage kid out here to Birdsong Farm to help out with the kennels? The kid says she's staying awhile."

"No, I didn't, but Mama just called me and she's up to something."

The assistant returned and mouthed, "She's called back, says she's coming over here."

"Oh, my god, no. Sunny, I need to catch Mama on the other line. Don't worry. We'll get this straightened out soon. Bye."

Maggie Lu punched the flickering line. "Where are you, Mama?"

"Near Memphis. My car's not running too good. Lord, it's hot without the air. This pay phone booth is worse, though. I've got a place to stay so don't worry about me hanging around. It's just that I need to talk to you about Tiffany. That's what they named her. I wouldn't have but..."

The child's name ricocheted inside Maggie Lu, the past flying right up to shake her. After taking a long breath, she said, "Mama, I'll meet you at that Krystal on Brooks Road where we used to stop when we were driving over from Mississippi. When can you get there?"

"'Bout an hour. I'll call you."

"All right." Maggie Lu dropped the phone in its cradle. She didn't wait for her next call.

*   *   *

The rush hour traffic was backing up near the Brooks Road exit off Interstate 55. Maggie Lu never left the office at that time of day, but all she could think about was diverting Mama's collision course reporting project away from herself. Maggie Lu's head sank against the headrest when she realized she hadn't asked her mama if the child was with her. Clamminess took over, even with the air vent pointed right at her. She inched down the exit ramp at Brooks Road, trying to decide how to handle this encounter.

At the Krystal restaurant Maggie Lu circled the lot,

squinting inside the plate glass windows, too much reflection. Slowing the car even more near the front door, she glimpsed the back of a woman her mama's height pushing through the entrance. Was a young girl in front of her? A horn honked behind her. Embarrassed to be caught gawking, she sped to the back of the lot. Spotting Mama's old Chevy Malibu with the convertible top down, Maggie Lu pulled in next to her unoccupied car and tried to walk casually near the restaurant window on the side with less glare. Too many tables were occupied to spend time foolishly staring through the window, ready to bolt if a child was with her. She had to go in.

Moving inside the icy air conditioning, Maggie Lu felt that the heat had left a film against her eyes. She blinked and moved toward the back of a lone woman with hair the color of Mama's. She touched her shoulder, then drew back with an apology to the startled stranger. Stepping away and near the door, she squinted toward a back booth. Mama sat alone bent over a notebook, her blonde-tinted hair pulled back in a ponytail, a lighted cigarette drooping from the side of her mouth. Just then her head bobbed up and she waved. Caught, Maggie Lu waved back, then plodded toward her. She slid into the booth across from her mama, recoiling from her smoky exhale. Mama stubbed out her cigarette.

"Maggie Lu, you are very professional in that business suit." She blew her a kiss across the table.

"Hello, Mama. You look frazzled. What have you got yourself into?" That familiar banter was their safest approach. Maggie Lu fidgeted with a small, battery-operated recorder in her bag. "Do you mind if I record?"

Mama chewed the end of her plastic pen a moment. "Wow, always in legal mode, aren't you? I've got one in the car, too." She gave her a half grin. "Sure, what the heck."

Maggie Lu sat the recorder on the table near the salt and pepper shakers and pressed the red record button. The cassette tape began to twirl. "State your name and the date." Mama complied and started in.

"Okay, here's where I am with this. I'm trying to get the *Clarion-Ledger* in Jackson to pick up my investigative piece on corrupt child adoption practices. Out of curiosity I decided to start with the Robinson Agency since that's the one Pearl used for your baby in 1977. I ran across Tiffany's case as one of several children placed through the Robinson Agency whose families were still making a yearly "contribution" to the agency. Might be a 'protection' issue, not good."

"My goodness, this is too much to listen to." Maggie Lu squirmed against the hard booth.

Mama was worked up. "Oh, there's more. I became suspicious of several adoption agencies who also were receiving yearly payments from the adoptive parents. Their adoption fees had long since been paid." Mama re-lit the cigarette from the ashtray.

"Whoa, that's quite a tale. Were the children threatened if there was nonpayment?" Anger crept in hearing the terrible consequences of Aunt Pearl using that adoption agency.

Mama's face, greedy with details, was unsettling. "I'm checking into that," she said.

Maggie Lu needed a break. Scooting away from her mama, she rushed to the counter, ordering a Coke to settle her stomach and a packet of fries, then looked over her shoulder. "Want anything?"

Mama stretched her chin forward, then smacked her lips. "Two Krystals and a big Coke."

Maggie Lu spread out the greasy food between them and layered a bunch of napkins on her lap to protect her suit.

Inhaling her cigarette almost down to the filter, Mama stubbed it out in the tiny metal ashtray on the table. A whiff of the melted edge of the filter caught Maggie Lu's nose. Mama picked right back up after a healthy bite out of the mini burger.

"My breakthrough happened when I started cross referencing the police officers who investigated the other adoption agencies receiving yearly payments as the same ones assigned to any complaints about the Robinson Agency. Their reports never presented enough evidence for indictments. I now had an excuse to visit the homes of adoptive parents who were disgruntled about these yearly payments. I have ten corroborative reports. I could file an indictment, but I wanted Tiffany's case to be part of it. Her parents were on vacation in the Caribbean, so I had to make an appointment about a month out."

"Mama, I'm not really in a position to examine the legal course of action."

"I'm not after that, now anyway. I could use some funds, maybe a place for her to stay. It's not all clear."

Maggie Lu cringed at involvement with both possibilities.

Mama resumed her story. "Only Tiffany and the housekeeper were home when I arrived. I was shocked when the housekeeper said both parents were still on vacation. She did remember that the family had discussed its ongoing payment to Robinson Agency to ensure the child's safety, but I didn't want to leave until I could meet Tiffany."

Munching some fries without tasting much, Maggie Lu glanced at the tape still rolling inside the recorder, nervous to hear such close-up details of the child's life.

Mama continued. "The minute I laid eyes on Tiffany, I could see you in her, those sparky gray eyes and high forehead, that wide mouth."

Maggie Lu took small sips of her Coke, savoring the little sugar burns in her throat. There were times she let herself imagine what the child might have looked like, but to actually hear of her appearance was unnerving. Maggie Lu leaned heavily on one arm until her hand felt numb against the bench seat.

"She was practicing piano in the adjoining room. I crept in to watch her. She smiled and asked where I was from. I thought saying I was a newspaper reporter might worry her. Instead I blurted out Crosston. Then I told her I might know some folks who looked a lot like her. She perked up at that.

"How could you?"

After flashing a roguish grin, Mama frowned. "I couldn't help myself."

"Oh, no." Maggie Lu coughed as the Coke went down the wrong way.

Mama was almost breathless. "That was last week. I received a phone call from Tiffany a few days later. She had found my card on their coffee table. Her voice was desperate for adventure. Could I introduce her to the people that looked like her in Crosston? That's when I admitted I was her grandmother. We just broke down and cried."

Mama's eyes moistened, then she blinked. Maggie Lu saw a different mother for a split second. She took a long drink of Coke, relishing the stinging liquid.

Mama kept on. "After we quit boohooing, she told me that her parents were gone a lot. She was lonely for family. I got right up from my desk and drove down to the coast to her neighborhood after telling her to pack a bag and meet me at the end of the block. I had her tell the housekeeper she was staying overnight with her best friend and wouldn't be home after school."

Now Mama listened to frightened children who wanted to be with family, not to Maggie Lu when she was her own kid. Maggie Lu moved toward the end of their booth, struggling not to bolt in anger, managing, "Lord, now you're the kidnapper. Mama, that risk could lead you into trouble."

"I was just caught up in the moment when Tiffany called me." Mama sighed. "I've got to get back to my story."

"She's at the farm, right?"

"Sunny must've called you."

"Yes, right after your call, Mama. It pretty much *is* her farm. Aunt Pearl left me just a few acres."

Eyebrows flapping, Mama oozed, "Really, Pearl did that."

Maggie Lu offered a faint nod so as not to engage her mama.

Mama pried a cigarette out of a new pack with her blunt fingernails and lit it, fanning the match out. "I told Tiffany I'd take her to Crosston. Good that Sunny was home."

Trying for calm, Maggie Lu said, "There'll be a missing person's report out on her by tomorrow."

Mama wagged her head. "I'm thinking the housekeeper will not overreact. I'll call her. I just worried from what Tiffany said that her parents aren't really with her much."

"And you believe this child that you've met once in your life?" Maggie Lu pushed against the table, trying not to let out a tirade about how little her mama had bothered to know her as a kid.

Mama blinked hard. Maggie Lu dropped her head, appalled that the child might indeed live in an unhappy home. She sighed and switched her worry to her cousin, warning, "Sunny has a tender heart; don't take advantage of her."

After wheezing at the smoke floating from Mama's pink lips, Maggie Lu refocused her attention. "Let me see that document Uncle Fred gave you."

Mama unfolded a sheet from a yellow legal pad holding one long sentence written by Uncle Fred. *I Fred Birdsong do solemnly transfer my rights and ownership to Birdsong Farm located in Bessieville, Mississippi, upon my death, to my daughter Sunny and my love, Beatrice Opal Hopkins.*

Maggie Lu's hands shook, so she laid the paper on the edge of the table. "There's no date, no witnesses, no notary. You have no rights to the farm. Aunt Pearl outlived him and willed what was left to Sunny and to me."

"Well, dammit," Mama growled.

Then Mama leaned forward, her eyes narrowed and unfazed. "I need a place for Tiffany. She needs to know our family, too. I've got to finish my work to expose the child endangerment schemes."

Maggie Lu tightened her shoulders and tried to regain a professional pose. "Do you want to file for temporary custody? Does the child want that?" She couldn't say her name. "The hiding won't work. She needs to be in school. Also you'll need a judgment against the parents."

Maggie Lu's blouse was sticking to her back and the grease in the air seemed to settle in every pore. A skinny teenager had dropped coins in the jukebox and Elvis began to sing "All Shook Up." What a ridiculous place to discuss these issues. Maggie Lu had suggested it, so she gave herself no reprieve. She glanced at the teen and immediately considered Tiffany, feeling uncertainty about the child's eagerness to leave her adopted family for unknown relatives. Mama was caught up in her reporting, not really knowing this child's motives.

Mama slumped forward holding her head in her hands. She lifted her head, tiny wrinkles gathering around her eyes. "I've got to work. I can't support a child, never could, though I should . . ."

Maggie Lu faced her mama. She couldn't believe she had to admit, "I am in agreement with you, Mama. We have careers. You've got to move her toward foster care or return her to her family."

"Well, I expected you'd give a little more thought to this." Mama sucked hard on the cigarette, and her cheeks held the smoke before releasing a gray cloud from her mouth.

Maggie Lu's mind drifted to this child now left out at the farm with Sunny, a new cousin to her, just like Mama left her with Aunt Pearl. Was Tiffany full of resentment that Maggie Lu had given her away? Now she felt all the guilt she put on her mama. Should she make amends and take on this child? Would the girl even like her? Legal complications began to tangle Maggie Lu's thoughts. She wiped damp palms on the napkin and checked the recorder. Why did she even want this evidence of a conversation with her mama?

Mama said, "You should take a few days off. Would you consider driving out to the farm? It might help us decide what's next for her."

"Us?"

"Yes, who else can help us?"

"Maybe social services." Maggie Lu took short breaths. "Why get Sunny involved?"

Mama clawed at her ear until it was red. "I saw in those adoption papers that the father had declined his right to custody, but Fred said that Pearl forged Karl's signature, thought he wasn't good enough to raise the child. The Dees were working people, good people, I thought. Fred must have mouthed off in town. Karl got wind of the birth, was shocked at the scheme."

"Karl came to Birdsong Farm looking for our baby back then?" Maggie Lu bit her lip in shock.

"Pearl told him it was too late, that the adoption had already gone through. Pearl got more money for agreeing to the Robinson Agency's demands."

Maggie Lu nodded. "The agency already had found a prosperous family?"

"Right, another part of the corruption."

Mama pushed back in her chair. "I know Karl's people. I'll find him. He followed you all the way to Pennsylvania when you went to school, didn't he?"

Maggie Lu nodded, uneasy to bring up the past. One of the reasons she had enrolled in college up there was to have a fresh start, and by winter Karl knew she was determined to stay. He left before she knew she was pregnant. They would be tied forever if she kept the child. She wasn't ready for either one. She didn't tell him.

Maggie Lu took a long breath. "I heard that he took over Dees Nursery and Hardware Store in Water Valley. The one his parents used to run."

Clenching her teeth, Maggie Lu immediately regretted saying a thing about Karl. Now Mama was trying to reweave the tangles. Maggie Lu had left the child and let Karl go and didn't want them in her life now. She pulled a tissue from her bag and found her checkbook. Blotting the heat from her face, she wrote out a check to her mama. "Will five hundred help you out?"

"Could you manage any more?"

Maggie Lu pushed the stop button on the recorder.

Mama pulled tufts of her hair over her reddened ear. Then her hand slipped across the table and snatched at the check while Maggie Lu tore it out of the checkbook.

As Maggie Lu slid out of the booth, her legs were unsteady. She could barely hold in all the anxiety. "Promise me this is the only night you and the child will spend at the farm. If you contact Karl, I don't want to be involved. Legally, I . . ."

Mama smiled. "You never saw us there."

Then Mama pushed the check in her purse along with her notebook. She strode toward the glass door, then turned. "Watch the newspapers."

Exhausted and uneasy, Maggie Lu watched her mama's red taillights slip into the traffic on Brooks Road just as she often had disappeared into the night.

In the Long Run

Maggie Lu swerved out of the Krystal parking lot and, by reflex, drove old U.S. 51 Highway all the way to Union Avenue, shock from Mama's fervor tightening her grip on the steering wheel. Her stomach roiled with anxious speculation. The stench of the greasy fried food saturating her business clothes forced her to lower the window. Trying to gulp city air was better than Mama's cigarette smoke drifting across her cold french fries back at the Krystal. After weaving her way into her 1920s-era neighborhood, Maggie Lu stopped in the driveway of her stone bungalow on Tutwiler and slumped over the wheel. Seeing Mama always exhausted her, a reason she never initiated the encounter. This time Mama had brought news that left Maggie Lu reeling.

She needed to clear her head. Inside she stripped off the garments that held Mama's smoke, kicking them toward the hamper. Tugging on a white t-shirt and blue jeans shorts, she jammed her feet into some new running shoes and began a slow jog on the sidewalk out front. She pushed hard to count breaths and to follow the path along the forest trail through an edge of nearby Overton Park. The cool evergreen breeze invigorated her pace until she emerged from the park trail to head home. Jogging in place at the stop light, her feet stamped harder in agitation. She made a wrong turn onto Eva Street, and her rhythm got ragged when Mama's conversation slipped back into her mind.

"Uh, huh," Maggie Lu remembered repeating to Mama's cajoling drawl across the table at the Krystal. Finally saying, "Why are you telling me this, Mama?"

Trying not to interrupt her jog, she altered her pace to avoid a limb across the sidewalk. Losing balance, she careened into a shrub and her shoe went soft. A dog hiding underneath the shrub yelped, somersaulting with a retreating bark. Maggie Lu gasped. What had she done? Sunny rescued strays, and now she'd stepped on one. Her cousin was miles away, but Maggie Lu called out, "Sunny, forgive me" at the flight of mangy fur. Her wobbly legs searched for a stride back toward the pavement.

"Watch out for the dog," came from somewhere nearby.

Her head jerked toward a voice on her left, but she couldn't respond. Sunset's shadows didn't hide the blue-jeaned figure with quick feet moving off the porch of the shingled house and closer to the sidewalk. Averting her eyes, Maggie Lu swerved away from the person into the street, accelerating her pace. Maggie Lu's damp shirt flapped chilly against her back, her mama's voice still buzzing inside her head. "You gave her life." Maggie Lu's fingers pressed hard into fists to make Mama's voice stop.

An achy embarrassment triggered Maggie Lu's gaze over her shoulder back down the street. Worry held her feet in place at the cross-street stop sign. She couldn't force a way home yet. Turning, she sprinted the two blocks back and stopped in front of the shingled house. The blue-jeaned woman gave a half wave. Unsure if she was hailed or scorned, Maggie Lu put tentative shoes on the sagging bottom step.

"Did I hurt your dog?" Maggie Lu choked out.

"Not mine, but strays got their rights. I can't take them all in either," the woman said, almost like a melody.

Maggie Lu inched to the top step awkwardly, swayed between each foot, then almost ready to turn, said, "I'm Maggie Lu. I'm sorry for the dog, maybe I could take it."

The dark-skinned woman pushed up out of a slouchy corduroy chair better suited for interior use. She was taller than she looked from a distance, her legs and arms thinner than most people her height. She pointed to a heavy Adirondack chair, her eyes expectant.

"I've got wine I could share while you think about it. I'm Pomona."

Pomona tipped the blue bottle of Riesling toward Maggie Lu, filling up a small jelly jar, and lit a few candles in a circle on the porch floor while the pink and orange skies faded. Maggie Lu slid back and deep down into the chair, wondering why she had agreed to sit on this stranger's porch.

Pomona leaned forward over the candles. "Did you say you were lost?"

"Kind of, just took a wrong turn, so much on my mind. My street is nearby, Tutwiler."

Pomona's brown eyes became flickering slits and her long limbs folded back away from the candles into the soft chair. She stared at the candles too long, then said, "I lost my dog a few years back."

Maggie Lu let some wine slip in and finally said, "How's that?"

"Been hard with no pup to help me through, but I'll always remember," Pomona said, holding out a shiny dog tag attached to a chain around her neck.

Pomona turned up the jar to drain the last drop of

wine, and then said, "I still worry, maybe my Pastorcita was a stray down by the beach after the hurricane hit, just waiting for me. I didn't try hard enough, but someone always comes along to care for the stray, right? You thinking about this one? What else is on your mind?"

Maggie Lu gazed at the shadow of the dog near the porch step. Worn by Pomona's eerie demeanor and the meeting with her mama earlier, she took in more wine, then said, "I've lost sight of things. Today my mama called and said she found the baby girl I gave away thirteen years ago."

Pomona held back, curled in her chair and nodding her head, waiting. "I've had no word from my girlfriend, disappeared shortly after we left Alabama. Don't know how I'd feel hearing about her years later."

Maggie Lu wondered uneasily about the friend's disappearance but couldn't think for long before her own worries surfaced again. Pomona generously removed an orange bandana from her neck just in time for the deluge of Maggie Lu's tears, saying, "You gave me time for my story of loss when yours has come to life again right here."

Squeezing the kerchief, Maggie Lu said, "I regret that I ever agreed to meet Mama at the Krystal and hear about the child."

Feeling dizzy and spent, her mind drifted to this child, Tiffany, now left by Mama out at the farm with Sunny, just like Mama left Maggie Lu there years earlier with Aunt Pearl. Was Tiffany full of resentment that Maggie Lu had given her away? Would Maggie Lu even like this child if she met her?

Maggie Lu leaned forward and set down the wine. "What was the worst part of your loss?" Maggie Lu needed to shift her worries.

Pomona wiggled her lips against her teeth. "Seemed like I had no choices after searching everywhere I could think to go. I know that's cold by what you've just said, but we do have to make choices to feel alive."

Rubbing her aching temples against the evening chill, Maggie Lu hung her head. "It's the living with them, those choices, living with what was true once and now might be a different truth."

Pomona pushed forward, blowing out the candles. "Did you still want the stray? I'm going to get you home now."

But she didn't. Maggie Lu woke up with the glare of early morning sun stabbing her eyelids. A dew-damp quilt and blanket Pomona must have offered kept out the worst of the chilly morning air. After Maggie Lu lifted her throbbing head, the rolled-up jeans jacket serving as a pillow dropped to the porch. From the jacket, Pomona's scent of pungent candle aromas lingered around her shoulders. Yawning, Maggie Lu gazed at the burned-out candles on the damp porch. Her lips pressed hard in disgust at all that she had poured out to this stranger last night, to this woman's dark eyes that flickered, maybe, with indulgence. Yesterday's stray had its nose tucked up under a brown paw, its body curled awkwardly into the corduroy recliner. Maggie Lu pushed forward and up out of the Adirondack and crept down the front steps looking over her shoulder, not wanting to rouse the stray.

But she did. Its spotted ear cocked. When the biscuit-brown eyes focused, a slow growl started. Maggie Lu forced her stiff legs to finish the stairs and her feet to remember the jog. The dog was staying put. It didn't want her. The chilly morning dampness prickled her skin but didn't penetrate the cold exhaustion she took back home. Would the stray later follow her scent?

Bea's Intrusion

In the next few days, sometimes Sunny was annoyed with Tiffany's being underfoot, then happy to have a little company and some extra hands to help out at the kennels. She hadn't meant to get involved so much with pet rescue, but her tender heart and Maggie Lu's financial encouragement helped her stay longer at her old home place. Now she felt more like herself at this rural place than at her city house in Memphis where Hamilton expected her to keep house and keep quiet.

Lately she looked forward to early morning walks with Tiffany and the skinny female bird dog and two scraggly terriers that she had just taken in. After this morning's walk, the kid stretched the lawn hose around the barn and let the spray out hard against the kennels' concrete pads. She giggled. "I'm spraying away the turds."

"You'll get too wet at this rate." Sunny twisted the outside faucet to lessen the water pressure. "Gotta scoop all them up in the red bucket when you're done."

It was mutual disgust. Tiffany wrinkled her face, and Sunny stuck out her tongue. Then they both laughed. "I may lose my appetite for lunch," Tiffany said. "What are we having?" Leaving Tiffany with her task, Sunny called over her shoulder, "I'll let you know."

Sunny slipped inside the kitchen, the screen door closing silently behind her. She'd forgotten to prepare lunch. At the farm she fell out of the domestic habits she kept in Memphis. She took the quickest choice and set to boiling eggs and stirring up tuna, sweet relish, and mayonnaise, rejecting the onion a child Tiffany's age probably hated. She edged around the stray calico cat who answered the tuna can opener's call.

Tiffany bounded inside the kitchen, letting the screen door shut nosily. "That smells fishy. I'm used to something hot." She disappeared into the bathroom, then returned with a frazzled rope to tantalize the cat. Tiffany slid into a ladder back chair by the sink, the cat stretching out by her feet. "Can I help? I know I'm supposed to offer, but I don't like kitchen work."

"It's nice of you to finally offer." Sunny tried for severity, but then smiled.

Her Maggie Lu-like eyes gave Sunny a start. Years ago she and her cousin had whined to her own mama in this very place about kitchen chores. Now Tiffany was repeating their same refrain. "Me either, give me a barn to muck out anytime." Grinning at Tiffany, so caught in deja vu, Sunny forgot to pull down her lip to cover her chipped tooth. "Doesn't your mama give you some kitchen work?"

"We have a maid."

Sunny stiffened. "Well, la-te-da and good for you."

"La, la, la." Tiffany popped up from her chair, making a tiny pirouette, and sang several verses of "Do-Re-Mi."

Sunny repeated the same lines a little off key, moaning, "I loved that movie."

"Yeah, we've got *The Sound of Music* video." Tiffany kept spinning until she dizzily fell into the chair, the old cat darting to safety under the table. Tiffany's playfulness might cause a scaredy cat to dart but it warmed the heart, too.

"So why did you want to come out to an old farm like this?"

"My parents just like going to the beach and resorts. They're so boring. You know I'm adopted? I don't have real parents. You and Granny Bea are real relatives, that's cool."

"You don't? How do you know?" Sunny wondered what Bea had really told the kid.

"Granny Bea said she didn't really know either, that is, where they are or anything."

Tiffany cocked her head at the new noise of a car motor rumbling over the gravel driveway. Sunny brought herself back to mixing tuna salad. After two days with Tiffany underfoot, she was glad to see her Aunt Bea's old Chevy pull up into the carport, the motor coughing before making a final whine, like Aunt Bea herself.

"Gotta be the fan belt, wondered if you'd broke down," Sunny shouted through the screen door.

Bea said, "That car is full of noises, but it hasn't quit on me yet. Had a lot of leads to follow. Am I in time for lunch?" She dropped a smoldering cigarette on the driveway and stepped on it as she climbed from the car. "Could use an overnight stay."

"Of course." Sunny tried to sound jovial while shuddering at the smashed cigarette. Careless habits worried her. She turned back to the boiling eggs, sliding their pan off the stove, and grabbed another can of tuna from the overhead shelf. She felt the cat's eyes penetrate her back, but didn't give the feline any satisfaction with a glance.

She didn't even remember the last time she'd spent

much time with this aunt, other than at her mama's funeral, and now lately Birdsong Farm had been mighty important to Aunt Bea. She offered her mama's room, then regretted giving her an ashtray so she could smoke inside the bedroom.

"I'm making fast headway in my investigations," Bea said.

Mistrust chilling her spine, Sunny added, "I hope it's over soon."

***

Sunny woke up apprehensive about Aunt Bea's snooping investigations and her own growing fondness for Tiffany. She knew she couldn't have this teenager for herself, but she began to think about trying to have a baby of her own again.

On the drive to Dees Nursery and Hardware Store last Monday, images of Tiffany ran through Sunny's mind, causing her to dawdle so much the store was closed when she arrived. She peeked at Karl inside, but something stopped her from knocking. She pushed the door open anyway.

She heard Karl say, "People have been talking ... my past might come back to haunt me and ... , uh, later." He hung up the phone quickly.

"You're after hours," he said, waving at Sunny.

The light caught the profile of his head. Sunny gasped at the recessed chin just like Tiffany's. The memories of Maggie Lu's relationship years ago with Karl flooded her mind. Sunny turned and hurried past the plants. "Gotta go."

Karl leaned over the counter. "You just came in to leave?"

"See ya," she called and scrambled into her truck, speeding all the way home to Birdsong Farm, panic gnawing at her throat over her discovery.

***

Sunny could see Aunt Bea and Tiffany were drinking from tall glasses on the front porch when she drove up the long driveway.

Running up to the truck, Tiffany asked, "What were you doing?" She glanced into the empty truck bed. "There's no dog food."

Sunny stammered for a story. "Got there too late. We'll just go in to Crosston tomorrow and stop at another store. We could eat out at Goody's Drive-In if you'd like."

"Yes, a drive–in is cool." Then Tiffany squinted at her. "You're all sweaty. Are you sick?"

Sunny offered a task in response. "There's enough food left in the barn. Go ahead and feed the dogs."

Giving a frustrated swing of her arms, Tiffany took long, dramatic strides toward the barn. A shiny silver bracelet sparkled on her arm. Sunny hadn't seen her wear a bracelet before. Sunny laughed, remembering her own teenage emotions, her fingers automatically circling her arm at the memory of a favorite bracelet she could only borrow. She had loved the engraving of animals frolicking across the gleaming band. She decided to wait to ask about the bracelet on Tiffany's arm.

Making her way through the kitchen, Sunny poured herself some of the iced tea in the refrigerator and plunked down on the wicker couch next to Aunt Bea on the front porch. She nudged the old calico with her foot. It lazily rolled over to show its white and yellow belly.

"Well, you look a little shaky there, rough day?" Bea struck a match off the floor and lit the cigarette bobbing between her lips. The calico leapt from the porch.

"Oh, you scared her."

"You and those animals." Bea let out a thin stream of smoke.

Sunny's hand gripping the cool glass, she took a long sip of tea, the ice rattling. She couldn't wait another minute. "Karl Dees is Tiffany's father, right?"

Bea stiffened. "What prompted that?"

"I saw him at Dees' store earlier and Tiffany's profile, that recessed chin and button nose, popped right out of him. He was in the shadows, so that's all I could really see." She looked directly at Aunt Bea.

Cocking her head, Bea was curious. "I didn't know you knew him. He was older than you, Maggie Lu's age."

Sunny was uneasy at where this was leading and wondered if Tiffany or Karl should know about each other. Was it her place to tell?

Bea cleared her throat. "Tiffany's home life is not the best. Well, that's what she tells me."

Sunny took more tea. "She says her parents are just gone a lot. I don't want to get involved." Sunny hugged her arms around herself, worrying that she might be getting too fond of the kid.

Aunt Bea tipped her head back for a long swallow of tea and set the glass down too hard. "Pearl told me long ago that Karl signed his rights away after the baby was born. Your mama was in the middle of setting up the adoption. Pearl might not have told him the whole truth." She inhaled the cigarette smoke deeply, then let out the gray mist in a rush.

An irritating tingle crept into Sunny's neck while she

mused over Aunt Bea's actions. She didn't like hearing her aunt talking about her mama's decisions. Bea never respected her mama, rest her soul, even though she was Bea's big sister. Sunny came to learn that those newspaper reporter jobs and her flings were always the most important to Aunt Bea.

Not able to contain her resentment, Sunny pulled back. "Where were you when your daughter needed help with that baby?"

Bea raised her palms, the long ash on the cigarette dangling from between two fingers. "Whoa, let's not go back in time here and stir things up."

Sunny frowned. "I was fool enough to think you really wanted to be in your granddaughter's life, but it's looking like round two of leaving a child out here on Birdsong Farm for someone else to care for."

"Why, you know I care for Tiffany, but I had to go to Memphis and then there was this investigative report to finish up. I thought you wouldn't mind her staying a bit. She loves her new cousin, Sunny."

"When will her parents be back home? She's missing school, you know."

"We'll be heading back to the coast soon."

The front screen door slammed. Tiffany was on the porch with them.

"No, Granny Bea, I don't ever want to go home. I'm having fun with all the dogs, but little Scruffy is yowling something fierce and . . ."

Sunny said, "Little Scruffy must be in heat. Go back and lock her in the milk barn." She flung her arm toward the door.

"What's *in heat* mean?"

"Desire gone wrong." Sunny laughed. "Go on."

Sunny and Bea followed Tiffany inside. Sunny slumped into a wingback chair and waited for Bea to pour more tea and for Tiffany to slam the kitchen door. She thrust a finger into the chair arm. "Aunt Bea, you better speak with Karl before saying much, if you know what I mean."

Bea propped herself against the kitchen door frame and sipped from the newly-filled tea glass. Her puzzled face turned red. "Yeah, okay." Then she grinned. "I've been over there. We had quite a talk about the adoption and maybe more."

Rubbing her temples, Sunny silently cursed her Aunt Bea's sly response. She was tired of her sneaky ways. Did Aunt Bea mean to get Karl to take the girl? She wished Bea would have never brought Tiffany to Birdsong Farm if she was going to have to leave in a crisis; that is, if Bea talked to Karl or to Tiffany about her investigation. Who knows how Karl would react to finding out about a daughter lost to him? Or Tiffany? Her longing for real family now might overwhelm her if Bea told her about Karl. Bea would do anything for a story, leaving torn emotions in her wake. Sunny flinched, knowing some other motives were probably stirring below Bea's surface.

Sunny wanted them all to pack up their messes. She looked around the room at pillows on the floor, Tiffany's backpack on the couch spilling out papers and small notebooks filled with her poetry, and her jeans jacket draped over the dining room chair back. Wiping her sweating forehead with her sleeve, Sunny crawled out of the wingback and upstairs to her room. She was on edge. She offered a dismissive nod to Bea. "I'm in need of a nap."

* * *

When Sunny returned from town the next afternoon, she found the room Aunt Bea was using in shambles and her mama's jewelry box tipped over. Tiffany stood in the doorway. "Granny Bea said I could have the bracelet." She stuck out her arm.

"That was once my cousin Maggie Lu's. She always liked the animal designs on it." Sunny balked at the thought of Tiffany unknowingly wearing her birth mother's bracelet. Did Aunt Bea know it had been Maggie Lu's?

"Oh, Granny said it had been hers, that your mama gave it to her, then took it back. Is it okay to keep?" Tiffany's gray eyes darkened. "What was your cousin like? Mama said she was dead, I'm sorry."

Stunned, Sunny sat down hard on the bed to catch her breath. She tensed at the thought of Aunt Bea's blatant lie about her own daughter and tried to remember to calm down.

"Yes, if she thinks it's hers, but your Granny should have asked first about going through my mama's jewelry box. You would never do that, would you?" Sunny pressed her hand hard against the bed in anger at Aunt Bea telling lies, even about her mama, then said, "It looks like she has gone through the whole box looking for something."

Tiffany moved away from the door. Hearing heavy footsteps, they both turned when Bea pushed into the bedroom. "Pack your bags, Tiffany. We've got to get back to the coast." Tiffany's shoulders tightened. "Aww, no, I'm not ready to go." She disappeared from the doorway. A loud door slam echoed down the hallway.

Bea whispered. "Sunny, I've confirmed that Tiffany's adoption agency is corrupt, and Karl admitted to taking a payoff to release his rights that Pearl helped initiate. He showed me the documents that I needed to corroborate my report."

Her eyes welling up, Sunny said, "Did you tell him she was here?"

"I told him I could locate her if he wants to meet her. I don't have any more time for him now."

"Does he?" Sunny couldn't hold back, her spirits sinking at the thought of Tiffany floating away from her into the arms of a legal morass.

"Yes." Bea was giddy.

"Oh, what about Maggie Lu?"

"When I went to Memphis, Maggie Lu said she wanted no part of Tiffany's life. She's dead to her, so that's what I told Tiffany." Aunt Bea's eyes were cold.

Sunny sank into the bed, Maggie Lu's response nearly smothering her. She could hardly look at Aunt Bea as she came to grips with her words. Sunny took in futile gasps, sickened with worry for Karl and for Tiffany over the trauma Aunt Bea was creating in their lives.

"Will she stay with her family?" Sunny tried to regain the conversation.

"I don't know, after all the scandal comes out, but I'm taking her back there for now. I've got to get in my reports."

Watching Bea's eyes flashing in the excitement of her discoveries, Sunny's stomach knotted in disgust. "You always put your job and yourself first, don't you Aunt Bea." It was not a question.

Bea stared back. "I just don't see it that way."

No longer wanting to face Aunt Bea, Sunny slipped upstairs into the hall, listening outside of Tiffany's door. Quiet was on the other side. Her hand stretched out to knock. Instead, she silently the door opened a bit. Tiffany stood before her, small and head erect. Sunny offered a tiny smile, wondering if their closeness would lead to a hurt neither would be able to bear. Sunny's hand still in midair, she reached out and touched the bracelet on Tiffany's arm, cool and smooth silver. She wasn't sure what she'd say.

Sunny's Confidences

Sunny waved to the waitress for more coffee. Karleen took a final gulp and pushed her empty cup toward the edge of the table next to Sunny's for a last refill.

"What do you actually want?" Karleen squinted at her friend across the table.

"After the tornado hit Birdsong Farm and nearly killed me last year, I've changed my ways."

Sunny loved her new dog rescue venture at Birdsong Farm, but her time there also provided a respite from her waning marriage commitments. She had a hard time saying no to many people, but after hanging out more with her friend Karleen at the coffee shop in Water Valley, she was gaining some confidence. Just yesterday she announced to her husband Hamilton, who maintained their home in Memphis, that she had decided to take in two more rescue dogs at her farm. Partly it was to stay away from home and Hamilton another few weeks at least. When she told him, Hamilton could only say, "Really," in a tone that Sunny let slip away when he ended the call abruptly.

"More dogs?" Karleen prodded her.

"Less guilt," was all Sunny could come up with.

"That's a start." Karleen nodded in agreement.

"You're loving all the work these animals require, or are you just needing more love?" Karleen flashed a grin and then motioned the waitress for the check.

Sunny's stomach was heavy from the two donuts and the pot of coffee she'd indulged in. She pushed back from the table, staring at her bulging jeans and wondered if Hamilton had ever loved her. Worse yet, she knew she had lied to him about being pregnant when they married. She was ashamed to tell Karleen about that desperation.

"I do love dogs," she said to move away from the discomfort.

Shifting in her seat, a jab of elation followed, remembering Tiffany saying the same thing, flashing those gray eyes. With Tiffany back in school on the Gulf Coast, Sunny was spending more time with Karleen, a good companion. Karleen had opinions about everything. That quip about needing more love made her edgy, but others made her laugh.

"And I care for dogs too, but I don't want the ugly ones you come up with." Then Karleen raised her palms and deadpanned, "Not ugly, no, maybe unusual."

Sunny stared at the jagged scar in Karleen's palm and wondered, "Accident?"

Karleen turned over her hand and winced. "Bad fight. I lost, got hurt pretty bad, did some stupid things, so I got out of Tennessee." Karleen's laugh was quick, then her eyes narrowed. "That's why I'm back home, lucky that Karl needed a hand."

Karleen worked at Dees Nursery and Hardware Store with her twin brother Karl but could always take a long break if Sunny called in time. Karleen was the only one Sunny wanted to tell her stories to lately, though the stories Karleen shared were always more exciting. Sunny leaned in to get a closer look at the scar.

"What kind of fight? That sounds scary."

Karleen slid her hand from the table. "It was a lesson learned, all right. No time now to tell all about that. Maybe later."

* * *

Sunny got up apprehensive on those mornings that she thought about going to Water Valley. She sat now in her denim shirt and jeans, but underneath was red lingerie. The silky fabric stirred her, making her feel not so alone even when she was by herself. She hesitated to talk about this fascination with Karleen.

She never wore the lingerie in Memphis around her husband Hamilton. He would think she was crazy. When they had been intimate, it had been a quick passion, fading into a boring routine. It had suited them both. She doubted her love for him more as time passed. Then came the real miscarriage, which shook them both into their own worlds.

Sunny had talked freely with Karleen, telling her sometimes she wished she would have a baby. She spent more time speculating on dating someone interesting even if she didn't divorce Hamilton.

"Dream big. It's your life," Karleen always said.

* * *

After their stop at the coffee shop, Sunny followed Karleen back to Dees Nursery and Hardware Store to pick up food for the kennel animals. She liked hanging out at the feed store. Karl could be playful or put her to work, if she was willing. Karleen offered suggestions for an herbal garden. Sunny admired the name plate on her desk, sharp white scripting, M. Karleen Dees. What was the *M* for? Was *Sunny* a real name? They both joked they didn't really know each other's whole names.

That was when she wondered if her Aunt Bea had even told Karl the name given to his child. Not long ago, after Aunt Bea had talked to him about Tiffany, Sunny was wary about what he might ask her. It had not seemed to affect her friendship with Karleen, but Karl was more moody. Sunny didn't want to talk about the situation. She fingered the potted plants but couldn't think where to plant them at home.

Karleen picked up a small, red geranium plant and tucked it next to the tailgate of Sunny's truck as she was leaving. "Just to add a little color to your day," she said, then blinked her long, soft lashes in a way that caused Sunny to linger and to wonder about the tingle behind her breastbone.

Karl's loud laughs pulled her away from worry, easing her into chatter of feed and animal nutrition. He didn't mention that evening when she'd let herself into the shop after hours, then bolted so unexpectedly. They both were probably edgier after Aunt Bea's visit. Karl was so nice to load the heavy bags of dog food into her truck. Sunny wondered if she'd like to work there with the two of them.

***

Two days later, with two new rescues causing her extra cleaning to do at the kennel, Sunny got to Dees' store right before closing time. She struggled at the locked front door, disappointment setting in. When she called for Karleen through the open gate and walked back around the outside through the line of potted trees and plants, she found her friend's tall frame draped over a lawn chair out back. Karleen was taking a pull from a flask of whiskey, her flip-flops propped on a wooden barrel. She jumped to her feet.

"Whoa, I wasn't expecting anyone, but I'm glad it's you. What can I get for you, Sunny?"

Sunny tugged at her collar. "Oh, sorry to bother you without calling."

Karleen snickered a little louder than usual. "Just me and Jack Daniels back here. Would you like to visit us?"

"I've never tried it, but I could."

Sunny felt a twinge of guilt even now from all her church upbringing about alcohol defiling her body. She'd learned to let it pass. She didn't want to drive right back home, but she was uneasy about seeing Karleen's altered demeanor.

Karleen ducked inside the back door of the store and returned with two coffee mugs, pearly beads of water still dripping from their sides. She poured a little whiskey into each cup and handed one to Sunny.

"Take a sip and let that heat slip down your throat."

Karleen stifled a laugh. Setting the bottle and her cup on the barrel, she let out a long sigh, her eyes fixed on Sunny's face. They both sat down slowly, at the same time, with the barrel between them as a table. Sunny sniffed the strong odor and dared herself to take a drink.

"I guess we knew it was just a matter of time," Karleen whispered as she put the cup to her own lips.

"You mean us drinking more than coffee? Sunny said, "What about Karl?"

"My brother leaves early most days, loves to fish. He's not gonna know about us."

"Us?" Sunny stuttered.

"Well, I kinda thought you dropped by late on purpose . . . uh, uh. You don't stay at home with that old husband in Memphis much anymore. We have spent some time together already." Karleen took another sip from the mug and her eyelids slipped down and shut her out.

Sunny felt her back dampen quickly at this kind of talk. Had Karleen really thought about her beyond their coffee shop chats? She tried to stop the tingle from behind her breastbone, then didn't.

"I do think about you." Sunny didn't know what else to say.

Focusing on Karleen's soft lips, Sunny let herself think about what they might feel like on hers. Surprised that she was thinking about a woman in this way, Sunny let more of the fiery liquid down her throat to keep the fantasy going.

Then the automatic nightlight clicked on behind Karleen. Sunny blinked and pulled herself back, releasing a tiny gasp. She straightened in her chair, feeling the damp lingerie pasty on her skin. She couldn't have intimate thoughts about a woman she had poured her heart out to. She had never felt more vulnerable.

"You okay?" Karleen leaned closer to the barrel table, sloshing the brown liquid.

"This stuff is powerful, makes you conjure up crazy ideas. Did you ever want kids, Karleen?" Sunny was letting the burning liquid help her toward an imaginary family.

Karleen leaned forward, a puzzled frown emerging. "Why are you talking like that now?"

"I don't know what came over me," she lied. "Well, I

do. I've been thinking about it more lately, seeing as my thirties are slipping by fast."

"That's not really what I had in mind to talk about. When you mentioned a baby the other day I didn't think you were serious. Kids would just be helping you spend your hard-earned money. You'd be stuck with Hamilton then." Karleen leaned back into her chair, a worried grin unfolding her moist lips. "I thought it was dating you wanted."

Sunny set her empty cup down on the barrel. "I better get back to the farm." Wishing Karl would come in with a string of fish and change the subject, she said, "Tell Karl I said *hi*."

Sunny hurried past the plants, banging into the gate. She turned with a weak wave. "I don't know what I think." She scrambled into her truck, speeding all the way home to Birdsong Farm, panic aggravating her insides over what Karleen must think of her. She pushed away at her strange feelings about Karleen.

* * *

Sunny could not muster the nerve to see Karleen again after their evening with Jack Daniels last week. Each time the phone rang, she let it go to voicemail. Now the jingle of the phone was insistent. Sunny had ignored Karleen's message earlier in the day. Maybe she was worrying too much about Karleen. She sighed, then pushed up from her wicker chair on the front porch, moving slowly inside to answer. She panicked at the familiar voice on the line saying "Sunny," but with anger in it.

"Karleen, what's wrong?" Sunny balked at her testiness.

"Karl's just beside himself, brooding over this daughter your Aunt Bea told him about. He said you knew about it last week."

Sunny sank into the closest wingback chair and tried to sound calm. "Not all the details." She tried to stall. Karl was more moody, fishing less since Aunt Bea's visit, but she didn't want to get involved. She barely remembered talking to him when she had gone to Dees' store Monday.

"Hold on, thought I heard a dog yelp." She was gathering her wits.

Karleen's voice trickled through the phone. "Sounds like a touchy subject, dogs attached."

Sunny laughed. "Just a yelp, no physical contact. All attachments are not necessarily sexual."

"Could be," Karleen was quick. "Did your door slam?"

"The neighbor's helping me with the kennels."

Karleen said, "Is something going on with you and Karl?"

Sunny didn't know whether to be flattered or feel smothered. "Going on?"

"Well, Karl got miffed about you and me drinking together, says lately he's feeling left out of everything. So was it Karl you were thinking about, Sunny? Were you serious about wanting a baby?" Karleen's voice was hard as a slap.

"No." Sunny touched her face as if Karleen was standing in her living room. She shuddered a moment, suddenly repelled by any speculation that she would be attracted to Karl. Her thoughts flashed back to a young Karl sitting this very living room waiting while Maggie Lu primped for their date. Even then she wondered what Maggie Lu saw in him.

Karleen's voice eased off a little. "I gave it some thought, didn't mean to put you down. We can talk later, unless you mentioned it to Karl too."

Sunny said, "No, uh, I stopped by late to see you

awhile ago, well, to say hi, and Karl was saying to someone on the phone that people were talking about him, his past." What had Karl told his sister about Tiffany?

"I'm sorry I missed you." Karleen's tone made Sunny antsy. "But I'm worried."

Sunny silently cursed. She wished she weren't alone so much at Birdsong Farm, but going to Water Valley might be getting her in some trouble she didn't know how to handle. Why had she mentioned a baby? Something else must be going on. She heard a long sigh. Sunny stared out the window and shook her head, then spoke into the phone, "Karleen, you still there?"

Karleen said, "Karl's feeling needy lately."

"I'm sorry I just ran out of the store and didn't chat with him, forgot something. He didn't mention it when he loaded the dog food in my truck last week." Fidgeting in her chair, Sunny got uncomfortable hearing about Karl's upset. She wondered if he was stirred up by the possibility of meeting the daughter he gave away.

Karleen sighed. "He's been acting different lately."

Sunny wondered if Aunt Bea's visit to Birdsong Farm with her foundling granddaughter had left a lot of tattered emotions behind. Karl was probably still reeling from Bea's news of this girl being the daughter he'd fathered thirteen years earlier. Sunny was disappointed in Aunt Bea's thoughtlessness.

"Poor Karl."

Karleen said, "Poor me. I need to get away for a little, going camping near my family's old farm."

Without forethought Sunny leapt at a change of subject. "Where's that?"

"Near where my hippie friends hang out at a farm up in Tennessee."

"I've never been camping, sounds like fun."

"What about old Hamilton? Would he care if you took off?"

"I'm not his thing anymore," Sunny blurted out carelessly. Her damp fingers gripped the armrest like it was moving, starting on the trip.

"You were never that blunt before." Karleen sounded delighted, then her tone shifted, "Oh, Sunny, I'm sorry y'all are having trouble. If there's anything I can do . . ."

Sunny worried what could happen alone with Karleen, but knew she wanted to see her again. "I will," she said, loosening her fingers from the chair. Then she remembered she couldn't leave the farm right now. One of the dogs was sick. "Might take a rain check on the camping trip." She talked quickly, not wanting Karleen to ask her anything else, not sure what would happen.

"I want to hang on, talk more, but I won't. Bye." Karleen sounded too calm. "I'll let you know when I get back."

"Sure, we'll do coffee," Sunny said evenly.

Queasy guilt gripped Sunny while she wondered what signal she had sent to Karleen. The whiskey had caused her to look at Karleen differently, but only for a moment. Talking about wanting a baby had been a stupid thing to say.

She looked around the room, imagining Karleen stretched out on the couch, their conversations going so funny. She listened to the dogs yelping to each other from the kennel. When Hamilton was here, the house had felt so empty and silent. Now the house was so messy, but so full of life after Tiffany's visit. Of course Bea's discovery of the child had started so much talk. Pressing her lips together tightly, Sunny slipped down in the wingback, confused about where the tingling behind her breastbone might lead her and all those confidences exchanged.

Running Away

Sunny picked up the phone and got an earful.

"I miss you, Cousin Sunny. I loved all the dogs in the kennels and staying with you at Birdsong Farm," Tiffany wailed.

"You can come back this summer. We'll even go with Karleen up to the Tennessee mountain farm where other kids live." Sunny tried to sound reassuring.

Tiffany's voice was tense in Sunny's ear. "You're my real cousin. Why can't you come down to Biloxi and meet my parents? At least talk to Mama, okay?"

Sunny felt a flash of panic. "Well, honey, I dunno."

Tiffany spoke in muffled tones that Sunny barely caught. "Mama, can I go back to Birdsong Farm this summer?"

Taking a deep breath, Sunny wondered about this parent that Tiffany had spoken about so few times. Quickly Sunny heard another voice on the phone. "This is Jane, Tiffany's mama. We'll be at the Bahamas casinos this summer." Sunny heard a strange giggle, then cough. Jane continued. "Y'all were good to her up there, said she had fun with her new relatives. It would be convenient for her to go back to that farm while we're gone."

Sunny hung on the phone in disbelief that Tiffany's mama was so willing for her to return to *new* relatives.

"Yes, Jane. So good to talk with you." Sunny kept an even tone though insulted at the label *new relative*.

Jane's voice trailed off. "Yes, of course. Oh, it would be nice to meet Bea. Tiffany will talk to you later. Bye."

Sunny hung up the phone, stunned at this encounter with Tiffany's mama. Then Sunny's mind started sorting again all that Aunt Bea had revealed about her investigation of the adoption agency scandal that led her to discover Tiffany's adoption. Finding Karl, Tiffany's birth father added ammunition to her aunt's explosive expose' that she hoped to present to the Jackson *Clarion-Ledger*. Aunt Bea seemed unphased when Sunny had reminded her of the messy emotions she'd be stirring up. Sunny bit her lip. Indeed, she and Tiffany had grown closer than she had imagined after Aunt Bea essentially left the girl on her doorstep for a week. Tiffany had called Sunny nearly every day since she left.

The next day Sunny listened while Tiffany told her she'd lost her appetite for a week after her Grandma Bea dropped her off at her parents' house in Biloxi. "I miss you and the farm," she repeated to Sunny. "Tell Grandma Bea to come over. She doesn't like me calling her much."

"I'll do what I can to reach her, honey. Got to go check on those barking dogs now." Sunny hung up the phone frustrated at the thought of calling her Aunt Bea but dialed her number. After a breezy hello, Aunt Bea sounded uneasy when Sunny announced that she had invited Tiffany to go with her and Karleen up to a farm in Tennessee in the summer. "Guess who Tiffany put on the phone in the middle of our conversation."

"You've talked to the parents?" Bea's voice was piercing.

Sunny groaned. "Tiffany put her mama on the line,

had no choice. They were planning a gambling junket about that time of year, seemed fine with it. Her mama wants you to come over. She hasn't met any of Tiffany's *new* family. I almost got snippy. We're the *old, original* family."

Bea gasped. "Did you say that?"

"Naw, but I struggled to hold back. You'll bring Tiffany back up to Birdsong Farm, won't you? Tiffany asked me to ask you. She'd like to ride up here with you. Call her, okay?"

"What about Karl meeting her?" Bea asked.

Sunny replied, "I don't know what'll happen. He talks a lot to his sister, Karleen, about Tiffany. I try to stay out of it."

***

Sunny didn't want all the anxiety about Tiffany to ruin her friendship with Karleen. When Karleen invited her to meet at the coffee shop in Water Valley, she was uneasy but wanted to make the trip. Unfortunately, Karleen was still worried about the effect of Bea's visit with Karl, so her conversation was the same as last time—but with a twist. Now Karl was losing sleep wondering about the lost daughter that Bea discovered. Karleen's eyes seemed frantic when she said, "Finally, he called Maggie Lu. I couldn't believe he said that maybe he and Maggie Lu should think about meeting Tiffany, being a part of her life. The call must not have gone well since Karl slammed down the phone. He just sagged into the nearest armchair and wept." Karleen shook her head and took a long gulp of coffee.

Sunny cringed at the mention of Maggie Lu. She remembered when she had casually let it slip to Maggie Lu that she liked having Tiffany at the farm. She was shocked at how harsh Maggie Lu was, her voice tearing at Sunny's feelings. Sunny moved her coffee cup between both hands before saying, "Maggie Lu told me to make sure I never mention her to that child."

Pushing away from the table, Karleen said, "I'm livid over the suffering Bea has brought on."

Sighing, Sunny agreed. "I am too, Karleen. Introducing Tiffany to the family has brought its share of problems, though I like the kid." She kept to herself the realization that Aunt Bea seemed more interested in her expose' than the sparks her discovery of Tiffany had generated between her daughter and Karl. Sunny hated to think about such callousness in Aunt Bea, but it was in Maggie Lu, too. Not wanting to stir up more animosity talking about Karl's dilemma, Sunny rose and patted her friend's shoulder. "We've both got a lot to deal with."

***

Early in the summer Bea called Sunny. "I got wind of a lead story to follow up in northwest Mississippi. I might have to spend a few nights with you to save money. I'll invite Tiffany to ride along. Y'all talked about a summer visit."

"Her parent's okay with it?" Sunny had not expected Tiffany's visit so soon. She and Karleen had been busy repairing the kennels and helping Karl out at the Water Valley store.

Bea's tone was unflappable. "The housekeeper said they were gone again. She'd let me know if I shouldn't come. Haven't heard from her, so it's a go."

Later in the week Bea honked her horn while coming up the long driveway at Birdsong Farm, then parking her

Chevy behind Sunny's truck. Sunny stood at the back door waving, making a quick list in her head of things not to talk about with Aunt Bea regarding her newspaper assignments. Tiffany dragged two big suitcases from the trunk of Bea's car. Bea sat in the car finishing a cigarette.

"Are you moving?" Sunny joked.

"A suitcase for each farm," Tiffany laughed. She dropped the bags and opened her arms toward Sunny. "Hugs, Cousin Sunny."

Sunny gasped at the tight squeeze and wound her arm around Tiffany, reaching a little higher to touch her shoulders. "You've grown a foot since I saw you last."

"Right," Bea muttered, leaning awkwardly as she pushed open the car door and dropped the smoldering cigarette butt into the driveway, smashing it with a grinding toe.

* * *

Late in August Sunny made a frantic call to Bea. "Tiffany's run away from the Roost farm. Karleen is searching for her now. My truck is acting up. Can you give me a ride up there?"

Uh, huh," Bea said. "I was on my way to Memphis anyway and haven't left Crosston yet. Might not have enough gas to get to that other farm." Within an hour Aunt Bea's old Chevy was speeding up the long driveway. Sunny had remembered to call the Adair boys to check the kennels the next few days. She threw a small bag in the back seat. After riding only a few miles, she wished even harder that the old Chevy had an air conditioner that worked. The drive across U.S. 72 seemed endless with the sweltering blasts of air sweeping through the old car. Bea pounded the steering wheel after they passed the Memphis city limits sign.

Sunny sat straight up. "What's wrong?" The front fender was tilting over on her side.

"Red warning lights are popping on. Something's wrong with the car."

"Sounds like a flat tire, that bump and the fender dipping like that."

Bea steered the Chevy into the parking lot of the Krystal restaurant. "I forgot to check the oil before I left. I hate to do it, but I'll call Maggie Lu to come help us."

Sunny stood outside the phone booth, fanning herself and listening to Aunt Bea talk.

"My car's broken down by the Krystal we ate at last time off Brooks Road." Aunt Bea shuffled her feet and tried to stretch the phone cord outside the stuffy phone booth. "Sunny's with me." *She's shocked,* Bea mouthed to Sunny. "Could you call a tow truck, maybe meet us for dinner?"

Sunny retrieved an envelope from between the car seats and a pen from her purse. She asked a guy in the parking lot the Krystal address and wrote it down, handing the pen and paper to Bea. Nodding, Bea scratched a phone number and a AAA number next to the address and hung up. She showed the numbers to Sunny. "Maggie Lu said these guys could help. I'm going to call as soon as you find us some more coins."

"Why didn't you tell her the reason we were here?" Sunny asked.

"Did you want to hear her meanness about the taboo kid?"

"No. We're all stressed out now with Tiffany in our lives."

"Stressed, right, losing time tracking my next news story, too." Bea said.

Sunny was beside herself ever since Karleen called

yesterday, admitting that Tiffany didn't want to leave the Roost farm to go home at the end of the summer. "Time is ticking away for finding Tiffany, too." Sunny's agitation was rising.

"Yikes, the kid latches on so quick." Bea had let her irritation slip.

Sunny raised an eyebrow. "No, it's worse than resisting. She's gone, run off with two teenagers."

Karleen's tone had been casual on the phone. Tiffany had made new friends with two older teens, Beck and Josie. They'd disappeared together, hadn't been seen since they didn't show up for supper. The teens were familiar with the area.

Sunny's response verged hysteria. "Keep up the search. I'm coming soon."

***

Sunny dug through her purse for coins, finally dumping the whole contents on Bea's car seat to retrieve the change. Coins rolled toward the crack where the seats came together. "No," Sunny moaned. Bea watched Sunny's arm scoot all the combs and brushes and tissues and no telling what across the seat and back into her cloth bag, then cinch it up too tight with a drawstring.

Bea didn't hold back. "Carrying all that junk reminds me of how Pearl used to lug a big purse everywhere she went. Are you turning into your own mama?"

Sunny's eyebrows wiggled. "We both wanted to have everything with us in case of an emergency." Sunny resented that Aunt Bea was still critical of her mama. Handing her the coins, Sunny said, "At least I have the money. Go ahead and make the AAA call."

Sunny paced until Bea returned to the car. "Yikes, I've

got to talk to Karleen. Maybe she's heard something." She almost ran toward the pay phone.

Glancing back, she saw Aunt Bea light a cigarette, slam the car door and lean against it, keeping her back to the phone booth. Did Aunt Bea really not care about Tiffany?

"No news." Sunny sprinted toward her aunt and sat hard on the curb next to the broken-down Chevy. "I thought leaving the Roost early to adopt another dog and take it home to my kennel would be a new attraction for Tiffany. She said she wanted to hang out with me at Birdsong Farm before going home. Now I wish I'd never left her alone with Karleen and those kids up at the Roost. The others living up there are stoned more than sober, fun, but in this case, no help."

Bea paced in front of the car, growling. "Don't mention Karleen to Maggie Lu. She wants nothing to do with that family. Plus, she'd freak out if she knew Karleen has been with Tiffany."

Sunny lamented, "Karl's scared to get involved. Maggie Lu threatened him."

Aunt Bea took a long drag. Curving her lips, she blew smoke rings on the exhale. "Maggie Lu's got her issues for sure."

After the AAA driver changed her tire and tightened her battery cables, Bea called Maggie Lu. "Could you swing by the Krystal restaurant? We're grabbing a burger before we leave." Aunt Bea hung up and grinned. "I'm glad Maggie Lu still comes when her mama calls her."

When Maggie Lu opened the restaurant door, Sunny waved at her cousin from their booth and nudged her Aunt Bea who was stubbing out a cigarette and taking a choky breath. "She made it."

"She actually came here." Sunny's voice cracked, still wary of Maggie Lu after their last conversation about Tiffany.

Maggie Lu gave Sunny a sideways hug and her mother a nod, before sliding into the booth seat next to Sunny, giving her a push for more space to get settled in. She said, "Y'all are a sight. Sunny, hanging out with Mama will keep you in trouble. What brings you to Memphis? I doubt that it is just to see me."

Bea sipped her Coke, then said, "I'm here on assignment for the *Clarion-Ledger*. I'm giving Sunny a ride up to visit some friends east of here. And, uh . . . I'm probably going to need a new tire. Could you spare . . . ?"

Maggie Lu leaned forward, looked hard at her. "Geeze."

Sunny dropped her head. "It's not money we're really after. We're going to search for Tiffany. She's run away."

Maggie Lu's eyes blazed. "This child shouldn't be in our lives. Mama, stop enabling this situation. Just call the authorities." Maggie Lu reached for Sunny's half full cup of water and gulped it fast.

Sunny's eyes were wet, but her voice was firm. "Tiffany wants to be in this family whether you like it or not."

Maggie Lu tugged at her collar. "I feel like you have chosen this child over me. So, okay. Just let me be."

"No, don't think that way. I don't want to lose contact with you." Sunny reached to stop the cup moving between Maggie Lu's hands.

Maggie Lu slid quickly to the end of the bench. She glared at Sunny and her silent mama, stood up, free from the booth. Then she dropped two hundred dollars on the table. "Good luck." Sunny gulped, watching her cousin stride away without looking back.

Aunt Bea stretched her arm across the table and

snatched the two bills, stuffing them into her purse. "Dammit Sunny, why'd you open up with that Tiffany talk? Maggie Lu hardly had time to sit down, nearly lost my chance for a little loan."

Sunny sniffed. "We used to be close. I hate to lie to her. I still want her to care for Tiffany like we do. I see that we upset her. Maybe she's scared."

"I've never seen her scared." Bea tapped a fresh cigarette on the table.

"You're not looking." Sunny said.

Bea took a sip of Coke and exhaled. "Now I'm just dropping you off up at the Roost this evening, got to get back here for an interview in the morning. You and Karleen will find Tiffany. I'm sure she hasn't gone far."

"No, I've got another ride. Karleen sent Karl up here to the Krystal to get me."

"What? How soon will he be here?" Bea scooted toward the end of the booth, clutching her purse as she stood up. "Make sure he just drops you off and gets on his way. Don't want any messy encounters up there."

Sunny nodded but felt a giddiness drifting through her. Tiffany might get to meet her daddy. She glimpsed a red truck pulling into the parking lot. Relieved, she rose and said, "Bye, Aunt Bea."

* * *

When Karl's red truck rumbled down Kudzu Road toward the Roost, the sun was dipping behind the pines. Their hour-long ride had been full of cautious conversation. Karl said uneasily, "I'll just sleep on a couch since I've never been out here, don't know these folks except by what Karleen has said."

"There seems to be plenty of room," Sunny said, happy that Karl was eager to stay longer than just dropping her off. He would help with the search.

They saw Karleen rise up from the swing on the front porch and give a little wave when Karl's truck lumbered into the yard. "I've missed you."

Sunny jumped from the truck and hurried toward the porch. "I'm barely gone a few days and Tiffany disappears. Gee, Karleen."

Karleen put up her palms defensively. "I know, I know, but she's with Beck and Josie. They know these hills. They'll be back after they've made their little protest, probably back by tomorrow." She nodded toward Karl. "Are you up to this, brother?"

Karl hurried up the steps toward the front door. "You know I want to see Tiffany more than anything."

Karleen nodded, then turned to Sunny. "Do you think I did the right thing, asking him to come?"

Sunny shrugged. "I'm torn. No telling what Maggie Lu might do when she finds out, but Karl cares and that's what matters to me most now."

"I care." Karleen tried to reach for Sunny's hand.

Sunny stepped back and wagged her finger toward Karleen. "And after what you've done, not watching after Tiffany, you shouldn't talk."

Karleen dropped her head. Sunny followed them inside. A bottle of Jack Daniels and a half full glass of the brown liquid sat on the table. "Care for a drink to calm your nerves?" Karleen said.

Sunny let the screen slam behind her. "No way."

Karl sat down heavily in a wooden chair at the table, saying, "Pour me a double. I'm pretty nervous about being here."

Karleen glared. "Pour it yourself, brother. You've been upset over this child ever since you heard about her."

Karleen grabbed her own drink and kept in step behind Sunny as she climbed to the upstairs bedrooms. When Sunny turned around, Karleen's lips turned upside down. "Baby, I know you're upset." She followed Sunny into her room. Sunny eased the door shut and softened inside Karleen's embrace, whimpering, "It's been such a long and worrisome day."

***

Early the next morning Sunny had Karl drive his truck up and down Kudzu Road. Jammed together on the front seat, Sunny and Karleen shouted out the window until their throats hurt. "Tiffany, Tiffany, please come home." Sunny felt a clamminess take her over again, imagining Tiffany and the other girls lost and confused. Karleen was quiet. Sunny kept regretting that she'd left Karleen with the responsibility for Tiffany. Finally, Karleen said, "I've never seen the other kids' mamas panic as much as you did when they did crazy things, went missing for just a half a day." Sunny frowned, wondering how often those girls disappeared without much concern from their parents.

When they pulled back up in front of the old farmhouse, they spotted Tiffany climbing between two strands of barbed wire that ran along the driveway, her jeans shorts and tie-dyed shirt full of burrs and tears. Two dark-haired girls a head taller than her appeared behind her.

Sunny punched Karl. "There she is." Karl gasped, probably overcome by the first glimpse of his daughter. Sunny jumped from the truck and ran toward Tiffany.

She held Tiffany close to her, sobbing. "Lord, I thought I'd lost you." Looking back toward the truck, Sunny smiled at Karl while he pushed the wet from under his eyes with his thumb. Karleen climbed out of the truck but motioned Karl to stay inside.

Tiffany, sweaty and giggling, said, "Cousin Sunny, come meet my good friends."

Josie gave a shy wave. Beck, the short-haired girl said, "Tiffany, you're sure lucky. Too many people want you. I'm jealous."

Karl stretched his arm through the truck window, his hand in the air for a minute like a goodbye and then he patted his daughter's head. "Don't be worrying everybody again, you hear." He cranked the truck hard and let it coast out of the driveway, leaving just a hint of dust in the air.

"Who was that?" Tiffany said. "Another relative?"

"The Lone Ranger," Karleen said with a smirk.

"That's Karl. Wave to him," Sunny said, relieved that he was not ready to meet Tiffany yet.

Tiffany wrinkled her brow. "But he's facing the other way."

"Wave, he'll see." Sunny said, knowing he'd glance into his rear-view mirror as he pulled away.

Ensnared in Crosston

The blue *Welcome to Mississippi* sign flashed by. Its swirling letters pulled up unwanted memories in Maggie Lu like weeds with the clod-filled roots attached. She bit her lip, cringing at the possibility of a chance encounter with Tiffany, now a teenager who might be roaming the streets of Crosston on a chance visit to Grandma Bea or Sunny. Sunny had created a bond with the girl that Maggie Lu wanted no part of, and she'd heard that Sunny had made friends with the father's family, the Dees. Keeping away from Crosston had been Maggie Lu's best decision for quite a while. Why had she let down her guard and agreed to return now? Maggie Lu swatted as a fly buzzed against her windshield looking for escape. She flinched, her foot pressing hard on the Z car's accelerator as if she suddenly realized she was not racing into the embrace of her home state but careening toward the menacing memories it held.

Maggie Lu hadn't visited Sunny at Birdsong Farm near Crosston since before her mama and cousin contacted her in Memphis on their way to search for the runaway Tiffany. Though Maggie Lu didn't want to be involved in the search, Sunny had felt the need to phone her that the child had been located. Maggie Lu cared for Sunny and would rather hear about her work at Birdsong Farm, pouring concrete flooring and expanding the old milk barn to create her kennels, such a bleeding heart she had for rescuing dogs. At least Sunny was keeping alive their childhood farm, which they'd jointly inherited. Although Maggie Lu appreciated that Aunt Pearl included her in her will, when Maggie Lu left the farm for college, she knew she'd never want to live there again.

Sunny promised her no guilty allusions to their younger years of dismay over their philandering parents, and no mention of Tiffany, if she'd come for a visit. Agreeing, Maggie Lu took Sunny up on her offer of supper and an overnight bed, pushing down the unease of returning to a home that would impart happy and often squeamish memories. As an adult she'd returned for the funerals of Uncle Fred and later Aunt Pearl, and made infrequent visits, preferring just to call Sunny for a chat occasionally.

Trying to shove away a bit of anxiety, Maggie Lu pressed the radio preset button for the WDIA blues station, releasing a retro tune, Elvis wailing the sad tale of "Old Shep." A tingle of loneliness slipped through her veins. She gripped the steering wheel tighter. If she let herself linger at Sunny's kennels too long, a sad-eyed pup might pull her in. Dismayed at all this vacillating, she tightened her grip, quickly dismissing any rationale for fitting a dog into her busy schedule. When the radio station went to commercial, the folksy announcer vied for attention while her mind flipped worriedly between work and visiting her cousin.

Passing the Crosston city limits sign began to pull Maggie Lu inside the fermented landscape of her youth, more anxious now of what was to come than when she had left Memphis. Besides returning to Birdsong Farm, an icy hesitancy began to stir at her decision to meet her law partner, Inez, at the familiar old building that housed Inez's law office in their hometown.

She was surprised how the shops around the courthouse square and the red brick Methodist Church felt as familiar as if she and Sunny had just passed through their doors as they so often did as teens visiting friends in town. Her Z car passed Baldwin's Drug Store before she recognized its flat storefront windows that merged into the long strip of stores on the west side of Waldron Street. Baldwin's used to have the best milkshakes ever. Got to make time for one, she vowed, but she cast a quick glance inside the open door. Were there familiar stares atop craning necks?

Downshifting to second gear, she cruised the Z around the square again, noticing cheap discount stores had snuck into the old Belk's Department Store building where she'd shopped so often with Sunny and Aunt Pearl—her own mama, the journalist, too busy chasing news stories to offer much concern for her wardrobe choices. Her resentment over her mama had lessened, but casual fits of bitterness arose when hearing Mama's blustery voice in a phone call right before leaving on this trip. Maggie Lu did not tell Bea how long she would be staying at the farm, but had Sunny? Pushing down a pang of distrust, Maggie Lu didn't want to think about the bond Sunny and Bea had forged over the girl, and now she shuddered when she heard the name, Tiffany.

Having a break in her court schedule in Memphis, Maggie Lu had agreed to meet Inez to consult on a case in the old Crosston office, saving her a long drive to Inez's larger Nashville office. Her Z halted for a wide-eyed woman with a familiar profile, both arms weighed down by heavy brown satchels. Inez mouthed a plaintive *help*. Maggie Lu quickly parked the Z and rushed over to lighten Inez's burden of legal satchels. Inez squeaked a breathless, "Thanks for coming here." Their blouses stuck to their backs, and their shoulders hung taut as they trudged the twenty-step staircase between two storefronts. Fiddling with the key, Inez managed to open the old half-glass door emblazoned in faded gold letters, *Attorney at Law*, Maggie Lu's deceased uncle's name now worn away from above them. Maggie Lu sentimentally kept the lease on this office that she had visited as a child, her Uncle Hugh always letting her lift the glass coverings on the bookcases and thumb through the thick law books pretending she was his research assistant. Now Inez made use of it, but Maggie Lu had not set up any space for herself since they opened the office.

Dropping their burdens in nearby chairs, they caught their breath and exchanged brief hugs. Sneezing, Maggie Lu swiped away a thin, dusty haze from an empty oak library table pushed up against the wall where two tall windows offered a view of the courthouse. She scooted two heavy oak chairs to the table and sunk into one, leaning back into the comfort of the strong wooden arms and squinting into the bright glare from the window. Stacks of thick law books in disarray were wedged behind the hazy glass of the barrister bookcases lining one wall. Her uncle had meticulously kept the law books in neat order. Wincing, Maggie Lu looked away with an edgy, "Let's get started."

Quickly emptying her satchel of electronic equipment and notebooks from several cases, Inez turned on the CD player, which emitted several coughs, static, and a woman's coarse, angry tone. Inez and Maggie Lu listened to the rambling exposition of Agnes Galatour, convicted of a seven-year-old murder of a woman growing marijuana on an east Tennessee farm. Their eyes widened as Ms. Galatour's voice rose.

"It was easy escaping out of that shoddy, old van during transit to state prison . . . I was mad as hell when I stabbed those women who testified against me during my trial . . . Karleen knows I meant business. She's said you'd help me deal with all this. It took them six months to recapture me." The pop of the player ended Galatour's monologue and brought silence to the room.

Maggie Lu threw up her arms and shook her head, uttering, "Unbelievable."

Inez shot back an uneasy frown. "I'm worried about some of this woman's associates."

Maggie Lu pushed up from her chair, saying, "Yeah, like Karleen Dees and those threatening her."

"I don't know her. Do you think I should proceed with this case?"

"You know her brother, Karl, my high school boyfriend."

Inez's mouth wiggled somewhere between a grin and a thin line. "Oh, yes."

Maggie Lu grumbled. "I know the whole family and want no association with them. I had no idea Karleen Dees was the friend of Sunny's that has been corresponding with this Galatour woman. I'm sorry I let Sunny coerce me into involving you in this case. Wow, no wonder you hated taking this deposition. That's enough for me to take in today. Why not work for a while on the other case documents that you brought. I'll be back later." Maggie Lu rose, giving Inez a perfunctory pat on the shoulder. "I need a break."

Fast out the door with Galatour's unnerving voice making her feel unsteady, Maggie Lu rushed down the twenty stairs onto the sidewalk. Yellow streaks flashed off the railroad track across the street, causing Maggie Lu to blink and nearly trip as her foot slipped from the curb into Fillmore Street. After a glance back toward the law office, Maggie Lu grimaced at Inez's outstretched fingers pressed against the upstairs window glass. She was sorry to leave Inez stuck, but she couldn't fathom involvement in the case that now pulled in Karleen and maybe even Karl, high school flame gone wrong. She did not wish to rehash that relationship with Inez. Enough people in Crosston knew too much of her business. She forced a frantic scan across the square. From the courthouse lawn, the metal confederate soldier facing north on his pedestal seemed to tilt his lengthy-barreled weapon her way.

A hand on Maggie Lu's shoulder caused a nervous twitch before she stared back at Sunny and heard her surprised quip, "That looked like you, so I thought I'd stop." Unexpectedly meeting Sunny in town made Maggie Lu's stomach lurch. She had counted on time to prepare for an evening visit at Birdsong Farm. She managed a cheery, "Fancy meeting you, cousin."

Sunny smiled. "Got a few minutes?" Her hand flapped toward Baldwin's Drug Store. "Want to head to our old hangout?"

"Sure." Maggie Lu hurried down the sidewalk. "Let's indulge." She pushed against the heavy glass door and waved her hand for Sunny to follow. Once inside, she offered an awkward hug and a quick, "Hungry?"

"Always," slipped between Sunny's jumpy laugh.

In a row of red vinyl stools perched on long silver spindles, half were occupied by plaid-shirted men leaning on the gray marble soda fountain counter. Some glanced over their shoulders nodding a friendly greeting to Sunny and offering a puzzled half-smile to Maggie Lu. Briefly Maggie Lu wished for the sociability of small-town life, then let her shell of independence and resolve re-emerge, a shield against a chance encounter. Hurrying across the black-and-white tile floor, she and Sunny each slid onto the cool vinyl bench of a booth near a back wall overburdened with grainy photos of local civil war scenes. Glancing across the myriad array, Maggie Lu said, "Crosston couldn't let it go, all the war stuff."

"History's important. Wounds are deep," said Sunny.

Sensing a good segue, Maggie Lu replied quickly. "Mine are too, Sunny. I had no idea that Karleen Dees was trying to help this Agnes Galatour, and that the crowd from the Roost was involved. You never mentioned her when you called me to help with this case. Inez just shared all the particulars with me, and she seems oddly shaken by it all. I want no part of it. You and Mama have chosen to associate with the Dees. I have erased my connection to that family."

Raising her hands, Sunny seemed about to push herself back out of the booth without another word, but an elderly waitress in a crisp, old-fashioned white uniform arrived at their table and offered a sugary greeting. Sunny leaned back into the booth.

"Chocolate milkshakes for supper," they said in unison.

"Y'all are a mess, never change." The waitress laughed, circling a 2 on her green pad with a swivel of her arm, her polished white shoes squeaking back across the checkerboard tiles.

A twinge of that kindness in the waitress's voice and

the memory of days she and Sunny had spent here made Maggie Lu soften toward Sunny, almost re-think feeling betrayed and almost let herself look forward to sitting on the front porch at Birdsong Farm in the morning. Yet a few minutes later she recoiled when Sunny straightened in her seat.

Pushing her chin out boldly, Sunny said, "Karleen is my friend. She feels that she has to try to help Galatour. Her brother Karl is not involved."

Maggie Lu was firm. "You know I don't want any association with the Dees family."

Sunny leaned in closer. "Karleen told me that Galatour went to Water Valley when she escaped on her way to real prison, tried to get Karleen to tell her where her accusers were since one of them was Karleen's friend and had stayed at Karleen's place for a while. Karleen is terrified of this criminal."

Maggie Lu reminded her, "Galatour *is* imprisoned for life."

Sunny's face fell. "She knows scary people who are not in prison. Some guys from Costa Rica came by Karleen's house in Water Valley. Karleen *has* to be sure Galatour knows she's trying to help her. Please, reconsider, Maggie Lu."

Scary people did not sound like an inducement to continue working on this case. Maggie Lu shifted in her seat and realized that Inez might have been threatened as well. She'd have to discuss all this when they met back at the office. Gaining her wits, Maggie Lu knew she would have to tell Inez directly that she wanted no part of this case.

The waitress delivered the thick milkshakes with straws tucked inside a whipped cream swirl on top. A moment later she returned with the frosty silver cylinders holding the additional portion of each shake. They both sipped in long silences, taking short breaks to refill their glasses from the cold cylinders. Maggie Lu tried to let the savory flavor cool her dismay over Sunny's request. Trying for a rapport, she thought of Sunny's constant dog rescue attempts. When she agreed to stay at Sunny's she'd promised no arguments. Yet learning of Karleen's involvement in this case, she felt blindsided. Finally, Maggie Lu drew in a noisy last pull from her straw, joking, "I never stop here at Baldwin's. It's all your fault I've finished this fattening thing." Sunny stuck out her tongue. "Serves you right."

Looking over Maggie Lu's shoulder, Sunny drew a loud breath, and Maggie Lu turned with a start, wary of who else could surprise her. There she was, her mama. Bea sent a tentative wave from one of the soda fountain stools, then scurried up to their booth and with an urgent, "I saw your car out front, Sunny," then a feigned wide-eyed, "What a surprise. My Maggie Lu is in town. Now I need to join you both." She slid onto the bench next to Sunny, leaning into her ear with a quick whisper. Her faded peasant blouse had a little rip on the neckline, frayed red threads dangling annoyingly, and her flowing skirt hem drooped at precarious angles. Sunny let an "Oh, my," slip between pale lips.

Fingers pressing hard against the table edge, Maggie Lu could only offer a stilted "Hello, Mama, what's this about?" Her nose wiggled against the aura of cigarette smoke that clung to Bea. With an urgent stare, Bea leaned over the table and said, "Once Sunny told me you and Inez might consider taking this Galatour case, I thought I better tell you I've been investigating Agnes Galatour since her escape from jail. What a coincidence."

Maggie Lu's shoulders tensed when her mama began to describe her attempt to get a big news story. Bea started in, "The police report stated that Agnes's guilt had been revealed at a funeral where she was in attendance." Maggie Lu nodded, uneasily watching her mama's excitement build in the retelling. Bea grinned. "Would you believe that Agnes gave the cops the slip on the way to the can? Lordy." Sunny sniffed. "She must've headed straight to Water Valley to Karleen's house after she escaped. Poor Karleen. She'd helped one of the accusers."

Bea brought up a crumpled pack of Marlboros to the table. Maggie Lu thrust out a hand. "Not in here." Glaring, Bea tapped one cigarette on the table, then let it drop, twirling it nervously. Maggie Lu slouched into the booth as her mama enthusiastically continued her journalistic narration. Sunny cut her eyes across the table as if to signal to Maggie Lu to let her mama finish. Maggie Lu pushed back in her seat and took a long drink of water, frustrated at the lengths to which her mama would go to report a story that had ties to the Dees.

"And that's only the half of it," Bea said, her finger pointing at Maggie Lu. "I been following the second Galatour case, after her capture, since Sunny had asked you and Inez to get involved."

Maggie Lu scanned the wall of battlefield scenes, feeling like she'd just endured the battle of Shiloh. "Oh, Mama."

Bea smiled. "I'm going to break the story tomorrow in the *Clarion-Ledger* about her capture and the menacing behavior toward Karleen and later Karl."

Sunny reached across the table and grabbed Maggie Lu's hand. "That's great news for you. You didn't want to take the case. Now that danger to Karleen is over with Aunt Bea's publicizing the case."

Bea said, "I didn't want Karl hurt either. He *is* my granddaughter Tiffany's father."

Wincing at the name, Maggie Lu stared at her mama. "I can't believe what you continue to unearth." Heat saturated her blouse as exhaustion from her mama's fervor began to sink into her bones. Hating the sticky entanglements that the Galatour case brought up, she wished she had not returned to Crosston. Pushing up from the booth, she said, "I need to get over to the office."

Sunny's eyes pleaded. "See you later at the farm?"

Maggie Lu stared at her mama a long moment. Bea tapped the unlit cigarette. "I'm just passing through. Y'all can have your time out there."

Relieved, Maggie Lu nodded and gave Sunny a quick good-bye wave, *later*. Struggling with the weight of the heavy glass door, Maggie Lu glanced back at the two women sitting below the array of civil war portraits. A tall, plaid-shirted man gripped the door above her hand, lifting the heavy weight. "Haven't seen you around here lately." His grin was curious.

Managing a weak smile, she tried to joke, knowing her past here would haunt her no matter what she did. "I can't seem to stay away."

Stopped by Shadows

A flutter of relief buzzed through Maggie Lu's head. She relaxed into the soft leather seat of her Z car, letting the wind swirl through her hair. The speed blurred her glances at the kudzu-covered trees, thick and mottled by late afternoon sunrays along U.S. 45 Highway. It was a familiar road to Sunny's farm, but their encounter at Baldwin's Drug Store earlier had enhanced her anxiety about their visit.

After leaving the drug store, Maggie Lu had a quick conversation with Inez about the Galatour case. They toasted their resolve with a shot of bourbon. Maggie Lu was pleased to have aborted the legal fiasco that Sunny had wanted her to resolve. *Aborted*, she wished that word had not popped in her mind. At least tension was barely teasing her neck and shoulders now. Another drink was all she needed to ease into an evening visit at the farm with Sunny, who promised not to argue but was sure to reminisce about their teen years spent together there. Maggie Lu was still making peace with that part of her life.

A battered yellow mailbox leaned nearly out into the road. Spotting *Tompkins* scrawled in funny red letters along its side bought a quick memory of the feisty neighbor often chatting in the school cafeteria and always welcoming her visits when Maggie Lu slipped away from Birdsong Farm. She flipped the steering wheel and maneuvered around the potholes in the long gravel driveway. She'd make a quick stop and then drive on to Birdsong Farm.

A stooped woman balancing on a four-pronged cane made her way out a wobbly screen door and lowered herself into a brown wicker chair. "Hey," she said, propping her chin on the rubber grip of the cane handle. "Do I know you?"

Maggie Lu stretched her neck out of her car window, saying, "Miss Edith, I was on my way to see my cousin Sunny over at Birdsong Farm and . . ."

"Oh, Maggie Lu get out of that fancy car, girl. Haven't seen you in ages. I'll fix you some iced tea." The old woman's step quickened, the cane feet tapping like a child's skip beside her when she disappeared into the house, her voice trailing from inside, "Just have a seat out there on the porch. My house is a mess."

Surprised at how shaky Miss Edith moved around, Maggie Lu thought she might go back and prop up that mailbox for her. She looked around the yard and under the porch for a pole or small board, with no luck. She mounted the steps. A musty smell touched Maggie Lu's nose when she edged onto a lumpy loveseat that might have once graced Edith's living room. Maggie Lu fingered the quilt of faded strips of pillow ticking and overalls fabric that stretched across the seats. A skinny man with big eyes, clad in overalls, slipped into her mind. "How's Mr. Kenny T?" Maggie Lu shouted toward the screen door. Maybe Edith's husband wasn't able to fix the mailbox either.

"Catting around, probably," came a sour response from Edith.

Maggie Lu's nose twitched—no longer at the musty smell but at the memory of Kenny T and her own Uncle Fred joking in the milk barn at Birdsong Farm about *moving up behind the girls at the factory and giving them a little pinch on the rump.* Maggie Lu bit her lip. Her eyes roamed over the weedy yard and stopped at a stack of rusty license plates piled at the edge of the wooden porch. Years ago, Edith had called her needing legal advice for her husband, who'd gotten mixed up in a petty theft ring.

Besides Kenny T's legal scrape, he and Uncle Fred had brought a lot of misery to their wives sneaking around with other women. She had never wondered before if these wives had their own secret dealings, unlike her own mama, Bea, who had always flaunted the attention Uncle Fred and other men paid to her. Maggie Lu's head fell back into the sofa. She was glad she'd had a shot of bourbon in the office with Inez. She'd like another. Turning toward the screen door again, she raised her voice. "Got any of Kenny T's whiskey on hand?"

Edith's cane was hooked over her arm when her back nudged the screen door, and she set two glasses of icy liquid on an old trunk that served as her porch table. Her eye lids fluttered when she chuckled. "The minute you mentioned Kenny T I was mad at him all over again. I dumped that sweet tea right back into the pitcher and broke into his stash of Jack Daniels." Edith pulled a little flask out of her apron pocket. "Here's a second drink, just in case."

"Wow, Miss Edith. I was just inquiring about his health." Maggie Lu cast an innocent glance, then turned up her lips in a slight smile.

She had always liked Edith, who had dished up generous portions at the high school cafeteria years back and had a joke or smile for those kids who'd say *thank you, ma'am, for lunch*. Edith would commiserate on the phone with Aunt Pearl when their husbands were gone. Maggie Lu sometimes hid in the dining room and listened to Aunt Pearl talk. "I love her girl staying here with my Sunny, but my sister Bea is heartless," Aunt Pearl had said more than once. Maggie Lu wished she hadn't learned later that Aunt Pearl had a pernicious side too.

These memories prompted Maggie Lu to say, "I was just thinking of how you and Aunt Pearl used to talk about your husbands on the phone."

Edith took a small sip and coughed. "Yes, we did. I sure miss her. Kenny T is just himself, you know. I'm glad to have a few young folks like you drop by."

Maggie Lu felt the liquor take her tongue. "Did you ever . . . think about another . . . man?" In an instant she realized her own feelings that she often pushed aside. A glimmer of desire lingered still from the most recent chance encounter she'd had with the fellow lawyer at the Tennessee Legal Convention. She blushed at the memory and flashed her eyes back to Edith to listen to her response.

Edith started to giggle. "Why honey, no one ever turned my head away from Kenny T, but Pearl got a little revenge."

Maggie Lu felt herself sinking further into the mushy sofa. She blinked at Edith. "What kind of revenge?"

Eyes alight, Edith started in. "Pearl's dead and gone, but your mama isn't. Oh, lordy, I'm sorry to tell. Pearl blackmailed your mama, told Bea she wouldn't leave you part of Birdsong Farm if Bea went up to Pennsylvania to visit you when you were pregnant or if she went looking for your baby girl later. Pearl kept all that money from the folks who paid to adopt your baby." Edith dug into her apron pocket and dabbed her nose with a crinkled hankie.

Maggie Lu leaned toward the trunk table wanting to reassure Edith that she'd already found the adoption papers and knew the sneaky details. Lifting her glass and swirling the ice cubes, she set it back down and brushed the wet on her cheeks with her own damp hands.

"I knew about it later, but I didn't know Mama cared what happened to me or the baby back then." Patting her stomach, which seemed to bulge with the swirling liquid, Maggie Lu fell back against the sofa, the loneliness of struggling with her college classes and her pregnancy bubbling up again. She watched Edith's mouth babble and tried to listen.

"Bea didn't want to be a grandma, if that's what you mean. Your Daddy cared but couldn't do anything, you know, in his situation."

"Did you know him?" Maggie Lu was surprised, gasping at the tingling breaths that floated up and down her throat.

"Of course." Edith blinked. "Leonard brought you over when you were little. Remember playing with our old dog Watchman?

Maggie Lu squeezed her eyelids tight and struggled for the memory.

Edith kept on. "He was underfoot here whenever he and Bea argued, but eventually I had Kenny T tell that older brother of his he couldn't stay."

"Brother? What are you saying, Edith?" Maggie Lu's mind unlocked an alert signal while a clammy hollowness filled up her body. "My daddy wasn't a Tompkins."

Edith waved a hand to grab Maggie Lu's attention.

"Now listen, Kenny T's mama didn't marry Lopez, but she gave the boy his name."

Leaning forward and her hand shaking as she tipped the glass, Edith let in a drink. Her eyes downcast, she began to rock back and forth, repeating, "What have I said. Oh, whiskey let out the wrong cat from the bag." Two of the rubber tips of her cane poked the side of the trunk, then shifted to the porch floor with incessant taps that began to annoy Maggie Lu.

"Leo Lopez was my daddy. I only remember a few fun times with him." Maggie Lu began pulling into her mind a fuzzy photo of a stocky man with one arm stretched across the shoulders of a skinny girl in summer shorts standing next to an old truck. In a tiny voice, she said, "I was six when he was gone. He died in a hunting accident, Mama said." Staring at the old trunk, she tried to imagine this new family connection.

Shifting around in her chair, Edith pounded her cane. "Hum, it wasn't no accident."

Her cane rocked while she remembered. "Early 1960s? That'd be about the time they sent Leonard to prison. He's not dead, honey. He broke parole every time he got out, eventually got in bad trouble so's Kenny T won't even visit him at Parchman now."

Not dead echoed inside of Maggie Lu. Her daddy was a horrible person sitting in a prison cell somewhere, but he was *alive*? Curiosity shot through her like she'd jabbed a finger in an electric socket. The warm liquor tinkered with her thoughts, sending flashes of an anxious drive to Parchman Prison Farm, then sitting down at prison phones and talking through a smudged glass barrier to a wild-eyed man in a striped prison jumpsuit who was her *father*. How many trips would it take to hear the almost forty years she'd missed out on? She gasped. What if he said nothing at all? Maggie Lu's fingers slapped the old quilt on the sofa to stop her raging thoughts. Dust particles drifted toward the worn porch boards.

A nervous Edith was pushing her thin lips in and out of her tiny round mouth. Catching Maggie Lu's eye, Edith took a shaky gulp of whiskey. "Oh, I'm swimmy-headed and must not be thinking straight. We ought not to be talking about all this family stuff. Lord, there's no accounting for what all's gone on."

Pulling herself up, Maggie Lu patted Edith's shoulder. "Don't you worry about what you've told me, Miss Edith. Why, you and I are practically related. A woman has to know she's got a daddy who's still living, no matter where he's living."

***

After churning over the Tompkins' potholes, Maggie Lu's Z car's tires whined against the hot pavement back on U.S. 45 and squealed at the turn onto Hollyberry road. The spinning rubber spit gravel as Maggie Lu downshifted into the long driveway that led up to Sunny's big white house. A sunset glow hovered over the fallow field adjoining the property. Sunny was on the front porch, her feet propped on a small stool. Her hand emerged from behind a book and waved. The Z car stopped abruptly behind an old truck, lurching Maggie Lu's torso like a rag doll. She opened the car door to a chorus of yelps and howls from the dog kennels next to the old milk barn. She pushed open the unlocked back door from the carport and darted into the bathroom off the hallway. After quick relief, she flicked on the light and stared into the mirror at a woman who had a daddy in prison.

Woozy from her Jack Daniels at Edith's, she filled a glass from the kitchen cabinet with ice and tap water and walked to the front porch. She couldn't wait to talk to Sunny. "Did you know my daddy was alive and that he's in Parchman?"

Dropping her book in an awkward reflex, Sunny could only ask, "Who is your Daddy?" Her green eyes shimmery in confusion, she stretched her skinny legs out in front of her and let her feet drop on the porch with a start.

"You mean my mama didn't tell you about Leo Lopez, since she tells you everything." A quick frown altering her face, Sunny said, "No, now don't pick a fight." Her hand waved Maggie Lu to a matching wicker rocker. "I'm younger than you, don't remember him, only you being so jumpy about the menfolk's guns and always repeating that your daddy died when he was out hunting."

Nodding, Maggie Lu splashed water from her glass, dousing the front of her blouse when she tried to gulp. "That's what Mama always said."

"Who said he is alive?" Sunny's voice was tinny.

"I stopped at Miss Edith's. She says my daddy, Leo Lopez, is her husband's brother and Leo's alive." Maggie Lu felt invigorated just saying all this out loud.

Sunny sprung forward with a start. "Uh, oh, my mama had a man friend named Hershel Lopez way after my daddy died. You and I had both moved from here. Any relation?"

"Whoa . . ." they both echoed, with a burst of surprise laughter.

Flipping back the rocker, Maggie Lu propelled herself toward the door in search of a drying towel and one more shot of whiskey. Making her way down the hallway of dusty family portraits of the unknown bearded relics and stone-faced women who preceded her mama and Aunt Pearl, Maggie Lu found the old liquor cabinet was moved behind a door. A quick sip burned while her eyes skimmed a wall with the high school pictures of Sunny and her. A shiny new frame with its glass reflecting a stream of light from the window across the room disrupted her reverie. So many changes today nagged at her nerves.

"I see you found the whiskey, must have been a refill from the looks of you," Sunny said, watching Maggie Lu sink back into the rocker and take a short sip. "Karleen introduced me to the strong stuff, so I keep it for her, but wine goes down easier."

Maggie Lu's neck fell into the soft headrest and her eyes squinted at the thin blue boards on the porch ceiling. Sunny's friendship with Karleen continued to be exasperating. An eerie suspicion pushed up into Sunny's reason for insisting that she spend the night here at the farm. "What's that shiny new frame on our childhood picture wall?"

Sunny tugged on her short hair, saying. "It's a new picture . . . I'm sure you'll like . . ." Then she began a long discourse that Maggie Lu let the bourbon blur, catching snippets about family connections and what it must feel like to not know your real parent, to be told that the parent is dead, and the shock of discovering the parent is alive and has not reached out.

Puzzled by the picture, Maggie Lu felt thoughts buzz inside a warm bubble, but she was cheered that Sunny held some sympathy for her and her lost daddy. A hint of a cool breeze drifted across Maggie Lu while she stared at the last sun rays stretching over the manicured lawn, almost catching a glimpse of two barefoot girls riding fat red horses bareback between the mimosas when they shared this home.

Tipping the edge of her rocker forward, Sunny seemed to be waiting for her to speak, but the bubble held Maggie Lu quiet. Soon Sunny left the porch and let the door slam shut, eventually returning with the shiny picture frame under her arm and holding an icy glass of whiskey that she clinked against Maggie Lu's glass on the table.

"Let's toast to loss," Sunny said.

Before Maggie Lu could raise her glass, Sunny gently laid the shiny picture frame in her lap. "This is your daughter, Tiffany. Both of you know loss."

Glancing toward her icy drink, Maggie Lu stiffened. Her eyes dropped to the framed photo and would not move away, stopping at each feature of the girl in the picture. The teen's sparky gray eyes, high forehead, and wide mouth were just like hers. Maggie Lu's finger almost raised to trace a cheek but dropped back to the armrest and gripped it tight. Shivering against the cool evening breeze, she felt the warm bubble burst inside. Her hand hurled the shiny frame out onto the manicured lawn.

Inside a startled breath, Sunny let out a little "Ohhh."

On reflex, both women's heads turned toward the yard, which no longer held any warmth from the sun. The frame rested a short distance from the front porch steps, a long gash across the glass that still protected the smiling young face inside the frame. Feeling a prickle from Sunny's watchful stare, Maggie Lu shifted in her rocker. Wanting to bolt down the steps and flip over the frame face down into the grass, Maggie Lu bent forward in her rocker, then pushed back, rocking uneasily over the groaning boards beneath her chair. *Not yet,* she thought.

Sunny bent toward her and said, "Tiffany thinks you're dead, too."

Dead, not dead vibrated while Maggie Lu tried to blink away what Sunny just said.

Finding Leo

"Leonard Lopez is in the medical unit," came with a thick southern accent across the speaker phone in Maggie Lu's office. The Mississippi State Penitentiary official told her that her daddy would be back in Unit 29, his home cell block, by the end of the week. She could go ahead and mail in a request for a visitation application to be accepted by the "the inmate."

Trying to keep the official on the phone, she asked, "Does he ever have any visitors?" With a start, Maggie Lu realized her daddy might have relationships with people she never knew. A list of questionable probabilities began to take shape in her mind—a wife, other children, in-laws. She complained, "I just found out he was there." "Uh, huh," came in a disbelieving tone from the speaker. Her hand tensed when she drew tight square boxes on her legal pad while trying not to sound defensive. The prison official could not divulge specific names, but after a long moment of fluttering papers scratching through the speaker, he admitted that a number of applications were in the Lopez file. He repeated the prison address and Lopez's prison ID number for Maggie Lu to send in her request. She felt a tinge of suspicion. Since Saturday when she learned her daddy was indeed alive, Maggie Lu had been determined to see him, but perhaps he might not accept her visitation application.

Her fingers dusted across the top of a small picture frame on her desk holding a black-and-white photo of a small girl and a stocky man. Her daddy, the inmate, was still out of reach. The dial tone buzzed into the room from the prison official's quick disconnect. She drew narrow parallel bars over the boxes on her pad and added a small face with bulging eyes. "Daddy," she said to the page.

Sliding a manila folder from her desk drawer, she flipped it open to the first page containing Leo Lopez's grainy prison mug shot. She thumbed the pages of criminal research she had already compiled including a list of convictions ranging from possession of contraband in prison, burglary, larceny, and jail escape to manslaughter. She stopped at the last page. His release date was blank. Did she want to lend her lawyerly skills? She closed the file and typed her request for a visitation application, then printed it on her legal stationery.

A week later when the fat envelope with the MSP logo arrived from Parchman, Mississippi, Maggie Lu's fingers were frantic, slicing the top flap with her letter opener. A hint of cigarette smoke slipped out with the bundle. Inside the two-page visitation application was a small yellow piece of stationary covered with tiny printing. *Dear Daughter, I was very surprised to get your application. Still feeling a little under the weather. Your mama told me you didn't care a flip about a jailbird daddy. Maybe she lied? I hope you come. I see you are a lawyer. Good. Signed, Your Daddy.*

That yellow sheet brought her a blanket of comfort. She had a daddy who wrote to her. Touching the small sheet transferred a cigarette scent to her fingertips.

Must've been something he and her mama shared, smoking. She'd have to ask his brand—no he'd have to buy them inside. She'd have to learn each step of getting to know him. A giddy child's emotion lightened her mood. What did he remember about her? A fatherless gap in her past might be filled in with his recollections. Would he have a sense of humor, or had prison hardened him? Maybe he only wanted her to visit to gain her legal help. Flinching, she held the little sheet tightly, trying to feel his every movement to form the letters on the page especially *I hope you come.* She smoothed out the visitation form and precisely filled in every line. Glancing at a calendar, she hoped to be able to visit him before long . . . if he allowed her to be on his visitation list.

Maggie Lu had been trying to contact her mama for a week, but Bea was not returning her calls. Leaving some angry messages on Bea's phone not long after Edith had told her that her daddy was alive was probably not the best way to find out the real motives behind her mama's deception. How to revisit? After dropping the visitation application in the mail, she'd try again. Mentally preparing a more contrite message, she pushed the familiar phone number but was disconcerted when Bea answered on the second ring with a tumble of words.

"All right, Maggie Lu. I'm sorry you found out the hard way about your daddy, but now Leo really *is* dead. I got the call this morning. I'm thinking it was gall stones that killed him. Do you want to ride down to Parchman with me tonight to handle arrangements? I might need a little gas money."

Eyelids clinched while tipping back in her desk chair, Maggie Lu searched for breath, her voice breaking with "Yes, Mama."

Bea's words rushed through the phone. "It'll take me a few hours to get to your house." With a click, her mama's voice dropped away.

As if she'd been punched, Maggie Lu doubled over in her chair and let out a long, shrill "Noooooo, Daddy can't be dead before he was ever alive to me." After a flood of tears, she laid her head on her desk, staring at the blurry black-and-white photo that held all she knew of her daddy. Now she'd have to rely on her mama's version of him.

***

The rumble of Bea's old Chevy Malibu brought Maggie Lu to her front door, travel bag in hand. Flinging her small overnight in the back seat awakened a small spotted terrier that barked defensibly. Bea threw up her hands, saying "I picked up this puppy for Sunny's rescue but didn't have time to drop it off at Birdsong Farm." Cigarette bobbing between her lips, Bea grazed the tip with the hot coil of the cigarette lighter, then gave her daughter a long stare, saying, "I wish you smoked." Maggie Lu frowned while the pup crawled along the console and wiggled into her lap when she sunk into the worn velour bucket seat. Cracking the car window to vent the smoke, Maggie Lu tried to calm the puppy prancing in her lap, its nose edging up toward the open window. "Did Daddy smoke when you were together?" Feeling edgy about the hundred-mile drive and now a puppy to wrangle, she tried for an easy start though her stomach held a heavy stone of resentment and disappointment.

"Yeah, we smoked out back of Cory's Hardware when he was on a work break. Lord, he was stealing even then. We thought it was fun to get a little extra money that way. He was a charmer, sang to me all the time."

Trancelike, Bea rambled out the memories of her early life with Leo, her voice giddy recalling backroad keg parties with Leo and his band singing under the stars. Eventually her tone became more moody, recounting a difficult pregnancy and small trailer living while waiting for Leo's short jail stints to lapse, too ashamed to change her mind about loving him. Flinching at her mama's mention of pregnancy, Maggie Lu let slip the question she'd held for so long. "I was difficult for you from conception?"

Bea's head swung toward her, wobbling pensively. "We all make mistakes." A nerve tightened in Maggie Lu's neck while *mistake, mistake, mistake* swirled through her.

With an occasional jolt hitting potholes that a weakened rear leaf spring couldn't bear, they sped along the two-lane U.S. 61 Highway through one-stop-light Mississippi towns, lingering between the flat, rich delta fields overflowing with rows of fluffy cotton bolls. Clutching the pup's warm body close, Maggie Lu held her tongue and listened until her mama said, "I just decided it was better for you to not get your hopes up of ever having a daddy. He was dead to me so he needed to be dead to you."

Spotting an orange Gulf gas station sign in the distance, Maggie Lu said, "Pull over, Mama. I think we all need some relief." When she opened the door, she wondered if she would get back in the car. Alert to the quick stop, the pup dashed through the opened door, its legs scampering toward the first grassy spot, and squatted for a long moment while a stunned Maggie Lu edged toward the tensed animal. Maggie Lu's hand extended slowly toward the wide-eyed pup while she tried for a soothing,

"Here puppy, come on now." Running around the front of the Malibu with leash in hand, Bea said, "Well, now we know it's a female."

Immediately the little dog left her wet spot behind and dashed around the back of the gas station, quickly halted by loud growling. In quick pursuit, Maggie Lu's foot slipped on an oil spot, slamming her shoulder into the station wall, and Bea scooped up the stunned pup, scanning for the source of the growl, and shoved her into Maggie Lu's aching arms. Legs wobbling her to the nearby picnic table bench, Maggie Lu clutched the dog and began to cry, shocking herself. "Mama, why didn't I ever have a dog?"

Dropping the leash on the table, Bea frowned. "I'm not even getting the relief the pup got." Then she paced directly into the station. After Maggie Lu attached the leash, the dog crawled beneath the table. Brushing her wet cheek with her hand while achy tingles burned inside her shoulder, she wished she had no weaknesses to show her mama, angry that some sadness within her crept out. She glanced down into the soft eyes of the pup when it whined, struggling to measure her questions about her daddy so her mama would not explode into her own woes with him, but instead reveal who he was.

Bea returned with a big bag of chips and two cans of Coke. She plunked down on the bench on the opposite side of the table, causing the faded umbrella attached to sway precariously. After a long swig of Coke, Bea tapped her can. "Loss. I didn't know how to help you with it so I tried to avoid it. Your daddy gone, a dog would eventually be gone, I was gone, working. That's why I just took you over to Pearl's, made it easier for you."

Tearing open the bag of chips, Maggie Lu watched the

brittle contents spill onto the rough tabletop. She dropped a few below the table to an eager pup. Crushing a few chips inside own her mouth, she said, "Easier for you, Mama."

* * *

The miles churned by, and the pup stretched its full fat body at Maggie Lu's feet, little whimpers sporadically slipping from between its pin teeth, a nervous back leg twitching through puppy dreams. Bea fired up several more cigarettes while she talked of her early news reporting days at the *Crosston Gazette*. Leo called often to dissuade her from dating other men. After graduation she'd moved back home but was stuck living with her parents. She was happy to escape to Leo's trailer. She married him because he had a cute little trailer and rented a wooded lot from a farmer just outside of Crosston.

"You married because he bought a trailer?"

Bea took a long drag on her cigarette. "Oh, it was close to family time. He was good when he was good."

Maggie Lu frowned. "Family time?"

Bea's mouth tightened. "Yeah."

Not wanting to hear details about her own daddy like she's heard her mama brag about with other men, Maggie Lu injected, "Why did the prison officials call you when he died? Weren't you divorced?"

Bea launched into the hassle she went through to get Leo to sign divorce papers and all the trouble he constantly caused her when he got out on probation even though they still shared a little fun. After a funny wink, Bea pushed down on the gas pedal a little too quickly, then eased off. Finally, when his brother Kenny T refused to help him out, she agreed to leave her name as his next of kin. After a big yawn, Bea complained that she would now have to deal with his estate and burial.

Maggie Lu leaned toward her foot, pressing into the pup's stomach and causing a little yelp. "What estate does he have?" Quickly she leaned down to scratch the pup's ears in apology.

Bea moved her lips back and forth a long time before saying, "He still owns that little trailer. Might be something in it."

Mama has lost her mind. Maggie Lu let those thoughts run through her own mind, but said nothing. Instead she picked up the pup and whispered in its ear.

Leo's Reflections in Prison

Leo Lopez watched the fluffy white clouds drift between the bars covering the window high above the foot of his bed in the infirmary of the Mississippi State Penitentiary. Breathing pulled constant pain into his chest and abdomen. He had not expected to see clouds again, at least from this side of the universe. He had hoped the attack would kill him.

Instead the burly guard, in a not-so-crisp uniform, pushed a wheelchair next to his bed, announcing, "A couple of gals here to see you."

Lurching upright, Leo said, "Who's that?"

The guard fumbled with a yellow form. "Says here Bea and Maggie Lu Hopkins. Before you can see visitors, you got thirty minutes to process to that unit. Want me to get that started?"

Tugging his hair nervously, Leo nodded. "Yeah, sure."

His eyes squeezed tightly together driving him to comprehend that his ex-wife and his daughter were both here . . . *together*. Gazing past the clouds and between the bars, he let in a memory of pacing the glittering white waiting room the day Maggie Lu was born, permitting that flutter in his heart to return for a moment.

Hoping not to make a fool of himself, he'd have to go through with it. He had responded to Maggie Lu's visitation request. He guessed Bea must've been contacted as his next of kin when they thought he was dead. Maybe the prison official didn't make a follow up call to let her know he'd survived—for now anyway. Uneasy about facing them, he doubted if they'd recognize who he had become. Glancing into the makeshift tin mirror on the wall, he ran thick fingers through black and gray spikes of thick, crew-cut hair and stared into deep-set light-brown eyes, then pushed his thin teeth down on his bottom lip, wiggled a bushy moustache, and touched his square chin. Pushing up with still-strong arms, he pivoted into the waiting wheelchair by his bed. A gush of heat saturated his head and neck while a jagged rope of pain from the lingering infection tightened around his insides, rocking him forward.

The guard stopped pushing his wheelchair and asked, "Are you going to hang on?"

Fingers curling around the armrests in determination, Leo worried that his visitors might not ever return after this visit. "Give me a push. I can make it to the visitor's booth."

A young woman with flashing gray eyes and a firm jawline was waiting on the other side of the glass booth. Hesitating a moment at the door, he watched her twirl strands of blonde curls around her fingers. Was this the same little girl who slipped away so quickly when he steadied her bicycle or played hide-and-go-seek in and out of the trailer? Gasping when his eyes met hers, Leo knew she was not really his daughter, but he had wanted her as his daughter, maybe because she was another part of Bea, if not of him. Did he hear Bea's disorderly laughter in the background? Gripping the wheels of his chair, he halted half-way into the booth, then looked down at the cracked tiles that began to slip and slide in puzzling patterns. A painful throb started expanding inside his head.

* * *

By the time Leo had realized that Bea had lied back in 1957 about when she had conceived this baby-to-be-their-girl, Leo was far too fascinated by anything Bea said or did. Smitten by her nerve and her laughter, he had never dated a woman who made him so happy with her praise and her passion but also worried him with her inquisitive, sometimes relentless nature. On the job Bea traced every aspect of a story, even on those small assignments at the nearby town newspapers. She left him with the baby when she could, and he thought he could learn to be a family man. He tried, but money came hard, and he wanted to buy her everything. Stealing at the hardware store was a lark for both of them. Her eyes lit up when he came home with a wad of cash gained from selling a few expensive tools she'd dared him to steal. He bought her a fancy ring and the little girl a tricycle. Maggie Lu's squeals riding the trike round and round the yard swelled his heart.

Yet after Fred Birdsong's truck tore out of their driveway one afternoon when Leo came home early from the hardware store, Leo had a jolt of recognition that he hoped was not true. He began to watch the stolen glimpses and the easy familiarity when they visited Pearl and Fred at Birdsong Farm. His heart saddened when he saw that Bea was infatuated with Fred Birdsong.

Eventually it seemed she didn't care if Leo or even Pearl would be disillusioned with her affair with Fred, if they let themselves guess.

Leo shuddered, remembering being so distraught that he hitchhiked to the Gulf Coast, walking the beach with his pant legs rolled up, kicking at the seaweed clumps, his damp tears mixing with the waves until he curled up under an abandoned tiki shelter in exhaustion. After a few hungry days he called Bea from a pay phone.

"Get yourself home. Your baby girl is missing you," was all he needed to hear.

Turning toward the beach he had spotted a couple of drunk teens who must've dropped keys right next to the driver's door of a rusty green Triumph TR2 sports car. With a quick sprint to the low-slung car, Leo scooped up the key ring and slid inside. The motor roaring to life brought a rush of nerves as he fumbled to find reverse. Exhilarated, maneuvering the long hood toward the street near the parking lot, Leo's hand rummaged through the gears until he'd found 5th and the powerful car propelled him desperately up the open road north toward Crosston and his family.

Rumbling into the dusty driveway after dark, Leo ambled up the block steps and left the trailer door swinging wide open when Bea flung her arms around him and passionately pulled him to the couch. "Sheesh," they both giggled to each other, trying not to wake Maggie Lu in her tiny room at the end of the trailer. Leo broke free of her embrace for a quick moment, tiptoeing down the hallway for a moody glance at the sleeping child before returning to Bea's sexy babble. An hour later the exhausted pair stood in the trailer's open doorway, and Leo flipped on the porch light to show off the sporty little car.

With a distracted gaze at the car, Bea sighed, "It will be fun while it lasts, honey."

Hesitating at her response, Leo shrugged, grinning. "It's too little. I'll trade it quick, get a shiny Mustang, way better than what you've been driving." Less than a month later, the police officer's heavy knock came on the trailer door.

* * *

After Leo served his time for auto theft, he returned to Bea and Maggie Lu at the trailer. He and Bea would sit on the makeshift porch perched on concrete blocks and smoke cigarettes while the little three-year-old girl played with her dolls in the front yard. Bea would talk of her latest reporting assignment. "I borrow a car from a high school friend for the longer trips. Wish you could get me a new one, but not like last time." Leo held back asking who these friends were, not wanting Fred's name to come up in the mix. He wanted to be with her and Maggie Lu more than he feared being hurt.

After too many reminders that she wished he could do better than to rely on the job back at the hardware and his brother for odd jobs, he thought she'd be excited that at least he was working, even if it was at Cory's Hardware.

One evening he heard her talking on the phone. "Can't come down to the garage for now, so I just can't repay you for the loaner car for a while, honey."

Tamping down his suspicion of another infidelity, Leo hoped to win her back, and he created a bigger plan so he could buy her a new car. He'd break into the payroll office and steal a few checks at the Chevy dealer one evening. They had refused to hire him full time so stealing would serve them right. He hadn't thought about how tricky it would be to cash those checks. Trying to cash the second fraudulent check down in Tupelo was a mistake that landed him a felony conviction. At his trial Bea's eyes were hard, and he knew he'd blown it big time.

When he returned to Bea two years later, she did not pull him into her arms but did offer him the couch. The child, Maggie Lu, was shy for a long time. Roscoe gave him all the dirty clean-up jobs at the Ford dealership, so some days he found buddies to fish with down along the Hatchie river instead. When Bea nagged him about getting a better job, and he had too many questions for Bea about her nights away from the trailer, Bea talked of letting Maggie Lu live with her sister Pearl. Leo's stomach lurched knowing... *The girl would live with her real father, Fred. I'll lose my little girl for sure.*

Leo struggled to think of what Maggie Lu really needed, but he made poor attempts at cooking, laundry, and helping with her school work. When Bea was gone, he took Maggie Lu over to his brother's for visits in the evening. Kenny T's wife, Edith, fussed over the little girl, and she baked brownies with Maggie Lu while he and Kenny T drank Jack Daniels and spun tales on the lumpy couch on the front porch. Their dog Watchman ran between the kitchen and porch when Maggie Lu decided to play hide-and-go-seek with him.

Sometimes when she got tired, Maggie Lu would crawl up in his lap and say, "I don't want to stay at Birdsong Farm. Didn't you always live with your mama and daddy?" That's when his heart would tingle at never knowing his real father. The day Kenny T's daddy died was the day Kenny T laid on the coffin and screamed, "I am the only true Tompkins boy to carry on Daddy's name." Then, glaring at Leo, "You're only a Lopez." Their daddy had tried to treat them equally, but Leo felt the sting of outsider when their parents argued and he was "just another mouth to feed."

By the time Kenny T let the brown liquid fill his glass for the third time, he'd always apologize for what he'd said at their daddy's funeral. "You are my true brother. Mama always said so."

Leo felt the liquor drag him to hollow places, saying, "With your wandering eye, you don't deserve a good woman like Edith, and I don't deserve the heartache Bea gives me with her wayward affections."

When the liquor finally silenced them into blackouts, he and Kenny T slept on the porch. Maggie Lu would still be sleeping in the big recliner with Watchman when he awoke. In the morning, while Leo and Kenny T gulped coffee and aspirins, Edith gave the little girl a spit bath in the kitchen and said, "I'll take you to your classroom and then I'm off to mine, working in the school cafeteria."

Many nights Leo slept over on his brother Kenny T's couch. He made it to work when he felt like it—or fished when he didn't want to darken the door of the Ford garage. One afternoon Roscoe called him at Kenny T's, saying, "I tried to give you a second chance. You've missed too much work. Don't come back." Eventually both Kenny T's wife and Bea told him he no longer had a place to stay.

Finally realizing he'd spent too many days fishing and dreaming of fly fishing in Montana with a skinny loser from high school and a bearded guy he'd met in jail, Leo let that desperate feeling slip in, deciding that a quick cash scheme could bail him out. Over beers by their campfire, the bearded guy goaded them, "We can only make it to Montana if we have some way to get there.

Maybe we could take down that little bank branch on the highway."

Uneasy, Leo scanned his mind for another site, then glanced over at the beat-up Ford pickup the loser had borrowed from his sister and said, "Why not hit the Ford dealer and steal a truck too?" Taking vengeance on Roscoe by robbing the Ford dealer sounded easier than a bank break-in—and more satisfying. Clanging beer cans over the fire, they all agreed. "Easy pickings, and we'll ride in style to Montana for that fishing trip."

The next night after the three of them forced Roscoe to open the safe in the accountant's office, Leo had tied Roscoe to a hydrolic lift that was holding a four-door sedan and left him there. He and the boys were flying high until he called Bea to brag about his stash. He couldn't believe Bea when she told him that the car lift had crushed Roscoe.

***

Approaching the visitor's booth, Leo hung his head, feeling the jitters he always felt when the terrible thing he'd done flashed through his mind. He hadn't meant to kill Roscoe, but that didn't matter. Everyone had turned against him, and he was stuck in Parchman. It had been a lonely thirty-odd years. Today something had changed. Those who had shunned him were now willing to talk to him. *Tap, tap, tap* on the glass booth window disrupted Leo's focus on the floor tiles. His light-brown eyes lifted and were met by quizzical gray ones. The young woman smiled and mouthed, "Hi, Daddy, I'm Maggie Lu."

Leo rolled himself further inside the visitor's booth. They both picked up receivers to speak to each other. Pulling his lower lip over the bottom of his moustache to hold himself in check, he could only blink back so much before he patted his eyes with his wrist and said, "You're all grown up, turned into a pretty gal."

Maggie Lu sniffed. "I'm so glad I found you. I just learned from Edith that you were alive . . . and were here. Mama told me you died in a hunting accident a long time ago." Her head went down, and her shoulders fluttered against the chair. He watched her grab a tissue, then two.

Taking a painful breath to quell a fiery anger at Bea's lie to Maggie Lu, he squeezed the receiver and surprised himself when he said, "Your mama was probably trying to keep you from being taunted by folks or feeling shame over a daddy who pulled off some crazy, mean crimes." A tight cord of pain cinched up against the shame he felt for his past. He took a long minute to stare at his feet, but Maggie Lu tapped on the window of separation, and her eyes were not harsh. His moustache wiggled, and he felt warmth rise inside his chest just as it had years ago when he watched her play and always wanted to look out for her. He gulped, "I've missed knowing you."

That's when she pressed those tissues tight and started asking him all manner of questions about himself. What he and Kenny T did as kids. What he liked to eat and watch on TV. Did he read books? What could she send him?

Mostly, he knew, she wanted him to remember what she was like as a child and how he had felt about her. Happy that she remembered the tricycle he bought, he told her about the old cars they took rides in though the countryside, letting the wind tousle their hair. Smiling, she said, "And we always sang "The Old Gray Mare" over and over when we'd see horses in a pasture." He could see in her face a few expressions that showed she was open to being close to him when he said, "We've got a little history, don't we?"

She nodded in response, and her eyes twinkled. "I loved being with you, playing games and singing when we rode though the countryside." Warmed by her reminiscences, Leo couldn't hold back, "Those memories keep me going."

His heart blushed through her laughter and flurry of questions, but he hesitated when she asked what prompted the prison officials to call her mama about him. He set down the receiver and twisted the wheel of his chair so that his back was turned to her. An officer nearby pointed to his watch. Time was short. Leo turned back his chair and quietly spoke into the receiver, "A guy punched me in the gut for taking a slice of bread that must've fell off his plate, I shoulda known better, got a ruptured appendix out of that dumb move. Back in my cell I went to hollering, and nobody came for a long time. I started to panic."

Surprised that her eyes were riveted on him, he'd nearly forgotten what caring felt like. Under his moustache, a little smile wavered while he continued. "I remembered you, writing for permission to come see me. I didn't want to die before seeing you. I was about to pass out from the pain when a guard showed up, and I asked him to call Bea, since she was next of kin in my paperwork. I wasn't sure I'd make it, but hoped she'd let you know it was kind of urgent for you to visit. I didn't want to be forgotten." Drawing a hand across his face, Leo wiped his damp cheeks, shame and sadness rocking his shoulders. "It's a hard life in here," he whispered into the receiver.

Shock was washing over Maggie Lu's face while a guard's voice boomed, "Time's up." Her shoulder twitched. Tight little lines formed around her mouth when she leaned forward. "I'm a lawyer, Daddy. I hope there's something I can do about your parole." She brushed her eyes with the clinched tissues and hung up the receiver. Stopping at the door, she turned, miming *I'm here for you.*

Leo nodded, then twirled his wheelchair around, pushing down a panic of freedom that swirled up into his mind. Outside these prison walls, would he still be her daddy?

The Last Ride with Bea

"What'd Leo have to say?" Bea tapped a cigarette on the car's dashboard before lighting it. Her mouth was curled in a way Maggie Lu recognized when her mama was trying to hold back before she unleashed a barrage of thoughts. Sticking an arm between the seats, Maggie Lu gave a pat to the sleeping little dog on the back seat when it raised a yawning mouth toward her.

Gazing back at the dog, Maggie Lu laughed. "I asked Daddy why I never had a dog."

"No, you didn't," Bea said, puckering her cheeks like mini balloons.

Choosing a guarded response, Maggie Lu averted her eyes out the passenger window. "Right, we talked a lot about old times, looked pretty sickly like he still had some problems with that emergency appendectomy."

Almost lightheaded, Maggie Lu's thoughts flew between her enthusiasm after meeting her daddy, unknown to her for thirty-something years, and her bewilderment tinged with anger at her mama for erasing him from her life with lies.

Bea lit her cigarette and, with lungs filled with smoke, let several smoke rings drift from her mouth toward the windshield. "Whoever called me from the prison thought

Leo was on death's door." She kept her gaze on the smoke rings. "Probably woulda made it simpler for all of us."

A vitriol flame singed Maggie Lu's throat. "Ouch, that's pretty dismissive of somebody's life."

Bea coughed. "Well . . . I dunno."

Struggling with the flame her mama lit inside, Maggie Lu started arranging the legal papers back inside a leather briefcase. "Don't say that. I'm glad to know my real Daddy."

"An embarrassment, an inmate . . . You gonna help him get parole?" Bea gave a quick shove to the legal papers sticking out of her daughter's leather case. Turning the key hard, she stomped the accelerator so the car engine roared, and she swerved the old Chevy furiously out of the Mississippi State Penitentiary parking lot, then north onto U.S. 61 Highway.

Maggie Lu tried to consider if she would be able to tolerate her mama for the one-hundred-mile drive back to Memphis. A sour saliva coated her mouth. "Yes, I've started to research his case. That's why we took the whole visitation time." Opening her window, Maggie Lu sucked in the cool evening air, but she would have no time to gather her wits.

"What'd he have to say about fatherhood?" Bea's eyes glided toward her.

"I was a kid when I knew him, that's it."

Maggie Lu pushed against an uncomfortable instinct raising up in her, that she knew so little of what being fathered felt like. Uncle Fred was remote when she complained to him or to Aunt Pearl. Later she'd hear him tell Aunt Pearl he *couldn't get close to the situation.*

Bea nodded. "That's all, huh?" Her neck snapped toward Maggie Lu. "What'd Leo say about me?"

Maggie Lu tightened her lips and briefly closed her eyes to hide her disdain. "Not a lot."

Bea huffed. Then the hateful words tumbled out of her mouth, Leo's petty crimes that she put up with for years until the last one that bumbled into a terrible accident killing Leo's boss. Bea's eyes dampened as she recounted the death of Roscoe, who she bragged had been very generous to her in ways she didn't want to recount. She had been grateful to Fred who'd helped her through some rough spots and to Pearl who'd agreed to let Maggie Lu live at Birdsong Farm for a long while so that Bea could earn a living tracking her journalist pursuits. "You were always happy out there. I could tell."

"Not quite, Mama." Squirming against the velour seat, Maggie Lu marveled at her mama's summation of her struggling life, sacrificially giving up her child to live at the farm with no consideration of her daughter's well-being or anyone else's at Birdsong Farm, except being googly over Uncle Fred. Suspicion of her mama's late-night rendezvous with Aunt Pearl's husband was something she had pushed down inside her for so long.

"Uncle Fred always seemed to resent me being at Birdsong Farm. Didn't you ever notice?"

Bea flicked her cigarette butt out the top of her open window. "Guess, he never liked Leo. What'd Leo say about Fred?"

"Enough," Maggie Lu ventured, hoping her mama would feel the heat.

Bea's eyes flared when she must've decided to no longer leave the unsaid in her life to Leo's interpretation. Dipping her head, Bea started, "I'm not going to lie to you. Fred and I were two peas in a pod. We never got over knowing that." Bea gave an anxious laugh, admitting that he was a scoundrel who beguiled her whenever she turned her attentions away from him. And she was obsessed with his willful attraction to her, answering his phone calls in the middle of the night and driving over to Birdsong Farm to pick him up at the end of the driveway, agreeing to park on every back road in the county like teenagers frolicking in the back seat. After a long pause, Bea told of the two separate weekends in December — years apart — that Fred took her to New Orleans for abortions. "He didn't want children, but we had you right after I left Ole Miss. He never let himself get close." Bea clapped her hand over her mouth. "I never meant to say that . . . he made me swear . . ."

"What?" The word echoed loudly enough Maggie Lu wasn't aware if she was repeating it in a dizzying sequence. Then a silent gasp ballooned inside Maggie Lu, thrusting her disbelief into a quiet, gushing drone while she rocked toward the dashboard with "Uh . . . uh . . . uh . . . no." She began to scan the shadowy fields outside her window and to hum a familiar childhood tune, "The Old Gray Mare". . . to push against an eerie memory of sloshing milk machines inside the barn at Birdsong Farm. Whenever Aunt Pearl sent her to call Uncle Fred for supper, she'd hesitate by the barn door, watching him detach the machines from the tethered cows. "Come in closer and feel the teats, gal."

Bea tapped a fresh cigarette on the steering wheel, saying, "That humming of yours is eerie."

Coiling fingers of one hand, Maggie Lu struck her own palm, each time with more fury, anger igniting into uncontainable pounding on her palm and thighs, then aiming a few blows to Bea's arm. "Oh, Mama, how could you?"

"Owww, cut it out before I wreck this car!" Bea shouted.

Maggie Lu's mouth contorted, her words edgy. "Uncle Fred—who hated me—is my father, too gross to *ever* believe." Her voice shook while a slimy worm of disgust began to throb inside her veins as she struggled to ask, "Why then would you leave me at Birdsong Farm?" The bitterness made her skin clammy and churned her stomach.

After rubbing her arm, Bea's thin fingers laced the steering wheel. "He wanted to help me get the stories that happened out of town so I could stay on with the *Clarion-Ledger*, promised to meet me places but couldn't always get away, said he'd try . . . to care for you. Anyway, it was a way for me to stay close to him. I wanted him more than I wanted anyone."

Maggie Lu felt herself being swallowed by the steamy velour seat, gagging at her mama's lustful pursuits with the despised Uncle Fred. "Pull over. This wretched news makes me sick."

Swerving into a weedy gravel driveway leading to a pecan grove, Bea reached across Maggie Lu and flung open her door before the car came to a stop. "Don't get sick in here."

"Mama, what are you doing?"

With a yelp, the pup in the back seat dashed between Maggie Lu's legs while she tumbled out on her knees and palms into the chilly air and heaved a bitter liquid, then rolled weakly onto her side. She glimpsed Bea making a fast walk into high grass, tugging at her jeans to relieve herself. Maggie Lu closed her eyes and imagined the contorted face of Uncle Fred glaring, flailing his thick hands above his head . . . *unwanted, unwanted* sinking deeper into her bones.

Maggie Lu pushed herself up to sit cross-legged in a patch littered with pecans. Glancing at the car with dread, she willed herself to finish the drive home. At a full-speed trot, the pup break-necked back through the grass toward her, toppling into her lap and covering her face with panting licks, its breath a mixture of sweet and foul remnants. She rose, lifting it up with her, and plopped onto the velour seat inside the car, shivering as she pulled the door to shut out the chilly breeze. Rocking the pup in her arms, she nosed its cool fur coat, letting in the comfort of its warm body. Making little whines, the pup wiggled in her arms while she echoed with her own slight crying moans.

Bea yanked open the driver's door and hunched over the steering wheel. "Y'all making a racket." Popping a cigarette between her lips, she took a long drag, letting the smoke drift out the open car door. She tilted her head toward Maggie Lu and slammed the door. "We've got to keep on," she said, cigarette bobbing while she backed onto U.S. 61. "What else can I say? Leo wanted you before you were even born. I thought I did too."

"*Thought*?" Maggie Lu heaved the word back at Bea. "It was family time, huh?"

Flinching, Bea nodded. "If you're a mama, you mean to care. You call it love. Sometimes you're not good at it. Now you wouldn't know that part. You made a different choice . . . putting Tiffany out for adoption."

Before she could bite her tongue, Maggie Lu spewed, "Get rid of it . . . your response to me over the phone. Years later you go find this child and just as quickly lose interest in her, leaving plenty of disrupted lives in your wake. All you're saying is you *meant* to care."

Bea ranted. "I guess my mama *meant* to care for me

too, but Pearl was her favorite and could do no wrong." She swerved as a spotted dog leapt out of a ditch, barking and chasing the front wheel before diving back into the dark woods. "You should blame Pearl for the whole adoption idea."

Maggie Lu lashed out. "Oh, I thought she was helping me. At least she seemed to care when I needed her. Why are you always so critical of Aunt Pearl?"

Bea's voice rose. "Always walking in the footsteps of know-it-all older sister Pearl. When I got out of Mama's house, I swore I would not take anyone else's blame ever again." She fiddled with a cigarette she couldn't light from the faulty lighter. "Why Pearl even named me Bebe, always mad she had to tend me and the house while Mama was always at DAR and Daddy running off to livestock auctions." The cigarette bent between her fingers, getting more and more pinched while Bea banged the lighter on the dash and reinserted it until the coil ignited. Jamming the fiery glow against the limp cigarette, Bea took a long drag. Releasing a steady smoke stream, she leaned toward Maggie Lu with a quizzical stare. "Looking back, I'm not sure why I let myself care for Fred, but I cared enough to keep his affections from Pearl."

Leaning back from the smoky haze, Maggie Lu asked, "Mama, who's next to be at fault?"

Bea straightened in her seat, accelerating through the next patch of open road, her words tumbling out in a higher pitch. "Well, Leo. I thought this trip was all about Leo, so now maybe you'll rethink his situation." Bea began to complain. "This whole trip was a big waste of my time since we found out at the prison gate that Leo had survived his surgery, no need for me to plan a funeral. He'll probably have you be in charge of his affairs now."

Maggie Lu retorted, "You should be glad you don't have to deal with him anymore." She listened to her mama turn toward jealousy of the relationship she would try to build with Leo, the man who wanted to be her daddy.

Bea repeated her doubts that she'd go back down to try to talk to Leo at Parchman. He didn't need anything from her now that he knew Maggie Lu was going to help him out.

Maggie Lu interrupted. "You hadn't been to see him before. I didn't think you two had much to talk about."

Bea finally admitted that she wished she'd had a chance to convince Leo to sell that old trailer and lot because she wouldn't be getting any proceeds now, concluding sourly, "I'll have to reconsider being thought of as his next of kin."

"Mama, it's my relationship with you that needs rethinking, and I haven't even gotten to know Daddy enough yet to determine if he's anything like you. That could be a bigger disappointment than all I've learned about you from this ever-so-long trip home."

Bea's fingers fluttered atop the steering wheel. The pup, after a long waking-up sigh, began to prance around the back seat. Maggie Lu reached through the front seats to pat the pup's side, reassuring, "Won't be long before we stop." Glimpsing the Memphis city limits sign, Maggie Lu swallowed the tension she had been riding with. Knowing she would settle into her own home soon was all she had left to do since these parents had left her with no family to speak of, other than Sunny. Not her cousin, her half-sister. The pup crept from the back seat across the console and into her lap, snuggling into her comforting pats.

When Bea stomped the brake hard in front of Maggie

Lu's house, Bea hunched over the steering wheel, saying, "That was quite a ride we had, huh?"

Bracing herself, Maggie Lu kept the pup under her arm. "I'm taking her home."

Bea tapped a fresh cigarette pack on the dashboard, saying, "Uh, huh . . . Could you lend me a little gas money?"

Maggie Lu dug into her bag and tossed a bill on the seat. "Probably my last one."

Bea nodded. "I figured you'd made up your mind." Jerking the car into gear, she fired up another cigarette, then tore down the street, taillights winking in disrepair.

Maggie Lu and the Pup

Well past midnight Maggie Lu was relieved to step onto her own porch and watch Bea's car disappear under the streetlights. Maggie Lu's neck ached from turning away from her mama's insensitive litany during the long ride, rubbery gum held tight between her teeth to tame her temper. Holding the stray wiggling against her, she smelled like a puppy. Unlocking her front door, she released the antsy pup from under her arm and flung her briefcase and bag on the couch. Still tense, she poured a glass of Cabernet and sat on the closest chair.

Allowing her only a few relaxing sips, the prancing pup trotted down the hallway and returned to a nervous circling near the front door. "No you don't, no puddles, Miss Cuddles." Signaling with both hands toward the kitchen, Maggie Lu flipped the deadbolt and chain and flung open the back door, running out into the yard to show the pup the preferred peeing area. Her stale gum sailed from her mouth between encouraging shouts. The pup bounded behind her and across the back porch toward the high grass near the rickety garage.

A flickering street light in the alley reminded her she needed to call the city for repair. Squinting into the yard, she eyed an overturned lawn chair and rusty barbecue grill leaning on a bent leg. Plastic bags were lodged in the chain-link fence near the alley. Frowning at the mess, she was surprised by her inattention. Late nights coming home from her law office, she trod the worn path from the garage, barely noticing the unkempt yard. Since moving to Memphis after law school, Maggie Lu spent much of her time at work.

She wished for a ball to throw to the pup but couldn't even remember the last time she'd played with a dog, often ignoring the dogs Sunny tried to foist upon her with a mocking tone, "A dog could love you, since you have no friends." What did Sunny know about her life, only the snippets she chose to share with her during infrequent phone calls. But what friend would she call to tell about the pup and her trip to Parchman and back? Her law partner, Inez, would not welcome dog talk but would definitely warn her about taking Leo's case.

Did she take the pup just to spite Bea, removing Bea's reason to deliver it to Sunny's kennel? Maybe she'd just let her guard down during the long ride, comforted by the pup's sweet sighs when she'd cuddled it near her. She doubted she could make time for a canine buddy, though it would instinctively offer more loyalty than Bea. Calling her *Bea* sounded right. *Mama* had an affectionate ring. When had Bea ever offered her any warmth?

Maggie Lu clapped her hands, hollering, "Cuddles," and enjoyed the pup's eager run and rollover at her feet, but after a quick pat, the pup scampered back into the yard. Maybe she shouldn't give any name to the pup yet. If caring for the animal didn't work out, she could always take her to Sunny's. Yet she felt a smile creep up after the pup's little yips at the noisy junker lumbering through the alley. The old car's backfire reminded her that

Birdsong Farm would probably be better for a pup than city life. The pup bolted in her direction. Allowing herself to enjoy petting the squirming pup that whined in delight at a tummy scratch helped to push back at her excuses again.

Squeezing her arms against the evening's chilly breeze, Maggie Lu paced the back porch. Cuddles, after some breakneck runs around the fence line, began sniffing inside the garage, not heeding Maggie Lu's constant urging to return. Eventually she called into the dark, "I'll go in and warm up with some wine. Let me know when you're ready to come in."

Weariness from the long day trip sinking in, Maggie Lu slumped into her soft recliner and enjoyed the rich taste of the Cabernet, wanting to dull the hours she'd spent in the car listening to Bea redefine their past, mostly Bea's own self-centered life.

Biting her lip, Maggie Lu questioned again why she always cringed when she heard Bea's voice on the phone, Bea only calling when she needed a favor or money. Whatever Maggie Lu gave in return was never enough to satisfy Bea. A burning resentment followed each encounter and left Maggie Lu feeling more alone. Tonight, the fury peaked inside her, and Maggie Lu felt her longing for a mother shift. She could no longer think of Bea as her mama, but rather a callous woman who seemed to never have time for a daughter anyway. Her eyes moved toward her legal briefcase on the couch, accepting her own conscious choice not to parent her own offspring. She had chosen to give her time to the law, a descendant she could accept.

She could do it, ignore Bea's next phone call and release any concern that would accompany it. Maggie Lu took another sip of wine and felt a flutter of new breath inside. After that elating thought, she worried that the ever-persistent and needy Bea would not stay away. Wheezing into a full burst of despair, she remembered a song about a troubling person who was like a boomerang, always returning. More wine until her head nuzzled the soft pillow in her chair and her eyelids drooped, halting a final sip.

A low howl broke into Maggie Lu's unsteady dozing. Blinking at the shaft of pre-dawn light that edged between where the vertical bamboo shades missed a slat, she leaned forward in her recliner and bent an ear toward the back door. A beeping garbage truck lumbered through the alley, followed by another howl. The pup that she'd claimed in a half-hearted rescue—where was it? Apprehension slipped in before she could climb out of her chair. She'd not braved the cold last night to wait on the pup to come inside. Was there a hole in the fence because she'd not taken care of the yard? Moving through the shadows, she flung open the back door and called, "Cuddles!" Hesitating, the pup limped a few steps from inside the garage, a front paw struggling against the grass unsteadily. Taking measured steps, Maggie Lu inched toward the pup and scooped it into her arms, its body shivering–or was it shaking in fear, unsure of her intentions? Maggie Lu whispered into its ear, "I'll take better care of you. I promise."

Repeating a *poor puppy* lament, Maggie Lu rubbed its head. Once inside, the pup squirmed against her chest. Under the harsh kitchen light, Maggie Lu saw a wad of green goo wedged between the pup's toe pads. Growling, the pup bared its teeth each time she tried to pull a few hairs away from what looked like her Clorets gum she'd thoughtlessly spit out in the yard. "What a dunce I was," she scolded herself. Growls turned into small cries while Maggie Lu couldn't think of anything to do about the wad. Placing the agitated pup on the linoleum floor, she quickly set down a bowl of water and a paltry bowl of Cheerios breakfast cereal and reached out warily, trying to coax the pup toward them. After a cautious glance, the pup hobbled to the bowls, lapping without interruption until the bottoms of both bowls were exposed.

Maggie Lu's rumbling stomach reminded her to empty the rest of the cereal into her own bowl. Munching at her kitchen table, she watched the pup sniff around the cabinets and behind the refrigerator before easing itself underneath a coffee table in the next room where Maggie Lu had placed an old blanket. Curling into a half circle, the pup licked its fur and continued to gnaw at the gum-encrusted paw before it gave into blinks and yawns, releasing itself into sleep. Maggie Lu stretched against the hard chair, flustered with her lack of sleep and the worry of what this little pup might need from her.

Tiptoeing across the living room floor, Maggie Lu chuckled at her newly found sensitivity toward the pup, not wanting to wake it. Unease flared over how to remove the painful gum. Letting the pup sleep was easier for now. She picked up the briefcase from the couch and crept down the hallway to her home office. Sunday was her catch-up day, but now she had her incarcerated daddy's parole to add to her caseload and a wounded pup to contend with. Sunny could help with the pup, but it was too early to call her on a weekend.

Spreading Leo's files on the big wooden table that served as a makeshift desk, Maggie Lu perched on a straight-back chair and flipped open the prison file. Leo's stern face stared back at her, but now she knew this face. She had watched its expressions change when he re-told tales of her childhood. Feeling this parent's affection, she immediately sensed what Bea had rarely offered her. She stared intently at probably the only man who really loved her mother, and maybe her, and wondered how he'd done it. If she helped free him, whom would he care for the most?

Tightness gripped her chest while she tried to pull up her lawyerly oath, her duty to try to help Leo. *I will use no falsehood nor delay any person's cause for lucre or malice.* Then she forced herself to read his thick file of parole rejections, the last one resulting from a conflict with another inmate. She would have to get more data on that one. The others were standard, Leo being a threat to society as a result of past offenses, declining lawyers, hmm . . . she wondered why? Leaning back in her chair, she searched the morning clouds drifting above her window, finally admitting to herself she would do the work but worrying what kind of Daddy would Leo be—or would a free Leo never be in her life at all? Eventually her hands flew into the air and she screamed, "I can't believe I'm putting myself through this!" A whine echoed down the hallway. Her hand to her mouth, she fumed, "I woke the pup."

She cast an annoyed glance toward the whimpers coming from the hallway. Closing the file, she cancelled thoughts of a nap and resumed her pup-tending role, dialing Sunny's number. With a start she realized she might adopt both Leo and the pup into her life when she said, "I kept the rescue pup that Bea was going to take to you before she got the call from Leo's prison."

Between bursts of "Really?" and "No kidding!" Sunny's chuckles grew louder in her ear.

Irritated at Sunny's recounting of her past excuses for not

having a dog, Maggie Lu interrupted, "I might have made a mistake. Already this pup got hurt last night. How do I tend to its paw embedded with a wad of chewing gum?"

Another little whine at the door turned her head. Cuddles hobbled into the office and tumbled over at her feet. She stared at the sticky paw. Listening to Sunny's method of gum removal made her squeamish. "Oh, sounds tricky, might bite me." Damp tingles replaced Maggie Lu's nerves hearing Sunny remind her she could just take the pup to a vet on Monday if she didn't want to try.

"Be brave, cousin," Maggie Lu heard. "The pup will be grateful."

Cuddles stretched and wagged its tail. Maggie Lu nodded., "I'd forgotten all about that feeling." Sunny urged, "Animals need mothering."

"What?"

Sunny said, "No experience needed . . . not as tough as you might think."

Maggie Lu cringed. "Don't compare this to child rearing. Okay, I didn't want that. Don't be hinting around . . . about the girl, the adoption. The next thing you'll bring up again is trying to get me to meet her."

Sunny's voice went low. "I put Tiffany's picture back on the family wall after you hurled it into the yard. She deserves an explanation from you, why you refuse to at least be a mother in name only."

"Leave it alone, Sunny. She thinks I'm dead, doesn't she? That's a relief to both of us."

Sunny said evenly, "You were ecstatic to find out that Leo is alive."

Maggie Lu's tone slipped. "That's different."

"Don't give me some of your legalese to justify . . ." Sunny was getting bumptious.

Maggie Lu tried to gain hold, but her voice rose a little lighter. "Although I was little, I remember when Leo was my daddy, living with Bea and me at the trailer."

Glancing at the folder on her desk, now she couldn't hold back. "I met Leo yesterday. I think I like him. I'm going to work on his parole hearing." Imagining Leo sitting next to her at a defense counsel table at the prison, and the parole board handing her his release papers, she took a quick breath to respond to Sunny. "I worry if he will stick around if I help him get released."

"Well now that's another sticky situation." Did Sunny chuckle?

Maggie Lu stiffened. "Puns are not what I need right now."

Sunny soothed, "You know you're my best cousin. I care."

Maggie Lu lessened her sharp tone. "I know, but now there's Leo in the picture."

Sunny urged, "Okay, what was he like? Aunt Bea thought he'd be dead when y'all got there."

Maggie Lu pushed down a resentment that Sunny enjoyed anything about Bea. Maggie Lu hesitated. "Bea woulda been happier if he was dead. She went hoping to get her hands on anything he still owned."

"Well, Aunt Bea might have a right . . ."

Maggie Lu cut in. "I don't want to talk about Bea. Leo seemed caring. I wish he would have been around when I was growing up."

After a long silence, Maggie Lu realized she was breathing noisily into the phone.

"Can't believe it's been twenty years since my daddy died," came from Sunny.

"Yeah," was all Maggie Lu could manage. Her heart

began to throb at the mention of Sunny's daddy. Would she ever tell Sunny that Bea said they had the *same* daddy? Heat mounting, Maggie Lu pushed past where she didn't want to go. "You would be mighty surprised if you knew . . ."

Sunny's voice was high. "What's that about? I know you had hard feelings against my daddy, but he loved us both. It couldn't be equal, with Leo being your daddy and all. Mama put your picture up on our family wall. I think you took the last family album."

"Your mama let me borrow it."

Sunny's words were so quick. "See if you can find it. Leo might be in there."

"They said my daddy was dead. So he probably isn't in there."

"That wasn't my daddy's fault. He let you . . ."

"He didn't let me do a thing. Fred Birdsong hated me because . . ."

Maggie Lu almost shouted, *he wouldn't claim me*, then took a hot breath, but a shiver stirred her thinking she'd be Margaret Lucelia Birdsong if he had. Distractedly reaching to cradle the pup in her arms, she was not ready to tackle the family chaos, still shaken by Sunny's reactions to her talking about Leo. She stretched toward a bottom shelf to pull over that tattered photo album Sunny reminded her about. The pup wiggled and slipped from her lap, crying as its sore foot hit the floor.

"Don't hurt that puppy just because you're upset."

"You know I wouldn't..."

"Well, I'm beginning to wonder who you can take care of or what both of us can do to each other."

Stretching the phone cord to balance the receiver, Maggie Lu squatted next to the pup, pulling it closer to her, and thumbed through the album. She stared at the last family reunion picture that included Uncle Fred and Sunny and herself almost twenty years ago, cringing at the shared narrow lips., Were their resemblances only from their mamas being sisters? Were there more hints of Fred in Maggie Lu? Had Sunny ever noticed? She decided to look more carefully at the big 8x10 family pictures hanging on the wall at Birdsong Farm.

Maggie Lu said, "I'm gonna bring this pup out to the farm before long, okay? I'll bring the album."

Sunny's voice had a twinge. "Okay, I hear what you are trying to say, so come whenever. Bye."

Maggie Lu let the phone drop into the cradle and said to the pup, "We're going to Birdsong Farm."

Revelations at Birdsong Farm

In the morning Maggie Lu couldn't wait to leave for Birdsong Farm, better that her cousin Sunny be surprised. Awakened early by puppy whines, Maggie Lu had her bag and the pup in the Z car before sunrise. After a speedy drive across U.S. 78 to Crosston and then a fast turn onto U.S. 45 South, her tires crunched up the long driveway at Birdsong Farm. Maggie Lu squinted at the familiar white bungalow casting its shadow across the dewy front yard. She stopped her Z car behind Sunny's truck, which sat in the carport. The pup bounced out of the open car door and raced to the end of its leash for a quick squat in a grassy spot near the carport, then began sniffing new terrain.

Tugging at the resistant pup, Maggie Lu tapped the back door, hoping to slip inside to get a closer look at the family picture wall before Sunny awoke. Surprised to find the door locked, she had to call out, "It's Cousin, are you up?" Soon Sunny, still in her plaid pajamas, slipped the lock, pouting, "You that eager to get rid of this pup?" Maggie Lu and the pup both pushed inside. "Aww, look at the sweet baby," cooed Sunny, bending down to let Cuddles smell her hand. After Sunny released the pup to run through her house, she shuffled into the kitchen. "Do you want coffee?"

"Definitely," Maggie Lu called over her shoulder while heading straight into the den right off the hallway. Fumbling for the overhead light, she narrowed her focus on the wall of framed family prints. Craning her neck over the desk toward the 8x10 of Uncle Fred and Aunt Pearl, Maggie Lu scanned Fred's every feature, his high forehead over those gray, piercing eyes, his high cheekbones and stern, thin lips. Her stomach lurched at having the same blood coursing through her veins. She glanced at her reflection on the glass covering Fred's photo and then shifted her eyes behind her shadow-self into Fred's eyes. Shuddering at the memory of his critical stares, she struggled with a queasy curiosity.

From the kitchen she heard Sunny cooing at the pup and heard its toenails clicking on the linoleum. Sunny's coffee preparations clattered down the hallway, but no tempting aroma drifted in yet. Taking a long breath, Maggie Lu had more time to scan the smaller frames. Her eyes glazed past a gold frame with cracked glass over the young girl she refused to claim. Only one picture of Fred on the wall showed a smile while he leaned with an arm against the white column of a building she recognized as the library at Ole Miss where her mama studied and Aunt Pearl and Uncle Fred only visited. That's the age he would have been when he impregnated Bea. When she reached to trace his upturned mouth, she wondered if that smugness had been captured by Bea's camera.

Sunny caught her in mid thought, popping in behind her. "Whatcha looking at?"

Maggie Lu drew back her hand. "Daddy . . . your daddy," she quickly corrected, feeling flushed looking into Sunny's replica smile, like Fred's when he was tentative. Wishing for more time, Maggie Lu gasped, "Where's the coffee?"

Sunny swung her hands in the air. "You are certainly irritating today. And so early." While Maggie Lu stood motionless by the picture wall, Sunny hurried toward the hallway, calling over her shoulder, "I'll get the coffee."

Maggie Lu took in tiny puffs of air, stunned at the heat rising inside her as her mind whirled with the unfolding reality that Uncle Fred was her father.

Sunny was robotic in her quick return, pushing on with, "The last time we talked, you said you were looking for pictures of *your* daddy."

"I am."

Maggie Lu's mouth moved, but no more words came. She tried to stall an upheaval of wooziness. Uncle Fred's big, wide face seemed to bulge from its frame, mocking the secret he had held about her. Maggie Lu's legs were springy, wobbling her away from the rows of frames. She needed more time to take in the eerie similarities that she imagined were leaping from his images on the wall. How could he both father her and not *be* a father to her?

Sunny's eyes narrowed. "Whatya trying to say?" She stood stock-still, holding a cup of coffee in each hand.

Maggie Lu's throat tightened into a squeak. "Your daddy IS my daddy."

Sunny's wrist quivered, sloshing hot liquid on her hand from one cup, making a cat-like "Yeow" that caught the pup's attention as it explored a corner of the room. Abruptly Sunny set down both steaming cups on a small table and perched on the cushion of a wingback chair, swaying angrily forward. Strands of damp hair sprung out from behind her ears while she swatted them firmly to her head and compulsively rubbed the brown liquid from her hand with a napkin. Her lips curled outward like a fish. "Are you crazy?"

Maggie Lu flung her arm toward the big picture of Fred. "Tell me you don't see me."

Leaning backward, Sunny said, "I don't even want to see you right here before me, acting this way." She pushed forward with a visible throb in her neck. "You came over here to do more than bring me a dog. You came for a fight, talking all this hooey."

The pup came bounding in between them with a whimper when its sore paw touched the table leg. They both reached for the skittish animal, but Sunny was first and pulled the furry bundle close into her lap. She was already mothering it. Red-faced and off balance, Maggie Lu thought she'd sink onto the floor. Instead she found the worn recliner, slumping into it, its legs screeching along the floor.

"You're wrecking everything." Sunny's voice dropped from angry to tired, sounding to Maggie Lu like her own voice, a similarity she hadn't noticed before.

"No, it was Bea that did the wrecking." Maggie Lu gulped the hot liquid, then fanned her tongue for coolness. "It was both of them, Bea and Fred."

Sunny clutched her cup without moving it toward her mouth and said, "Sneaking in here, you're actually claiming Fred? Why can't you let Leo be your daddy?"

Remembering Leo's parting wave at Parchman, Maggie Lu's face melted, but her eyes flew to the wall absent of his photo and a scowl emerged. "So you believe me?"

Sunny held up her palms. "Stop right now. Don't go too far."

But Maggie Lu set in. "Bea was talking nonstop on the trip back from Parchman. It slipped out. She claimed she didn't *mean* to tell me."

A stunned Sunny, with a chiseled face that Maggie Lu had not seen before, leaned forward. The only sound was the pup's panting as it squirmed for a new position in Sunny's lap. Then Sunny finally found her voice. "How does that help you or me? I knew Daddy ran around on Mama. She knew that Aunt Bea and Daddy had something going. I might have some more siblings out there, but I don't want to know about them."

Maggie Lu pressed her hands into her thighs. "Truth, I just want the truth about who I am."

Shaking her head, Sunny said, "You're still Cousin. Don't you get it? My daddy and your mama led crazy lives and didn't think or care who they hurt. I've tried to push the hurt away. You've made it worse."

Maggie Lu felt flustered. "Bea did it."

Sunny pointed an angry finger. "Now *you're* doing the hurting." She blinked hard. "Why did you feel the need to tell me? You want to be as cold as your mama?"

Sunny's words sent a jolt, causing Maggie Lu to not hold back. "You've felt Bea's coldness too, right?" Maggie Lu now sensed that Sunny struggled with what Bea offered her, too. Maggie Lu felt her brain freeze and her own thoughts about Bea harden and her wonder about Leo melt into disarray. Would Bea remain only a thin sheet of ice between all of them?

Like Bea, Maggie Lu knew she couldn't hold her tongue. "By knowing, maybe I'm clearer on my anger at Bea and Uncle Fred. It's not just about her neglect, but she put me in this house with *him*. Your daddy *knew* me, but he was ashamed, and I soaked up that shame, unknowingly, with his every glare." Maggie Lu knew now what was not nice about herself—she wanted to drive a wedge between Bea and Sunny.

Sunny wiped her eyes with a stained napkin. "I see that Aunt Bea was chasing her career back then. We both have our rejections, Maggie Lu. Remember my brother died, and I was never the son Daddy wanted."

Maggie Lu's eyes moved over the picture wall to the baby Sonny, who died as a toddler. She skipped over to the frame with the cracked glass that she had angrily thrown into the yard, her finger jabbing at the scarred portrait of the young girl, Tiffany. "Why have you and Bea tried to force this child back into my life?"

Sunny's eyes were squeezed shut. "You know I wanted a child and couldn't have one."

Maggie Lu blurted, "I didn't *mean* to have that child." Jostling her cup back to the table, she felt she'd edged herself too close to a subject she didn't want. Maggie Lu pushed hard against the soft recliner.

Sunny's words flew out. "Your daughter, Tiffany, is family. Her adopted family was not enough for her. She loves visiting Birdsong Farm. She loves us for finding her." Sunny's shoulders shook in between loud gasps for air.

The pup tumbled to the floor, carrying Sunny's napkin down the hallway and back, tearing around the room and barking, mimicking their voices. Sunny reached under the table to quiet the pup. "I know Aunt Bea doesn't care as much anymore about her grandchild. She's busy. I hoped you would . . . care more. I simply wanted Tiffany in our lives."

Shuddering, Maggie Lu said, "Right, just like Mama, I don't want to tend children."

Maggie Lu glanced out the window toward the still-creepy milk barn full of memories of Uncle Fred's beckoning her inside. She could not grasp parenting, barely making a home for herself in Memphis. Sunny had made the farm a family gathering spot and made it her own with the kennels. Maggie Lu watched the pup lick Sunny's outstretched hand and let itself be cajoled into her lap.

Sunny curled into her mama's old wingback and closed her eyes. "I don't need a sister, Maggie Lu. I need us to be close just like we always were." The loss was in the room with them. Sunny squeezed the pup to herself, tutting, "Are you all I can trust?"

Maggie Lu ached from knowing the path Bea and Fred had pulled them into. The outsider, Maggie Lu realized that knowing the truth made her somebody else. She extended her hand toward Sunny and the pup. "Trusting is hard, cousin."

Sunny's Pursuit

Sunny couldn't stand to watch Maggie Lu's leaving. She stooped to pick a stray dandelion from her front yard. Still she caught a glimpse of her cousin's Z car creeping down the driveway, then making a gravel-spitting turn onto Hollyberry Road. She stuck the dandelion behind her ear, hoping to make it to the porch where she flopped down into the squeak of her mama's old wicker chair, leaning her head nearly into her lap, feeling drained by their long talk. After tears and shouting, Sunny was grateful that Maggie Lu had finally come full circle and realized their lifelong bond should not be in jeopardy because they had crazy parents.

She rocked for a little while like her mama had done so often, sometimes almost trancelike. The family secret Maggie Lu had delivered pulled up scenes of a younger Mama and Daddy sitting at the kitchen table silently or raising their voices in the carport and then going silent when she ran by. Their adult lives were going on behind their "parent lives," selfishly ignoring their impact on their children.

Interrupting her thoughts, the stray pup Maggie Lu had left with her scratched at the screen door. Slipping inside, Sunny bent toward the pup, the dandelion falling from behind her ear to the floor. "Cuddles, you've got some nerve giving Cousin an excuse to come over here." She plunked a scoop of puppy chow from the pantry into a plastic bowl. Hesitating in front of the kitchen window near the sink, she saw the new bird dog she'd rescued chasing a ball around its kennel like her daddy's old Spot used to do long ago. She'd make a place out there at the end kennel for Cuddles soon and add the pup's description to her pet adoption list she published in the *Crosston Gazette* every week.

Slipping two coffee cups into the pile of dishes in the sink, she flinched again from this morning's heated talk when the coffee had burned their tongues and then grew cold from distraction. Glancing at her reflection in the window, she saw her mama's features inside her own, maybe less of her daddy's. Did her mama stare out this very window into the adjoining field, trying to stuff down the hurt her husband's philandering had caused her?

***

Sunny hadn't realized she'd moved away from the sink full of dirty dishes until she had crossed the threshold into her mama's bedroom, a place she rarely entered. Cuddles barked and leapt against her leg. Although her mama had been dead a number of years, Sunny had made few changes to that room, not ready to claim every room as her own in this farmhouse she and Maggie Lu had inherited, the house she took refuge in from her floundering marriage to Hamilton.

Sunny's stays were initially temporary, settling back into her childhood bedroom upstairs. When she first left her husband at their home in Memphis, she thought she'd take a break from their anguish over her miscarriage, find solace with some animals at Birdsong Farm. After years of traveling back and forth had passed, her desire to resume her life in Memphis was waning. Yet every few weeks Hamilton filled their phone conversations with his golfing scores and headaches from his insurance office until he was hurried off the phone by his rude secretary. The familiar tone of his voice kept her listening yet offering distracted replies to his news until she eventually interrupted, pouring out rescue animal dilemmas, which he mostly responded to with useless advice. She began to think he was probably sleeping around, maybe with that secretary, though he wasn't one to let his eye wander toward every attractive woman who crossed his path. Maggie Lu had opened the embarrassing wounds of her daddy's womanizing, but Sunny hoped to at least think of Hamilton more kindly. At least he talked.

She reached for the cordless phone in the den and called his number. "Hamilton."

"Hello Sunny," he said absently.

Sunny couldn't hold back. "Aunt Bea told Maggie Lu that she and I are sisters."

"Your daddy? Well, we knew he was not...faithful," he said too quickly.

Sunny flinched. "Are you seeing anybody?"

"We're not divorced," he said evenly.

"You're not admitting anything," she prodded.

His tone switched to critical. "Do you want to admit anything?"

Feeling flushed, Sunny spat, "This is how it always is with us." She tried to hold back an avalanche of discomfort. "I can tell we're starting our own separate lives for real."

"Time does that," Hamilton said flatly. "I've got to go."

The phone still heavy in her hand, Sunny couldn't imagine the secrets Hamilton now kept. She stared through the bedroom window out toward the driveway where looming live oak limbs were skewing the sun's rays into phantom shadows that seemed to creep toward the window. She had never been afraid to stay in the big farmhouse by herself. Today she felt more alone than she had when she and Hamilton first agreed that being apart might be better. Hadn't they meant only for a while? Her fingers tingling from gripping the cordless phone, she jammed it back onto the base unit. She focused on the tiny bits of sun outside her mama's bedroom window.

Chasing a yellow tennis ball past her, the pup scooted under the bed in her mama's bedroom adjacent to the den, then began to whine. Dropping to her knees, Sunny peered under the bed at Cuddles, who had ensnared herself between two large boxes wedged under the box spring. Tiny bubble-brown eyes blinked above a nervous pink tongue. She gripped the edge of one box and tugged it toward her, making a wider space to grip the panting pup's bony sides and pull it free, enjoying gleeful face licks from the pup. Sunny tugged the remains of the old box closer, spilling out an assortment of jewelry boxes and scarves and a few red hats. She pushed her fingers between the soft scarves and inhaled a whiff of the stale Avon perfume her mama had always worn. Her cheeks dampened. What had her mama done when her daddy was so often gone? Had she put on her finest—and in later years, her red hat—to join other ladies who no longer wanted to talk about their husbands, but maybe about another interests? Sunny's interests were rescuing dogs and spending time with Tiffany and Karleen, stunned that she'd finally admitted it.

Sunny opened a long red shoe box that was sticking out from the torn larger box. She did not recognize these glittery pink pumps, but the soles were worn enough that her mama must have enjoyed them. She placed one shoe next to her and was about to remove the other, when instead she put her hand into the shoe and felt the shape that her mama's toes had made. She imagined a smiling Pearl in glittering shoes twirling with a shadowy escort. A resentful pang pinched her stomach. The shoe flipped on its side.

Cuddles darted beneath her knees, snapping her teeth around the end of the toe of the pink shoe. Sunny lunged, catching the canine thief. A folded yellow sticky note was lying on the floor. It must have dropped from inside the shoe. Sunny unstuck the note smudged with a dirty thumb print and read its shaky script. "Call me at 286-2777, Hershel." Temptation prompted her to call the number, but with a deep breath, the revelation came that she was not ready for another emotional jolt this afternoon.

Cuddles sprinted back into her lap. She wrapped her arms around the panting pup and dipped her head to listen to its heartbeat, whispering into its ear, "Do you think you are so cute and special?" After its little whine, she could tell that Cuddles wanted to be a house dog. The last house dog at Birdsong Farm had been her mama's tiny chihuahua skittering around the den and settling itself onto any cushion it chose.

The sentiment accompanying that vision surprised a laugh from Sunny. Her mama's little chihuahua had snapped at her ankles with a not-so-friendly first greeting on one of her visits from Memphis to Birdsong Farm. "Brownie was a gift from a friend." Her mama returned a dry smile but offered no responses to Sunny's further prodding. Sunny could never get over how people and their dogs were always so alike. It was part of the wisdom she used for arranging adoptions. She had to see the person and the dog together.

Now she thought it strange that her mama had accepted a dog when she'd never wanted one in the house before. As teens Sunny and Maggie Lu had begged for a dog other than one of Spot's bird dog puppies, to which her daddy had already assigned either hunting jobs or price tags. Sunny glanced toward the end of the bed, the click of Cuddles' nails clawing up the set of little wooden dog stairs. Brownie was often lounging at the foot of the bed, especially during Mama's last year, when she was so haunted by dreams of the dead toddler brother that Sunny would drive the two hours from her home to spend the night. Who came when she could not? Who had built these little stairs?

Sunny dropped the pink shoes back into the large box, her foot giving it a final shove back under the bed. Stretching as she rose from the floor, she realized that her mama had secrets like everyone did. Pearl's backhanded love, *those shorts look darling even if your legs are a little thick,* had always pushed Sunny closer to her daddy. Although she was hurt by Maggie Lu's revelation about her daddy, Sunny now sensed the curiosity Maggie Lu must have felt about a newly discovered father, enough to make her examine all his photos on the picture wall in the den. Sunny twirled the yellow note around her finger and called the number.

A long "Hellooooo" came in response.

"Is this Hershel?"

"Why?"

"I just found your number among my mama's things. Did you know Pearl Birdsong? She passed away in 1987."

"Why?"

"Are you Hershel?"

"Daddy's at Crosston Senior's Home now. Don't know if he'll talk to you."

"What's his last name?"

"Lopez."

The phone clicked in Sunny's ear. A stream of chills saturated her body.

***

When Sunny's truck lumbered into the only parking space in the lot next to Crosston Senior's Home, a stooped-shouldered man dressed in a loose-fitting gray jogging suit waved toward her as he was ushered off the front porch by an exasperated attendant. She followed them inside and inquired at the reception desk for Hershel Lopez. Offering a patronizing smile, the receptionist replied, "It's the dinner hour. Did you have a reservation to join him?" Flushed, but determined, Sunny nodded and moved quickly in the direction of a Dining Hall sign.

She spotted the gray-suited man smiling at her and asked, "Do you know Hershel Lopez?"

"I do." His milky blue eyes seemed to flicker. "But I'd enjoy your company, too."

Sunny squirmed, shifting in her sneakers. "I need to . . ."

"Another time, then," he said, offering a slippery grin while he lifted a finger toward a thick-shouldered man in a red shirt and blue jeans huddled over his dinner plate at a small table. Moving past her to a nearby table, the gray-suited man eased into a chair next to a thin woman in pink, saying, "I'd enjoy your company, too."

Amidst clanging silverware and a mix of steamy odors, Sunny threaded a path through myriad round tables encircled by an assortment of gray-haired seniors. Slipping into the open seat across from red shirt, she asked in a low voice, "Are you Hershel Lopez?"

His small eyes cast a puzzled stare and his cheeks flushed. "Who wants to know?"

Sunny's lip tightened. "I'm Pearl Birdsong's daughter. I thought..."

A thick brown arm reached across the table toward her, then both arms floated over the table in a rhythm only he must have heard. His wide lips moved with the rhythm and then opened to a smile of even yet slightly stained teeth, saying, "She was a wonderful dancer."

Hershel's right arm began to twitch. A tall, uniformed woman stopped at the table. "Never seen you here. If you're helping him with his dinner, sit on this side of the table."

Sunny nodded, moving closer and handing Hershel a piece of corn bread from his plate. His hand wobbled it toward his mouth. The tall attendant turned away.

"Damn disease," he said. "Glad Pearl didn't see it."

"Then you knew her?"

"Very well." He almost sighed. "You favor her."

Sunny's back warmed at his affirmation while her throat tickled.

"How did you meet Mama?"

He scooted his chair backwards and frowned. "Fixed a big water leak out in her front yard." His arm twitched until he grabbed the armrest. "Your daddy was dead by then."

Picking up utensils from her side of the table, she leaned forward, pushing aside bits of macaroni and cabbage on his plate while busily slicing his wedge of catsup-soaked meatloaf into tiny squares. Sunny babbled, "I'm not accusing..."

Hershel gave her a long stare. "We treated each other well."

Realizing her slicing flurry, Sunny dropped the knife and fork. "She didn't mention . . ."

Hershel pulled his chair closer to the table and spooned the meat unsteadily, his neck bent closer toward his plate, speaking maybe to himself. "We kept things to ourselves."

Catching her breath, Sunny spied the key on the table next to his plate. Did he ever have a key to her mama's house? A worn tab inscribed *Lopez* was attached to the key ring by a beaded chain.

"Do you know Leo Lopez? He was married to mama's sister Bea."

"My cousin," he said, continuing to chew. "In jail, couldn't help it, kinda like me being here." His head rose and an awkward wheeze sputtered from his mouth. His deep brown eyes absorbed her disjointed query. "Why did you come, girl?"

Her gaze shifted to his plate, the aroma of over-baked macaroni and soured cabbage saturating her nostrils. She squirmed against the hard chair to stave off a dizzy embarrassment.

"I wanted to know more about Mama."

His eyes glittered.

She guessed that Hershel could not tell her what she really wanted to know about her mama. They had kept that to themselves.

Edith Tells on Pearl

Sunny gunned her truck past the wobbly yellow mailbox covered with *Tompkins* scrawl and stopped just short of Edith's front porch. The old woman was stretched out on a mottled quilt covering a lump of furniture. Her face peeked from her mass of gray hair with her large eyes staring quizzically. "Here's company. I'll declare."

Sunny eased up the wooden steps and sat on the porch's edge, cooing, "Miss Edith, it's your neighbor, Sunny. I've got to talk to you about Hershel Lopez."

"Kenny T's not here and wouldn't want to say much about that Lopez family. He just left for Crosston." Edith laughed while tamping her palm against a trail of drool from her lip. She leaned forward, her cheeks beginning to redden. "I can't tell on those folks, almost dead or surely gone."

Sunny's stomach lurched. She had counted on Edith's help. She gazed at the folded skin hanging beneath the old woman's chin, wondering when Miss Edith had turned the corner to elderly. She shifted her attention. "Did you know any of the Lopezes?"

Edith squinted like she saw some of the family right before her. "Kenny T's mama . . . was a pistol, though she never married one of those Lopezes."

Edith leaned forward, whispering that she wished her

husband's mama had not fooled around with that Lopez man, Luis. Sunny pulled her chair closer, glancing to see if someone else was listening. Edith said that Kenny T's mama claimed the child, Leo, was the result of a one-night stand with Luis. He didn't hang around, so she was quick to get Kenny T's daddy interested in her and have his baby too. Edith was adamant, though her lips quivered, that the woman was not a typical mama, instead wearing low-cut gowns even in her old age. She heard tell that his mama was friendly with another Lopez brother, even after she married Kenny T's daddy. Sunny held back a chuckle while Edith forgot any promises she had made about not talking about the dead.

Edith paused. "I always wondered if Kenny T inherited his mama's wandering eye."

With an exasperated look, she told Sunny that liaison with Luis Lopez brought to their door through the years a set of Lopez relatives that she never did approve of, especially when Kenny T got lured into their ploys. Squirming to free herself from the low couch, Edith gave an indignant stare and said, "Leo was always a schemer. He's in Parchman prison, you know."

Sunny nodded. "Maggie Lu was amazed when you told her about Leo even still being alive." Smiling at Miss Edith's direct admissions, Sunny scrambled to bring the conversation closer to details related to her mama. "But what about Hershel? I think my mama knew . . ."

"Was so good of your cousin, Maggie Lu, to come by." Edith's eyes fluttered. "Now I shouldn't talk about Pearl, rest her soul." She pulled at the flour-stained apron that half covered her plumpness and fidgeted with a little string hanging from the quilt she was sitting on. "I'm hungry. I've got some cold biscuits and ham left. Can I fix you a plate? I like to eat with somebody." Grabbing her 4-pronged cane, she pushed against it enough for leverage out of the couch. "Got to let out the dog first."

A new dog? Sunny didn't want to ask. Worrying Edith might topple, Sunny jumped up and reached toward the cane, wrinkling her nose against a whiff of the many meals cooked that stained Edith's apron.

"I couldn't believe Pearl had a house dog, talked about that little thing like it was a human," Edith called over her shoulder as she let the screen door slam.

The set of dog steps next to her mama's bed flashed into Sunny's mind.

A few minutes later Edith returned with two glasses of iced tea, a plate with two biscuits precariously balanced on top of one glass, and her cane swinging from one arm. A silly grin crept across her lips. "I plumb forgot Watchman died a while back. That recliner he slept in will flip open just like he always left it." She set a tea glass and the biscuit plate on a little trunk. She held the other icy glass to her forehead. "Let me clear my head, honey. Did you want a biscuit?"

Glancing at Edith's soiled apron, Sunny shook her head. Taking a glass of tea from the trunk, she slipped into a nearby lawn chair, hoping it wouldn't fold up on her. How feeble Edith was. Silently she chastised herself for not stopping by more often. She watched Edith bend over unsteadily to pluck a biscuit from the plate before lurching back onto the couch.

"I know you all miss Watchman."

"Kenny T could talk to you about that dog all day."

Sunny's ears perked up. Could Kenny T tell her about Leo's cousin Hershel, too? She held that thought but knew to change the subject. "Who gave Mama that little dog?"

"Her dog was Brownie, or was it Blackie? No, that was my cat." Edith scratched her ear.

Sunny tried again. "Do you remember a broken water pipe in Mama's front yard?"

"Kinda." Edith's brow curled while her cane tapped like a memory walking. "Yep, Pearl was frantic. A fella and his son, yes that was Hershel and Junior, drove all the way out to Birdsong Farm and fixed it." Edith sniffed into a hanky she pulled from an apron pocket. "You know Pearl showed another side of herself after your daddy died."

Heat flashed up Sunny's back, embarrassed at what her mama might have done, but kept on. "How's that, Miss Edith?"

Sunny wasn't ready to admit yet that she'd found a note from Hershel in her mama's bedroom yesterday and that she'd met Hershel yesterday evening at Crosston Senior's Home. She wanted to hear more. She dug back to the past. "I was surprised about Mama getting the dog. She talked about her lunches in town with the red hat ladies. I was in Memphis more then."

Munching the biscuit, Edith sank back into the couch with a dreamy gaze at the porch ceiling. "Hershel loved that dog and thought she would too. I bet I wrote that in my little notebook, stuff I'm curious about."

"Kinda of a diary?" Realizing Edith's memory seemed to slip, Sunny was glad Edith had written down anything about Pearl and Hershel.

Edith pressed her lips. "Now I can't tell all."

"How did they meet?"

"While the boy worked on that pipe in the front yard, Pearl let Hershel come inside that first day. They drank wine. They put on the record player. Oh honey, she couldn't wait to call me. And she told me way more than she should have. No wonder they went dancing and down to the casinos all the time."

Imagining her mama amidst the glitter and clang of a casino on the arm of the stocky man she had met recently unnerved Sunny. She held the icy glass of tea in both hands and took a long drink. "Casinos? Where?"

"Backwoods places, but Pearl would say around Biloxi. Hershel knew some high rollers, maybe some relative of yours got mixed up with them. Didn't your mama's sister Bea look into all of that for the *Clarion-Ledger*?"

Sunny stiffened. Back when her Aunt Bea rolled up to Birdsong Farm on a road trip from Biloxi with her newly discovered granddaughter, Tiffany. Sunny had been so excited to welcome this young cousin into the family. Immediately a wave of sadness caused a little sliver of ice to catch in her throat. She missed their times together. Tiffany hadn't called or visited in a while.

Sunny hadn't realized how uneasy it would make her feel, her mama's role in Tiffany's illegal adoption by the Biloxi couple who were professional gamblers. Did her mama and Hershel really have dealings with them?

"Did Mama mention their names? Did they have children?"

Edith spoke cautiously. "`She might have mentioned their daughter who was often left with the help, but Pearl didn't judge them right off."

Sunny marveled that these friends might actually be Tiffany's adoptive parents, the ones that Tiffany had wanted to leave and find her "real" family. Unsure how much her mama ever told anyone outside of the family about her role in Tiffany's adoption, Sunny asked quietly, "Did Mama ever mention that niece who was adopted by a couple in Biloxi?"

Edith waved a frantic arm. "Now I didn't say Pearl was laying claim to her, if that's what you mean."

Sunny blinked and tried to ease the tension. "So these were Hershel's friends?"

Edith slurped her tea and set it down with a grin. "I knew Pearl was mighty fascinated with their fancy clothes and boats and carefree friends."

Sunny didn't hold back. "Gamblers?"

Edith sucked in her cheeks with a big nod. "Gosh, their picture was in the paper when they won those big jackpots at Beau Rivage casino. Pearl and Hershel were in the picture too, all of them whooping it up, holding big cardboard checks." Edith's cane began tapping again.

Sunny gasped. Her mama might have left her a secret jackpot. All she'd found yesterday in her bedroom was a note in a shoe. "I never heard about that prize."

Cane stopped, Edith's shoulder slumped forward. "They didn't make it home with the prize money, had some kind of key to a villa instead." Edith was quiet, her eyes shifting out beyond Sunny's shoulder. Sunny watched her expressions slip in and out between her moving lips until Sunny said, "I can't hear you, Miss Edith."

Edith sipped her tea and rested her chin on the handle of her cane. "Pearl told me that right after that picture came out in the newspaper, they gave Hershel access to this villa and took his winnings, bad advice that ruined their good times near the coast."

"Bad advice?" Sunny repeated, her mind spinning into visions of out-of-control slot machines and money and keys floating above Hershel's head just out of reach.

Edith's breath was noisy. "Your Mama was confused about it, talked about moving to a villa somewhere south for the longest time until she kinda turned on Hershel. I haven't heard tell of him since your mama died."

Keeping her eyes steady, Sunny wondered if Kenny T knew where Hershel was or had visited him? Sunny gulped the last of the iced tea and shook the ice cubes around the glass, her hopes of fortune murky. She felt sheepish acting like she knew nothing of Hershel, but now she couldn't wait to return to Crosston Senior's Home to ask Hershel about a villa.

Edith cocked her head to one side. "What's wrong, honey? Do you want more tea? I didn't mean to go on so long . . ."

Sunny squeezed her eyes into a pleasant gaze. "Thanks for giving me a visit. You were such a good friend to Mama. Now I better get myself to town." Easing out of the wobbly chair, Sunny was full of Lopez history and her mama's diminished hopes, but she knew there must be more that Hershel and maybe Kenny T could tell her.

Still on the Hunt

Mesmerized by the late afternoon parade on U.S. 45 Highway of farm trucks and tractors towing trailers coming from the fairgrounds, Sunny was stuck in the Tompkins' driveway, hunched over the steering wheel of her truck. She couldn't decide whether to go home and ponder all that Edith had said about her mama and Hershel or drive straight to Crosston Senior's Home and ask Hershel about the Pearl Birdsong that he knew and what happened between her mama and him.

With an exasperated "Damn" she fell back against the seat when she glanced in her rear-view mirror. Edith was on her front porch waving her hands over her head. Slipping the truck into reverse gear, Sunny backed down the driveway, stopping abruptly a few inches from the porch. "You okay, Miss Edith?"

The old woman crumpled her apron between both hands and shook her head. "He ain't there no more."

"Who?" was Sunny's exasperated response while she surveyed the yard.

"Watchman. I know he's dead. But he always loved to jump into the back of a truck no matter where it was going. The old dog loved a ride, wind in his ears."

"Yes, he's dead, Miss Edith." Sunny tilted her head to one side, trying for a caring smile.

"Oh, you're right, but he still comes if I need him to." Edith motioned her with a *move on* wave. "Not like Kenny T." Her laugh was sour.

Flinging a hand in response, Sunny eased her truck on up the driveway, mixing in her mental debate about her mama with concern for how long Edith had been seeing the otherworldly. Then she gasped. In a flash of fading sun on her windshield, a rusty truck swooped into the driveway toward, her head on. Spraying a flurry of gravel, she jerked her steering wheel, swerving into some weedy grass, and stomped her brake. With a squeal of brakes, the rusted heap lurched to a stop next to her truck. Kenny T pushed a little striped railroad cap to the back of his head and leaned out his window, eyes focused in a long stare. "Is that you, Sunny Birdsong . . . whoever?"

"You always drive like that?" Sunny fumbled to calm herself and glared at the old man.

Edith's husband was showing his age. Sunny gasped at his twinkly blue eyes sunk deep into his thin face, ignoring his reference to her unknown married name. "Yep, I'll always be a Birdsong." Her eye caught a little red smudge, lipstick maybe, at the corner of his thin lips, her breath tightening with the rumors she'd heard of him chasing women who worked at the mill. Unconsciously she pushed a finger at the edge of her own lips.

Kenny T cocked his head so his cap slipped down over one ear, his gaze trying to creep past her façade, seeming to size her up. "What you and Edith been chawing about?"

Looking him in the eye, Sunny put it simply, "Talking

about the Lopezes." She couldn't resist, picking up the pace, "Met Hershel Lopez recently. I heard that he and my mama got pretty close until he won some property down south." Sunny's heart stirred faster and her hands held a damp, tight grip on the steering wheel. She couldn't believe she blurted all that at once to her old neighbor. The warm exhaust from the trucks floated between them.

Kenny T tugged at his cap. "Cut off your truck." Sunny hesitated at his abruptness. Maybe she'd angered him. His truck went silent and he leaned further out of his window. A little vein over his eye began to throb and his thin lips started moving in a speedy cadence someone might use who had a story to tell. Sunny leaned her head against the frame of her open window, curious but uneasy at what the old man might disclose.

His eyes softening, Kenny T nodded. "Good times with Hershel, never as foolhardy as brother Leo. We were daring boys, stealing watermelons and hurling toilet paper through the branches of trees on the courthouse lawn." Clearing his throat, he began again, "As for your mama . . ." but faltered into ". . . my mama was . . . enough said, my mama. She'd say we both had a spark to us that the others didn't."

Sunny remembered Edith's worry that her mother-in-law and her husband shared a wandering eye, but Sunny kept to no expression.

A little laugh forced itself from Kenny T's throat. "Your daddy, Fred, pointed me in some bad directions that Hershel warned me against, but you don't need to hear that."

Sunny raised her head in alarm, nervous that she might hear more about her daddy than she cared to. She looked oddly at Kenny T and wondered if there were a pack of adulterous men who strangely found camaraderie. She insisted, "No, I don't. I want to hear about Hershel."

Kenny T frowned. "Hershel never recovered from his wife dying. Had to raise his boy, Junior, worked all the time..."

Sunny's fingers drummed on her dashboard while she searched for a way to stop Kenny T from revealing personal details about this man's early life. After hearing about Hershel's struggle, she wondered if she should even make a return visit to the senior home to talk with him. "Kenny T, did Hershel go willingly to Crosston Senior's Home?"

"He's had his ups and downs. His shaking condition worried his son, Junior." Kenny T sniffed. "I hate him being there." Sunny watched Kenny T suck in his breath and maybe wipe his eye. Kenny T said, "He cared about your mama, but winning that villa messed things up. I never knew why."

Sunny couldn't hold off a frown, disappointed that Kenny T rambled on about more than she needed to hear, but not enough about what she wanted to know. She had to talk to Hershel.

"Gotta go," said Kenny T, cranking his truck. Making a hurried tug on his cap, he pointed and Sunny turned to see Edith waving her arms from the porch at the end of the driveway. "I don't know if she's calling me or Watchman."

Then Sunny had an out-loud thought. "Could I help Edith by giving her one of my dogs at the kennel to foster?"

Kenny T shrugged, flattened his tone, "Might have to get me a new one."

"Dog?"

"Woman." Kenny T's head spun toward Sunny. "Just kidding."

Sunny shuddered at his steely blue eyes and jerked her truck into gear. She tore through the gravel driveway, barely stopping by the mailbox before waving down the traffic to let her in, and made a fast left turn on to U.S. 45 Highway toward Crosston.

***

Glancing at the truck clock, she pulled around back of the Crosston Senior's Home. She knew she'd nearly missed the dinner hour. Sunny grabbed a mashed-up straw hat from behind her seat to help her slip by the reception desk guard and pulled it low over her eyes, swearing as she slammed the truck door. Once inside, she dashed past the reception desk into the dining hall, scanning the remaining gray-haired occupants lingering at random tables. Her eyes stopped at a familiar red shirt, the same one Hershel had worn yesterday. Sunny glided between the tables and touched the old man on the shoulder. "Mr. Hershel, it's Sunny. Can we talk again."

The old man's dark eyes locked a hollow gaze while he steadied himself against the table, then a flicker appeared, and the corners of his thick lips shifted upward. "Company again, okay, but let's smoke."

Sunny followed his shuffling steps down a short hallway and outside to a small fenced patio. A man with milky blue eyes offered a slippery grin as he edged closer to a plump lady releasing smoke rings from her small, oval mouth. Hershel shook a little box of Tiparillo tiny cigars at Sunny, who waved him off with a "not my brand" chuckle. After Hershel's wobbly hand finally touched the end of his cigar with a flame, they settled onto a bench. After a few puffs Hershel tapped the cigar on the edge of the bench to release the ashes and said, "Your mama was a lovely lady."

Sunny gripped the edge of the bench and leaned into a whisper. "Why did y'all break up?"

Hershel wagged his head. "All in the past, girl. That time was just a fog. Why are you so like a dog with a bone?" He took a longer puff on the little cigar and rested against the back of the bench.

"Because I want to know more about the last years of Mama's life." Sunny pressed down an ugly guilt. She had made excuses when her mama begged her to extend her visits from Memphis. She'd tired of hearing about the red hat ladies and had not paid close attention to her mama's excitement over traveling with friends whose names Sunny didn't recognize. Sunny resented her mama's nightmares about the lost babies, nightmares that prompted call to Sunny for comfort in the middle of the night. Now Sunny wondered what else had really haunted her mama. Glancing at the little cigar, Sunny wished for a minute she could take a puff. "I am a little nervous asking you about Mama."

With a quick glance at Sunny he said, "Since Pearl and I were older when we met, there was more to figure about how to get along." He rested his forearms on his thighs, and his words took off in a steady breath. "I thought I'd swap some of my casino winnings with my friends. They offered a nice little riverside villa in New Orleans. Pearl was mad about the lost money, got into it with my friends. Kinda put me in a rough spot between them."

"Mama could argue with a vengeance," Sunny agreed.

Hershel kept at it. "Gosh, my friends shut down that

villa talk quick once they heard Pearl's last name. They realized her connection to their adopted daughter, Tiffany. She was Tiffany's aunt. They lit into her about the terms of that adoption she cooked up back in 1977."

Her mama's tangled role in Tiffany's adoption skewed Sunny's thoughts. She blinked herself back, shifting her head away from the smoke curling from Hershel's cigar. Her stomach lurched, beginning to regret what she'd come to learn about her mama. She tried to quiet the conversation, saying, "That adoption is all past history, over and done."

Hershel looked up for a moment. "The whole argument made me sick."

Sunny opened her mouth and closed it without a word, shock building against her ribs.

Hershel went on. "When we got home, I talked Pearl into having a big vacation at the villa. It was right on the Mississippi River. She only liked the view, hated the rest. It *was* an old stucco condo, and the papers to it were messed up. She didn't like that a bit, thought we'd never get any title to sell it." Hershel tried out a laugh and another puff on his cigar. "She was a fussy one."

Sunny smirked at the word *fussy*. Her mama sounded downright cantankerous.

"I started to go down there without her, met up with my Biloxi friends—she would no longer speak to them—and I made some good fishing buddies. I hate to say that your mama showed another side when it came to money. That hurt me." His dark eyes searched her face. "I couldn't get a deed to the place so she could sell it. I didn't try to find us somewhere better."

Feeling like she stirred a sticky nest of emotions in Hershel, Sunny wheezed, "I don't know what to say."

A flicker passed his face. "Pearl was a fireball of emotions. Sometimes I couldn't get over to Birdsong Farm fast enough for her when I'd get home from work. We'd have wine . . ." His eyes shifted. "Other times we'd go to dinner, and she'd get into money talk. I was uneasy with the two sides of her. I didn't want to develop two sides of me just to be with her."

Sunny hesitated. "She had nightmares. I wonder about all that she couldn't resolve?"

Hershel's voice got quiet when he told of her mama's confessions. "We kept some things to ourselves." Some things he wouldn't repeat for "a daughter" to hear, but Sunny pressed him until he admitted, "She thought you loved animals more than any human."

Sunny didn't suppress a smile, affirming what she had often only said to herself. She didn't want to stumble on a part she might have played in her mama's unhappiness. Was she part of a nightmare her mama would never reveal? She said, "She was critical of my ways. It was hard to love her."

Hershel's eyes stayed locked on hers when his voice shook. "She *was* lovable."

Sunny tried to know more. "Did she think you loved her?"

Hershel set his jaw. "I look back at that little golden time we were enamored, but our ghosts had a stronger hold on us. Your daddy didn't commit himself to Pearl. My wife was the world to me. After Pearl and I were spending more time, we knew we weren't a fit. We began to drift apart." Hershel grimaced. "The last few months, I didn't answer her calls much. I let the time get between us."

Sunny sniffed, "She scared me with her nightmares. I answered her calls, but I felt helpless." Sunny recalled being awakened by a voice that didn't even sound like her mama, bawling loudly in the early morning hours, calling out for a baby son, long dead. Sunny shifted toward Hershel. "Did Mama talk about my brother, Sonny?"

His response was quick. "For a while I thought he was still alive." Then Hershel's neck swiveled abruptly. "She wanted a son very much, no offense."

Was Sunny trying to regain her footing in her mama's memory? It was too late. They both knew Pearl better than Sunny had wanted to admit.

Hershel stared down at his feet, his left hand clenched. Sunny watched the tip of his little cigar send a curl of smoke between his fingers. In that moment she wanted all that she'd heard about her mama to go up in smoke.

***

It was dusk by the time Sunny turned down Hollyberry Road and into the long driveway to the big, empty farmhouse at Birdsong Farm. Did she glimpse a ghostly flutter by the curtains in the front bedroom? She cut the engine in the carport and leaned against the truck door, drained from her talk with Hershel. Yelps from the pups in the kennel greeted her while she climbed from the truck. She turned on the outside lights so she could fill the water and kibble bowls but didn't linger with hugs and pats for the animals like she usually did. Emotions raw, she knew the dogs would sense them if she touched their bodies.

Exhausted, she turned to face the house and walked through the twilit hallway, hesitating at her mama's bedroom door. Inching inside, all the talk had kept her mama close. She almost stumbled over the little dog stairs by the bed before sinking into her mama's stiff rocker in the corner. Wiggling against the rigid discomfort sent the rocker backward. From the throes of the rocker, she stared at the white chenille bedspread, almost glimpsing her mama's thin hand reaching from underneath it.

Sunny listened for words the room held. Little breaths into the phone . . . *I am your mama . . . Sunny . . . why aren't you here . . .* had left Sunny always clutching the receiver with inconsolable excuses, exasperated by lost sleep. When she did make her way from Memphis to Birdsong Farm, she perched on her mama's bedside, enduring her despairing lament . . . *Punishment must have made me hard.* Sunny gripped her thin hand when she wailed over . . . *lost babies.* Could her mama have really cared about Sunny's own lost child? She never knew. On some nights when she had visited the farm, Sunny was awakened by her mama's sobs . . . *Are you waiting for me, my baby boy?..* but sometimes her mama emitted a growling roar . . . *My son is not here to take care of me.*

Memories of her mama's earthshaking, angry voice shook Sunny still. Sunny curled her fingers around the chair's armrests and rocked, forcing herself to listen more to the creaking floorboards beneath her. Tears dampening her cheeks in the moonlight couldn't lessen the questions about her mama that still lingered, couldn't release the despair her mama had passed to her.

Moving On

No one who had lived or lingered at Birdsong Farm could forget the place. Harboring one view of Birdsong Farm were those who spent part of their lives there, and though they might be tempted to turn on Hollyberry Road and gaze at the white farm house, they knew they'd never stay there for long. Birdsong Farm had formed a part of their lives, but they didn't want their lives marked by its shadow. Others could not resist returning if for only brief visits, others were lured to stay, tempted to create something new on those troubled yet fertile lands.

Leo

Leo Lopez pressed his forehead against the steamy bus window on the day he was let out of Mississippi State Penitentiary at Parchman on parole. He had a one-way bus ticket to Biloxi. When Beach Boulevard curved and he caught sight of the expanse of beach along the Gulf, he begged the driver to stop right there instead of taking him to the bus station. Once his feet touched the sandy beach, he took in salty breaths of ocean air, almost feeling his feet lift from the ground, so magical.

The sand blown from the beach crunched under his shoes while he hiked up Main Street to his rooming house where he found an envelope with his name and a key on the counter, a staticky TV drifting down the hall the only sound to greet him. Hiking to the third floor, he was winded, his shirt collar sticky when he jiggled the key and flopped into a sagging chair and propped his feet on the limp mattress. Orange haze dusted the room, the warmth and open expanse without bars causing his eyes to flutter against the late afternoon light until sleep overtook him.

By daybreak he went back on alert each time sporadic footsteps hurried in the hallway and overhead. Not used to trusting anybody around him, he bounded down the steps and halted, waved over to the counter by a stooped woman who confirmed his name and pointed to mailboxes behind her. He nodded his understanding with squinted eyes. He backed outside onto the sidewalk, a sharp glare of sunlight striking his face. Blinking, he took in the faint salty breeze. Munching on an apple from his pack, he stopped a few blocks down at a hardware store and bought fishing gear and a pup tent. After a long walk along the beach, he set up the tent on one of the lots cleared by a long-ago hurricane across from the Gulf. He couldn't stay closed up in his room just yet. He spent his next free nights listening to the waves break uninterrupted by footsteps or anyone telling him what to do. He would have to think on how to live the free life again.

Days faded away before he called Maggie Lu. "I'm breathing free air thanks to you. The room's got a great view, no metal rods," assuring her he found the room she rented for him but not revealing his tenting alternative. Taking in Maggie Lu's urging for him to come to her house in Memphis, he tried to keep his voice steady. "I'm better off on my own for a while, got some prospects for keeping fed." Her tone, almost plaintive, caused a flare of guilt in him, but he said, "It's not the time for me to learn to be the daddy you'd expect. I'm not the same fella as when you were a little girl. I've got to find my own way."

He knew he'd eventually take a break from the beach and visit his hometown, Crosston, but didn't mention his plans. After Maggie Lu told him that his cousin Hershel was living at Crosston Senior's Home downtown, he'd have to prepare for that reunion. Didn't sound like Hersh would be up to a game of pool and a shot of whiskey at their familiar haunt, the old Roadhouse.

It still hurt him that his brother Kenny T and his wife Edith had cut off all communication with him when he was sent to Parchman. He'd asked a lot of them a number of times so he tried to understand but thought he just might drive up to their place for a quick "hello." He wouldn't drop in on Sunny at nearby Birdsong Farm. Maggie Lu's cousin wouldn't remember the times he and Bea came by on the weekends for short visits with her parents, not after all these years.

On her last visit to Parchman, his ex-wife Bea was still civil, so he was okay with her still living in his old trailer outside of Crosston. The trailer wasn't worth enough to fight over, and he wasn't sure she'd welcome him if he showed up. He'd have to figure a drop-in when she was off pursing one of her reporter stories. He left something there before they sent him to Parchman, and he needed to get it.

Maggie Lu

When the streetlight flickered against the window over her desk at home in Memphis, Maggie Lu blinked at the hours she must have spent lost in thought. After all her worry about establishing some kind of father and daughter relationship with Leo, she hadn't heard but one peep after he was freed, a noisy, quick phone call. She tried to understand that he just wanted his own life back without complications. She worried about his ability to legally provide for himself but decided not to offer to be on call if he needed her attorney services again. Disappointed that her hopes for being reacquainted with him were dashed, she seesawed between raw feelings and freeing gasps of pulling back. At least she'd freed him.

Pondering that Leo chose to distance himself didn't take away her childhood affection for him. In her unease, Maggie Lu's mind jumped to her recent discovery that Uncle Fred was her real father. She let her anger roil since Fred was already dead, and she couldn't give him a piece of her mind about not claiming her as his own. She was no longer stuck in her dark feelings of abandonment. Knowing that Fred and Leo were both troubled men, she realized what little they'd offered her eventually lessened her need for fathering.

She didn't need mothering either. On the last road trip with Bea, visiting Leo in Parchman last year, she'd cut that motherly tie. Maggie Lu could no longer tolerate Bea turning a blind eye to the hurt that her indifference had caused in Maggie Lu's life.

Since she'd lived with Aunt Pearl, Maggie Lu once thought she seemed to offer more motherly concern than Bea had. Maggie Lu let her thoughts run on, tracing rifts that never healed before Pearl's death, feeling her anger toward Aunt Pearl's role in her own child's adoption flare almost into a headache. Maggie Lu rarely let herself consider if she really had wanted Karl Dees' child or

Aunt Pearl's offer to raise their daughter while she finished college. Maggie Lu brought her thoughts back. Adoption outside the family had seemed to suit them all at the time.

Maggie Lu pushed against her swirling ideas and knew it was time to leave this family behind, put herself in new surroundings. First she'd have to tell Sunny of her latest plans. After endless rings, Sunny picked up. "Leo's going his own way, doesn't need me, so I'm striking out with a new job in Chicago."

Sunny's voice was resolute, "Oh, so far away. Okay, sounds like you've got your mind made up. New work might suit you, though I'm not sure about living up north. Get yourself a nice place. Call me when you're settled in." Maggie Lu almost floated from her chair with relief at not to have to visit Birdsong Farm again anytime soon.

Talking to her law partner, Inez, did not go as smoothly. Inez's voice was tense. "Are you joining a new law firm?" Maggie Lu tried for a calmer tone. "I just need a change in the work for a while." Eventually they'd agreed that Maggie Lu take a leave of absence from their Memphis firm. Now Maggie Lu scribbled the last two lines confirming her leave in a letter to Inez, making her departure official. She placed a copy of her Legal Aid Society of Chicago acceptance letter in the same envelope, just to make her intentions unmistakable.

Leaning back, she glanced out the window and up toward a bright full moon, its gleaming surface mesmerizing. Stretching her arms out toward the silver orb, she felt the same giddy freedom that Leo had mentioned. She padded down the hallway toward the kitchen and poured herself a glass of wine to celebrate.

Sunny

At Birdsong Farm, morning sun fell on the worn, wooden floor next to the rocker that held a dozing Sunny. She awakened from dreams in the rocker as if it was still rocking her, full of recollections that her mama's former man friend, Hershel, told her about their time together. She had hoped for a glimpse of more joy in her mama's later years but heard that her mama was more obsessed with money and land and loss.

Yelps from the kennels outside shook off her tired dreams. She grabbed a plaid jacket by the back door on the way to the barn. She flung open each kennel to release her latest brood of rescue dogs into the large, fenced side yard. She scooped kibble into each bowl and refilled the water bowls, the energetic dogs leaping on her legs to greet her. Staying a few moments to receive her individual loving pats, the excited dogs nipped at each other, then ran headlong around the fenced perimeter. Sunny propped against a fence post and took in the crisp morning air, occasionally reaching down to offer another pat when a dog stopped at her feet. Hamilton would never understand what beginning a day with the dogs meant to her. She frowned into the sun but no longer missed her husband's groggy morning laughter over coffee, his playful picking at her boring everyday breakfast of cereal and fruit. She didn't wonder if anyone else was sitting across the breakfast table with him this morning. She knew she was strong enough to stop thinking like that.

Now she often shared meals and laughter with Karleen. She might be in love. They had grown closer than she could have imagined working with the dogs together at Birdsong Farm. When Tiffany came for a visit, she altered their routine at the farm and was not as reliable as when she was a younger teen, but her affection built at Birdsong Farm through the years was strong. Sunny would always welcome Maggie Lu's daughter as her own to the farm they loved. She doubted Maggie Lu would ever feel at home at the farm but hoped she'd not stay away too long, maybe even be willing to meet Tiffany one day. At least Sunny knew Birdsong Farm was home.

Tiffany

In her early twenties, Tiffany hated all the turmoil in her adopted parents' lives but took for granted her bank account their gambling winnings supplied. They only expected a call every Sunday. They were used to her frequent trips to Birdsong Farm during most of her teen years. She still loved spending time with her cousin Sunny and the rescue dogs but didn't want to follow Aunt Karleen's lead, thinking like a businesswoman about the rescues. She didn't tell her parents that lately she earned extra money and spent some of her favorite time with her real dad, Karl, at his hardware store not too far from Birdsong Farm.

When she did come home to Biloxi, she'd go to the old part of town and visit the housekeeper who so often had been her parental companion. Some evenings she'd camp on the beach, picking up with beach bums or vacation junkies, enjoying the tales they spun that were far different from her own experiences.

One evening, back on the beach in search of a blanket she'd left earlier in the day, she tripped over a fishing line stretched out on the beach. Snapping the line, she picked up the fancy pole attached to it. An old geezer came at her, hollering, "Hey, fishing is my livelihood."

She thrust the pole back at him, shivering against the night breeze and backing away.

He stretched forward, made a closer look, quieted, then said, "You forgetting the chill comes in after sundown? Dressed mighty thin. Come warm yourself at my campfire."

Tiffany edged toward the inviting blaze, strangely fascinated by his change in tone when he gave her his name. "I'm Leo." Crouching down and holding her hands out toward the flames, she responded. "I'm Tiffany."

Settling onto a log, Leo started rambling, "Not had anyone to talk to for a long time." Tiffany warmed to listening. "When I was younger than you, I was fishing with my brother, Kenny T, down the road from Birdsong Farm, got some good eating. Not bad luck here. I'll be hitchhiking up to Crosston before winter comes."

"To do what?" Tiffany knew Crosston. Leo didn't slow, like he'd set his mind to telling. "To make amends with my ex-wife Bea or at least stay in our trailer when she is off reporting stories for the *Clarion-Ledger*." Tiffany's back straightened. "What was her name, Bea?" Leo nodded and kept going. "If not, I already have an offer to go to Memphis and live with our daughter, Maggie Lu."

Stunned by these familiar names he was saying, Tiffany fell back, her elbows sinking into the cool sand, and stared directly into the campfire. She felt the full heat of her neediness to know about her family. She caught her breath, then let it go. "I have a Grandma named Bea who works for the *Clarion-Ledger*. My grandma told me her husband was dead, her daughter, too."

Leo's brows wiggled. "It's a common name, Bea."

"Grandma Bea took me to meet my cousin Sunny who lives on Birdsong Farm, near Crosston."

A Lineage of Deception

Leo started gathering his fishing poles into a pile next to him. Now, not looking her way, he said, "The Bea I know had a sister, Pearl, at Birdsong Farm."

Tiffany dug her heels out of the sand where she had planted herself. This old man might know her own relatives. She leaned toward the fire to catch his attention again. "Listen, my Grandma Bea told me long ago that her only daughter, Lucelia, was dead." Was her full name Margaret Lucelia? Was this stranger the only one to tell her the truth?

Tiffany asked, "Have you ever heard my name mentioned at Birdsong Farm?" She could hardly hear her own words. The name Maggie Lu rang in her ears. "Does Maggie Lu have other children?" If Grandma Bea's daughter was alive, Tiffany had a *real* mama somewhere.

Leo's eyes moved in confused glances before he curled up by the fire without saying another word. Staring at his limp form, Tiffany felt as full of heat as the campfire before her. Her body shook as she stood, then forced her steps away from the campfire. The chilly ocean breeze ruffled her hair and pierced her thin wrap. She'd lost the warmth fast, the mist mixing with her damp eyes. She had nothing to warm her but a volley of words. Which ones were lies, which ones true?

The next morning Tiffany returned to the burned-out campsite. She had to know more. She spotted Leo setting up his fishing lines down by the beach. She ran toward him, her bare feet kicking up sand. Breathless, with arms stretched wide, she declared, "You're my grandfather if you were married to Grandma Bea Hopkins."

He held his hands up, stopping her when she was suddenly in front of him. "You got the right Bea there, but I wasn't her daughter's real daddy. We're all dead to

Bea whether we are breathing or not. We can't tell you a thing about your lost mama. No use worrying over knowing that now."

Tiffany's throat felt dry. "But you said you could live with Maggie Lu if you wanted."

Leo shook his head. "We've cut each other loose."

Tiffany's eyes blinked back a hard stare. "I want to know my real family."

His eyes changed, locking directly into hers. "If you've got folks, real family, up at Birdsong Farm, that'd be a fine place to stay put." Leo took a step back and started turning his reel to pull in a catch, making a final, softer glance over his shoulder. "Let me be now, girl."

Her excitement dashed, Tiffany cast a long gaze out across the breaking waves, mesmerized by the whirr of Leo's fishing lines and the nauseous emptiness taking hold of her. Her fury mounting, she spun around, her feet running, pounding the wet ground, desperate and uncertain which way to go now. Her gasps increased and burned her throat, and the sand slapped the back of her legs until she stopped to avoid what she thought was some little kid's leftover, half-gone sandcastle. Gazing as the waves crept under its edges, weakening the sandcastle walls, she pondered with whom was she the most angry.

Within the week, Tiffany roused Karl with incessant pounding at the front door of his Water Valley home. She doubled over, searching in her purse, screeching, "No key!" When Karl clicked the lock, Tiffany pushed through the door. Her hair tangled, her eyes flaming a glare, she pounded his chest. "I have a mama somewhere. You never told me Maggie Lu was alive." Stumbling backward, Karl held up an arm in defense while repeating, "Who told you this? How could this be?" Legs buckling, he collapsed into his recliner. Leaning over him, Tiffany continued flailing her fists until her legs wobbled and her body crumpled onto the rug in front of him. Her knuckles pounded his bare feet.

Cursing, "Dammit girl, stop," he swiveled his legs onto the armrest and his head fell onto his knees. He pushed out a moan that frightened her. His breath was shaky. "I can't give you a mama. The woman didn't want me either." Tiffany's neck strained upward, eyes squinting to face him, blinking under the harsh ceiling light. He pushed a palm under his chin and his stare bored into her. "We're better off without her." Tiffany gasped and leaned her head against his leg, gritting her teeth against the pain of her search for her real family. Who would help her find the illusive Maggie Lu?

Bea

When Bea heard Tiffany's voice on the phone, she wished she'd hadn't taken the call. Tiffany's guttural moan ground into her ear. "Why didn't you tell me Maggie Lu is my mama?" Bea lurched forward, sputtering excuses and grabbing a tissue to absorb droplets on her flushed temples and forehead. She had kept a distance from her granddaughter for a few years, not to get muddled in Tiffany's obsession about her "real family." Now had someone betrayed their secret? She blared, "Just hold on now, Tiffany. Calm down enough to talk to me."

Cigarette! Bea propped the phone on her shoulder and reached for a cigarette to set fire to it, then noticed the lighted cigarette resting on the edge of an overflowing ashtray and winced. She inhaled deeply and closed her eyes against Tiffany's rant. So loud and panicked, Tiffany's voice was like fire through those mean little holes in the phone.

Anger kept Bea's office chair rocking while she belabored feigned confusion in response to Tiffany's hysterical claims of learning her birth mother was alive. Tiffany's tone wavered in her ear when she couldn't remember the man's name on the beach who talked of Birdsong Farm. Keeping an even tone, Bea said, "Probably that stranger was a drifter from Crosston." Her ear hurt but she tried to soothe Tiffany. "Remember the family you know here is all there is . . . Sunny, Karl, Aunt Karleen, and me."

Bea forced the receiver off her ear, a little safe distance, and glanced toward her desk calendar, knowing she had to wrap up this call or it was going to delay her scheduled interview with an ex-MBI agent who could give her the goods to finish up her latest expose for the *Clarion-Ledger*. Tiffany's outrage reminded her of her daughter's temperament. Bea's own tie to Maggie Lu was frayed after that trip to Parchman to see Leo. She hadn't even known Maggie Lu was moving to Chicago until Sunny told her. Maybe Bea didn't need to keep Maggie Lu's secret anymore. Could anyone discourage Tiffany's pursuit? Scanning for a way to stop Tiffany's fury, she stuttered. "Well, I dunno . . ." A few short breaths came through the phone. Then "I don't believe you, Grandma." *Click*. Bea's feet hit the floor, and she slammed the phone down. She fired up another cigarette and blew a little smoke ring. Her family was going up in smoke, but she had a big story coming that would probably clinch the Pulitzer.

About the Author

Maryann Hopper is a writer and a storyteller who grew up in Mississippi. Her first collection of short stories, *Missing the Magnolias*, was an audio book. Her second collection of short stories was entitled, *Don't Let the Flies In*. Both were independently published.

She was selected for the Tucson Festival of Books Masters Fiction Workshop in 2015. Her short story, "The Losses Go Deeper," won honorable mention in the Lorian Hemingway Short Story Competition in 2016. Her short story "New Brunswick Enigma" was a finalist in the Lit/South Awards for Fiction in 2022. She has written non-fiction articles as part of Womonwrites' Southern Lesbian Feminist Activist Herstory Project that were published in *Sinister Wisdom* 2014-2022. "My Croning," a chapter from her memoir in progress, was included in the anthology *Crone Chronicles 20-20: Intimately Inspiring Glimpses into the Lives of Wise Women 52+*. She has a master's degree from the University of Memphis. This work is her first novel. She lives in Marietta, Georgia, with her partner, Drea Firewalker, and their two housecats, Kali Sue and Littlecat.